GOTCHA!

Babe Toner

Order this book online at www.trafford.com
or email orders@trafford.com

Most Trafford titles are also available at major online book retailers.

Print information available on the last page.

ISBN: 978-1-6987-0152-3 (sc)
ISBN: 978-1-6987-0151-6 (e)

Trafford rev. 05/21/2020

www.trafford.com

North America & international
toll-free: 1 888 232 4444 (USA & Canada)
fax: 812 355 4082

1

My father was a computer programmer with a doctorate and worked for one of the largest and most famous New York banks that moved to Newark Delaware. They did it for the tax incentives and not worrying about what lives might be disrupted by all of this. The employees needed a job and they would have to get used to our slower ways down here that they didn't live under in New York. My parents really loved their jobs and I suppose they loved me, although they forgot to tell me that they did. I was walking around wondering is this how the other kids are treated by their parents.

My mother taught nursing at the university, and loved it very much I guess she could use her position to take a leadership role and maybe even use some of her political beliefs and mold a new movement with these first time away from home babies. She certainly doesn't try to find out how I am thinking or how I view the world and if the truth be known she wouldn't know how to have a one on one with me, they were a strange couple. I guess you could say that I was busy being a pain in the ass and in the way to them. They tried to hide it but they didn't try hard enough because I could only conclude that they didn't care what I thought of them just don't bother them.

They put me in a private school in Newark that had everything a person would need that wanted to learn something different or be somebody in a higher position and they turned out some great leaders in a lot of fortune five hundred companies. The school is the best kept secret in the country I think it was the atmosphere and the location out of the city that relaxed the students and let them learn their subjects easier. It didn't matter that I was away, my parents never had time for me because they always brought work home and it kept them busy most of the evening and they never knew I was around. That didn't bother me; I knew they loved me they were just caught up in their career building jobs and sometimes I would get in the way, if the truth was known it was probably most of the time. I was the son that they didn't realize they had in their world they were living in and how I came about is a mystery to me.

I was tops in my class but I loved computers and digital cameras and I am learning all that goes with it. I am hoping someday that I will be able to use this knowledge and make a good living from it. When my parents were doing their work at home and when I had some free time, I would get myself a small camera and a telescopic lens that can help me take some long distant pictures. I learn something new every day and I didn't tell my parents what my plans were, he would teach me on occasion all he knows about the computer and I want to take my computer classes at the university someday and prefect my skills. My father told me I was leaps and bounds ahead of people my age or even older?

By the way my father's name is Michael Smith and my mother's name is Mary and my name is William Smith. We live in the woods north of Newark that is very hard place to find. The deer don't have any problem finding it because they eat all our shrubs every year even though we live next to this huge game preserve they prefer dinner at the Smith's and eat anything that looks green, they even tried to eat our artificial Christmas tree that my father would put out on the lawn as far as we're concerned they are a public newsiness, and living next to a game preserve you would think that it would help us and our shrubbery. We must have better food to eat, and they pass all of that untouched by human hands food on the preserve to eat at our place. Hell, they even bring their children and show them where they can eat around the clock and never be touched.

We talked about putting up some deer fencing ten-foot-high, it would be an eyesore and the neighbors would bitch to the county about our high fence or what they would call a spite fence so we decided against it and avoid starting a community property war with our neighbors.

When I see the deer, in the yard eating our shrubbery every now I'll hit them in the ass with my high-powered BB gun and they leap in the air and leave faster than they came. The sting of that BB shot has them jumping anything that is in front of them, no matter how high. Now if their children look like they were in trouble, look out because they will plow their way through anything that is in their way just to help them get untangled and rescued off the property. I have tons of birds that come to eat the birdseed that I put out for them and the squirrels. I enjoy watching them I have learned a lot from their behavior . They don't need to be fed in the summer because there is an abundance of food all around especially the game preserve next door, they have everything over there. I will say that I haven't seen any Buffalo or any wild horses yet but anything can happen around here next to the woods, I am just being funny, just deer and Canadian geese is our main visitors. The deer don't make any noise but the geese do, even at their different altitudes they fly and I love it when they do there calling, there is not that many animals that try to talk like they do. I know they are saying something, it's usually the one out on the point that makes the most noise and brings them over our house into a landing in a pond nearby.

I am a freshman in high school and freshmen where I go have to live on campus their first year, I know that sounds crazy but there you are. it is very safe and secure and it didn't bother me being away from home and it didn't bother my parents as well, the relationship works best when we are not around each other. I can't make it any better so I am not going to try and fix it, I didn't break it.

I find myself observing people and all the different things they do; no two people are the same. I see some people sitting on benches talking to themselves and some smiling and laughing I have even seen some very sad and troubled ones and some having a very angry conversation with themselves. Some women smoke but mostly men. Very few pipe smokers and at least fifty present read a magazine or a newspaper, the other 50% are with someone and in a lot of cases it's the opposite sex. I noticed that their conversation seems to be that one of them is serious and never looks happy. To me it was more fun than going to the movies. I take all of my pictures of people that have some interesting behavior and sometimes they are on the phone talking to someone. I guess I am easily entertained by doing these observations, to me like I said earlier it better than going to the movies.

There are times when I am not observing people and that is when the weather is freezing, I prefer my equipment to be exposed to the warmer temperature and sunny weather. I think when I get my license, I can go around to some different places providing my parents let me use their car or they might get me one of my own. I think they will get me a clunker rather than me use there's, we'll see.

One of the girls in school has taken a liking to me because she says that I am a computer whiz and she wants to be one too. I don't think she knows what it takes to be a computer whiz, take it from me I have spent a lot of years on the computer for too many hours to add up. Her name is Pat Weber and she wants me to show her some things about the computer that will help her in college. I don't know if I want to spend some time teaching her about the computer and get tied down to teaching and not perfecting my own skills. Because for me to get a computer science degree I will have to be able to score in the middle nineties to get a scholarship

She said she has good snacks thinking that I would like that and get me to teach her about the computer. I told her I like snacks too and what she doesn't know is that I would like to snack on her. She doesn't know how I feel about wanting to snack on her but I think that she knows that I am no different from the other guys who at our age who have a one tract mind and girls can only find that out by dating. She asked me again to help her out, I think that this is a good opportunity to see how far she will be willing to go to keep me coming back. I said ok when does she want me to come over. She said how about Friday evening around 7 o'clock. She said she has her own computer in her room and that's where we will be spending most of our time. She said that she will tell her parents you are coming so that is one hurdle out of the way because we would be spending all of our time in her bed room. I had to keep from smiling after hearing that. Pat was the head cheerleader and she was the tallest cheerleader we had. She would knock your eyes out when she started doing her cheers, her short skirt suited her well and to think she wants little old me to spend some time with her in her room training her to be a better computer operator, I hope I don't look that weird, like a nerd or something. I am no different from any other young blooded American boy in a room with a hot chick who likes to kick her legs up in the air, that invited me there to help her.

I told myself to take it slow and easy and she will take care of me and my needs, I hope. I was kind of nervous walking up to her front door not knowing what was going to happen. Like, are her parents going to be nice to me and make me feel welcomed or not hide the fact that they don't trust me alone with their daughter in her bedroom. I hope they will remember that I was invited there by their daughter.

Well here goes I pressed the door bell and it opened a few seconds later? It was Pat and boy did she look good; she took me to meet her parents who were getting ready to go to the neighbor's house for bridge. The father Michael said that Pat is looking forward for you showing her some of your computer skills. I don't know that much but I am willing to teach her what I know. Michael said that Pat is very impressed with the way you use your computer in school, he told them she is too kind.

The mother Mary who is a perfect copy of Pat or should I say that Pat is the perfect copy of the mother. The mother knows how she was at Pats age and is well aware of how Pat is going to use this time alone with me. That is something that I will never know but I bet she was hot just like her daughter. I came over with good intensions and I am flattered that she asked me to help her. The father said they will be back by 11: o'clock. Pat took my hand and took me to her bedroom and she sat at her desk and turned on her computer, I wanted to make a funny so I said, well that's a beginning and she said you ought to see the rest she can do on the computer. I told her I thought she would be out on a Friday evening rather be stuck in her room with a computer geek and her reply was and I thought the same about you and went on to say, if she wanted to be out on a date tonight she doesn't think she wouldn't have any problem finding some stallion to go out with. I told her that Friday is just another day of the week for him and that makes it less complicated for me. She told him that Friday is a big release for a lot of people that don't have big plans like I do.

I don't date that much and I know it's because I spend too much time on my photo skills and computer skills. She wanted to know what are you doing with photography and I told her collecting candid pictures of people in different places and how predictable they are and that allows me to take great pictures. I love looking for that one picture that turns out to be great? I will have to recognize it when I see it and shoot as many pictures I can.

"What do you do with all those pictures?"

"They don't take up that much space on a disc and I can store thousands on a Turbo USB stick."

"Do you have any storage sticks?"

"I don't but I can get some when you come over again. They seem to be the thing to have when you want to save something other than it just being on the computer"

"If you don't know what they are you won't be able to know where to go and get some."

"That's true."

"I will get a couple and show you how to store information and find the right port to put them into."

"That sounds really exciting; I can't wait to see that and how it works."

"I asked her if she has Microsoft word."

"No, I don't, I don't even know what that is."

"Tomorrow I want to take you to Best Buy and have your parents buy you the latest version of Microsoft word and all the other things that I will recommend that you get."

"I'll be real happy if you come with us."

"I will be happy to because it wouldn't be any fun having to go back and exchange some things when we could have gotten it right the first visit. I hope your mother will understand that you need this to enhance your knowledge of the computer systems and a lot more, you will be surprised to see what I am going to teach you."

"I can assure you I am open to anything new that you want to show me and I will be the best student you ever had."

"That's good that you have an open mind and are looking forward for me being the teacher, you will be my first student."

"I can assure you I am looking forward for this experience for a long time and you will be my first teacher."

I had left before her parents came home and this was very hard for me to be in the same room with her, I think she would have done anything I would have asked her to do. Pat saw me in school the next school day and asked me if I was available for going to Best Buy and getting those computer programs Saturday. I said I was and does she want to meet me there or does she want me to come to her house and we can all leave together in her car. She thought it would be better going in her car. I told her I would be at her house at 9: o'clock. She asked me if I could come over Friday night again. I said, "What no date again and I don't think she liked that remark.

"I have a date with you so quit worrying about my dating, I date when I want too and who I want to and right now I am tied up with the rather nice computer buff who I waited all week to see him again."

"I am sorry if I upset you."

"You didn't upset me at all, I just want you to feel more comfortable around me, you have a lot of good attributes that I like in you. You don't have to make wise remarks to me because you have me up on some pedestal and you don't see yourself getting up there with me and you feel uncomfortable with me wanting you to be in your company. A girl would be crazy not wanting to be with you."

"Ok, I was just seeing how you think and now you told me and I will be more confident with you, and I think you will like it and relax a little, I am sorry for not showing more confidence in myself."

"Does this mean that you will be taking advantage of me because you're helping me with the computer?"

"To be honest with you the thought has crossed my mind the more I 'am around you I love my chances of taking advantage of you not knowing how you're going to respond."

"Good I will keep an eye out and see what you have in mind and what advancements that you will be making towards me."

"Nothing that you wouldn't approve of."

"I am anxious to meet with you Friday evening if you still want to, we can call it our date night and we can be very happy together for the night."

"Of course, I am looking forward to it, you do realize that computer knowledge doesn't happen overnight, it's a long process and one you will never forget. Do you have a good memory and are you able to recall from that memory when you want to because working with computers you will have to be able to do that a lot and the more

you have to use your mind the better it will start to recall different terminologies a lot easier and you will notice the improvement almost right away?"

"By the way my parents are going out again and they are leaving me all alone with you, I think they trust you more then they trust me."

"I think you will find out that I don't bite and if I do, it will be very gentle and some people would call love bites that might be in some private places not to be seen just by anyone."

"If you keep this up, you'll be talking dirty to me next and I will get to see the other side of you."

"Only when it's appropriate and I have time to back it up otherwise talk is cheap and there is nothing cheap about me."

"Well then I will have to see what I can do about that."

"It sounds like you have a plan."

"All girls have a plan."

"What is your plan with me, do you have one?"

"That's for me to know and you to find out."

"I think you want me to make some moves on you and then you will either accept them or reject me and depending on how you feel about me and how my move makes you feel."

"You'll have to wait till Friday to find that out."

"Do you think we will get any computer work done?"

"We'll see how it goes, but in all likely hood we probably won't get that much computer lessons done that night.

"I'll tell you up front that I was surprised that you latched on to me by stepping over all the other computer buffs."

"Don't be, you are the best catch out there and take it from me there are a lot more girls that would like to have you come to their house for private computer lesions that you might not be aware of. I hear what they say about you and I knew I better get a move on

before they entice you into their bed room to help them improve their bedroom computer skills"

"I can assure you that you are the best catch out there too and I hope I can live up to your expectations."

"We'll just have to wait and see."

William saw her in school Friday and he asked her if it was still on for Friday night and she said nothing has changed, 7:30 is fine with her. William was getting scared about what could happen between them. He knew that she would have to approve of all that goes on. It was time for William to leave for Pats house; his mother gave him a ride. He rang the doorbell and Pat answered it and said, "You're early" and William said he was anxious he's been waiting all day to come here tonight, she told him he just missed her parents and that her mother agreed to buy her that computer program you recommended so it looks like were on for tomorrow. She took him up to her room and closed the door; he noticed her cheerleader outfit hanging on the back of her door and it looked like it just came back from the cleaners. William asked her if it was her cheerleader outfit. She said it was and asked him if he would like to see her in it.

"Sure, if you want to."

"I don't give private showing for just anyone, I want you to see me close up like no one has ever seen me before."

"Well I am honored to be the first."

She took the outfit off the hanger and laid it on the bed and she started taking off her clothes until she was down to her bra and panties. The panties didn't hide much, it's hard to hide that patch and how good she looked in her panties. she put on her little skirt first and then her top and she asked William if he liked what he saw. He told her that he loved what little he saw and she asked him if he wanted to see more and he said why not. She took off her top and stood there in her bra and reached behind her back and undid her bra and held it up with her arm. She slowly lowered her arm exposing one boob at a time. What a picture this was she had two perfect boobs and walked over to Michael and she told him he could touch them if he wants and boy did, he want to and also kiss her nipples and made them rock hard. She got real close to him and she kissed him with an open mouth. He knew that this was going to lead to something he hopes she can handle all this touching and kissing.

William got the message to do what he wants and see what it will take to get that skirt off, the way she was breathing it looks like it will be soon. I found the skirt zipper and slid it down until it fell on the floor. She slipped out of her panties and he immediately went right for the forbidden area looking for the forbidden fruit. She was moaning a lot and it didn't take long to find the right entrance. I better be able to keep moving on or I will have a bad night.

She told him that it will have to be this way until either she can go on the pill or he will have to settle for her assistance. William told her that she will never get pregnant this way. She said good then if you're happy I am happy. William laid her on the bed and he put his finger in her and she came right away, in fact she came another time. She said that she was very happy how it went this evening and he made her feel like a lady. She asked him how did it go for him and he told her she was great and she said good then I want to do it again; it took longer the second time. They laid close together She held on to him for dear life, she has never experienced anything like that in her life. She knows now that she can't live without him.

She said she couldn't wait for her mother to get her a prescription for the pill and hoped that she will go along with it.

"Just like that your mother is going to take you to a doctor and get you a prescription that will prevent you from getting pregnant and condoning you having sex with other guys. This is what mothers have to decide on these days so the pill is the only answer there is in these cases or have a pregnant daughter still in high school."

"No, not with anyone else just you, it is easier for me to have relations with you safely, rather then I get pregnant out of wed lock, the pill is the easiest solution. This is the solution that a pill is worth a pound of cure. They don't want me to get pregnant at my age."

"How will they know we want to have sex?"

"Look for thousands of years this has been the number one problem between a boy and a girl and besides my mother was my age once and she had the same problem to contend with and it looks like they worked that out."

"Can I ask you if you love me, because no woman will have sex with her boyfriend if she didn't feel some love for him?"

"She waited a split second and said that she loved him the first time she laid eyes on him and I have been carrying around this feeling of how I felt about you until now and I do love you with all my heart and you can have me all you want I'll never turn you down for sex any way you wanted to know how I feel and that's how I feel about you."

"After tonight we will never be the same again, we just consummated our relationship just like we were on our honeymoon."

"I think we better get dressed even though my parents won't be home for at least another hour and a half, it won't hurt to play it safe."

She rolled over on top of me and rocked on my penis until he was rock hard, she squirmed for a while and shouted out she loved me. William knew this girl can't get enough of him. They both got dressed and they kissed for a while and William said we better turn on her computer and she better put her outfit on the hanger and put it on the back of the door where it was hanging. Things were never going to be the same between them she will always want William to give her a good screwing. She rinsed her mouth with some mouth wash and she sat at the computer and told William that she will never forget this evening. You gave me what every woman wants, a good screwing by the man they love very deeply.

William told her when she gets her new program, he will be able to set up a lot of storage in her program. He told her that this is a long process that will payoff later down the line. She told William that she wants to be good at it like he is, that is what attracted me to you. William told her when he was younger and all by myself, I played with my computer day and night until I got good at it and now that I have perfected my skills, I am playing with you. she told him that all good things come to those who wait and I have been waiting for you a long time and you have made me feel like a woman should feel after being with the man she loves.

She was very interested in his photography adventures when William told her that she will have to spend some time on the computer before she can come in with him on his photography studies. He told her that he will teach her how to be a good photographer and better still how to identify what makes a good picture and how to pick a good subject. She couldn't control herself she just wanted to kiss him. Just then they heard someone call out Pat we are home. They both looked over the room and found everything to be ok. The bedroom door opened and her father asked them how's it going and they both answered very good, William is a computer genius and William responded, "I wouldn't go that far."

"He's modest; take it from me he is."

"Ok he's modest; I want to know if you accomplished anything this evening on this computer of yours."

"Tomorrow when I get my new computer program I will accomplish more. William and I will be seeing a lot of each other from now on and he's my boyfriend you might say that he is exclusively mine, we are going steady"

"Well William how does that sound to you."

"I couldn't have said it better, thinking that he knows everything that goes on between to young people because he probably did it himself."

"Oh, I know what ever Patty wants Patty gets, if it's good for her and her future years in college then she can get most anything she wants, thanks to you for taking an interest in her."

"I am sure it the way she wants it makes it hard to turn her down. The living truth of that is I am here aren't I and what I am teaching her here will go a long way in college. There are a lot of students that want to take computer science classes that can't pass the entrance exam to get in the class"

"I think your right because by the time she gets to college everything will be done on a computer and there has to be someone that can know everything about it that a company needs to stay ahead of the competition. These collages know this so they offer the best that's available to the best who can qualify that can open up new worlds for them."

William stood and shook Mr. Smith's hand and he told Pat that he would be here in the morning around 8:45. She said that her and her mother will be waiting. She told William that she would walk out with him, when they got outside, she told William that she hopes her father will get the picture about them being inseparable from now on. She knows that her mother will talk to her about it and she'll let me know what she says. It was hard for them to say goodnight after the evening they just had. She stood outside the front door with him and told him that she loved the way they made it tonight. William said he was going home to rest and be Smith when they meet in the morning. William put his hand in her panties and she squirmed until he felt her twinge. She started crying and she told him that she loved him with all of her heart and she always want to be with him.

William wasn't gone that long before her mother came up to her room and she said your father said that you were proud to announce to him that William and you will be seeing each other as much as you can and that you will be going steady with him, that being the case you two will be inseparable.

"I did say that and I meant it, I waited a long time for someone like him and I am not going to give him up or our time we can spend together."

"I guess you know that when two young people see each other as often as you say you will be doing will only end up in bed with the man you love and you getting pregnant because you didn't take any precautions."

"It looks like to me that you are thinking more about this than I am."

"That's why I want to make an appointment with our family doctor and have him subscribe some medicine for you to take orally every morning without fail. It is widely known as COCP (Combined Oral Contraceptive Pill.) It will keep you safe from having any accidents when you're with William, heavens only knows what you're going through when you're with him."

"To me it seems like your condoning me having sex with William is that what you're saying or am I misunderstanding why you want me to take a pill?"

"Not at all, I know I can't stop you from having sex so I'll do the next best thing and get you a prescription that will make it safe. I 'am too young to be a grandmother and you are too young to be a mother so I want to prevent that."

"What's this doctor going to say when you march me in his office and want him to prescribe me the pill for a fifteen-year-old girl."

"I can assure you that he will understand, this is for your own good. There wouldn't be any young girls pregnant in high school if their mothers took an interest in their daughters like we are doing with you, are we clear on that? Girls are vuln Abule to a young good looking guy that seems to be going to the top, they want to hang on as long as they can, even if it means having sex with him on demand with no protection and getting pregnant before they had a chance to start their life"

"I am really thankful that you are my parents and that you care what happens to their child. You don't have to be a genius to see that it is impossible to keep two young people that are in love apart, nothing has worked over the years so the pill prolongs the inevitable. The pill doesn't keep them apart it only keeps the young girl from getting pregnant and once the sex starts there is no stopping it. Am I getting that right because nothing works but the pill?"

"I'll let you know when your appointment is, I don't know if he will give you a physical or not so be prepared for the most that can happen on this appointment and you can't go wrong. It might just be a non-evasive checkup to see if you have any blood pressure problems, that seems to me that is what going to happen."

"Mom did you ever take the pill when you were dating daddy. How could we not want each other when you were alone with him? Surely you must have wanted him in the worst way."

"No, I saved myself for our honeymoon and not on the back seat of his car looking up at his dome light. I am proud of you mom but today these circumstances are different no one is saving anything for their honeymoon, why wait."

Pat had no way of knowing if her mother was not telling her the truth. She did know a lot about conceptive measures. We had the time of our lives last night without a pill, her mom didn't know that and if she did, she would have a heart attack. Pat thought with this pill I will finally get to feel what it's like to have him inside me. She couldn't believe how good it felt and how they try to keep them apart for as long as they can knowing that these kids will screw on top of an ant hill just so they can get that loving feeling. If you want my opinion the mother is doing the right thing, her daughter is far too intelligent to be going to school pregnant and her baby's father has plans to go to college and he can't take on the role of being a father at this time in his life and there you have it, the woman loses once again.

2

William got up early Saturday morning and he was going to make sure he would be there on time. He walked to Pats house it was just a couple of blocks away and he rang the doorbell, Pat answered it and she had a look about herself that could only come from a contented woman. She stepped outside and gave William a big wet kiss and told William that her mother had a talk with her last night and she is going to take her to our family doctor to get a prescription for the pill. William said that was fast and she said thanks to my father who I set up to tell my mother what I told him but only the way a scared father can tell his wife. Pat took William out to the kitchen where her mother was finishing a cup of tea. Her mother offered me a cup and I said I have already had my one cup this morning.

Her mother stood and took her cup and saucer to the sink and asked are you two love birds ready to go. William almost shit his pants after hearing that from Pats mother. When they got to the car and William didn't know where to sit so, he chose the back seat and leave Pat up front with her mother. That was definitely a class decision on William's part. We got to the store just as they were opening and we walked to the computer program isle and William found it right away having been there a number of times, it was windows 10 or the latest one out for windows. I took Pat to the backup section and he bought a 128 GB/go turbo 3 and a couple of 5g backups. She would need a HP 3 in 1 printer, fax and copying machine with a built-in scanner and plenty of paper and printing ink. He wanted her to have all she needs to be good at it and learn all the things that are necessary to be a good computer programmer.

William got her a six pack of copy paper and a document shrewder and one nice paper cutter, one more thing a pack of Kodak color picture printing paper, not the gloss paper because it smears if it isn't totally dry after it's printed. William totaled it up in his mind and figured there was almost a thousand dollars there. The mother never said a word the whole time Pat was loading up the two shopping carts. William told Pats mother that the startup is often a shock. I told Pat that she didn't need anything else; she might have to get a bigger desk later on for this stuff to sit on. The mother was happy that her daughter had something that would occupy her after her school work is finished and now William will take up a lot of her time.

They rolled up to the checkout register and the count Michael came with $737.50 Mrs. Jones gave the cashier her Visa card and they left as fast as they came. Pat is excited that William was going to teach her how to get these items working. There was plenty of room in the trunk and the ride home was fast. Pat helped William carry in the items and they did it in two trips. The mother disappeared and left them alone, it was never going to be a good idea to leave them alone in their minds. Pat told William when she sees the doctor how will he give her the instructions on what the pill prevents and what can happen if you stop taking it. She is sure he'll be very professional about it, trust me we will both know all about this pill before that day is over.

William let Pat down load the Windows program, he just guided her through it he had her physically do the download. Every chance they could get they would touch each other that made them very aroused. As long as the parents are home nothing was going to happen. Pat thought that pill can't come soon enough for her; she never dreamt that she could want someone so bad; she hopes that it not showing knowing that the mother isn't missing anything that what goes on between the both of them. She is a knock out now at fifteen what will she look like at age twenty. I think she will want to marry William when the opportunity comes after college. You have to give the mother credit for seeing this so soon and Pat telling her father that William and her were going to be inseparable, it was Pat that made all this to happen and making them think that it was their idea.

They spent hours getting everything set up and William made Pat do it all hands on. So now it time to teach her a lot of things that she will need to know to work the programs successfully. There was a soft tap on the door and it was her mother asking them to come down for lunch. She made some soup and some grill cheeses. Pats mother was very interested in William and his parents; William is so far ahead of her thinking that he knew what she was going to ask him before she did, by the time he was finished answering all of her questions she really liked him and was happy for her daughter. William thanked her for lunch and they went back to her room setting her system up and running. William closed the door and Pat turned around and started kissing him and William's Oliver started to get hard.

William put his hand down her panties and he ran his finger over her opening and touched her boat and she almost fell over. William told her they should stop and that they will have to wait for a better opportunity. She told him that she was tingling all over and she will wait because she doesn't want to get caught, they will have a good thing going soon and they can screw without a rubber and she will live for the day that she can have William every day if she wants him. William said that they have everything installed now and they should take a break and if she wants, they can pick up where they left off today. Pat said let's do something different like a movie or spend some time in the park. The way she wants to screw all the time the park would be very entertaining, there are some good spots where there is some privacy but it's still out in the public.

William liked that idea and he told Pat that they don't have any transportation and they will have to have a ride from her parents. Pat didn't like that idea and said why don't you take me to your house and show me your set up tomorrow. I'll tell my parents what we're doing Sunday, I am sure she will think it will be ok. William knew his parents will be too busy to take any notice of them being in his room and maybe they will go out somewhere. Pats mother dropped them at the movies and she said she would pick them up in front at 9:30. They took a seat all the way in the back there were people all around them doing everything but having sex so William couldn't take her panties off, someone with a sensitive nose would easily pick up the odor that comes from a woman that is being aroused. Mrs. Weber was right on time and she said that she had some snacks for them when they get home; they sat at the kitchen table and talked about the movie; Pat was happy to be alone with William even though it was at the kitchen table where nothing can happen.

It was hard saying goodnight to Pat she walked him to the door and let him touch her where it counts and he told her that tomorrow they might have a better chance in him penetrating her than their first time. He told her that he was just going to let it soak. She asked him would it hurt and he said that the pleasure will outweigh the pain. He told her the only thing that will hurt is when I have to take it out. She was hot just listening to William say those things to her. Pat went to bed wishing for tomorrow to come fast and it did she jumped into the shower and went down for breakfast and told her mother again that she was going to spend the day at Williams and work with his system to get familiar with how a good working system operates.

The mother being a worry wort told her to be careful and Pat asked to be careful of what. Her mother never answered her and put the breakfast dishes in the sink. Pat was no dummy she felt the vibes and knew what she was alluding to. She walked down to William's house and rang the bell. William opened the door quickly and pulled her in and said, "Guess what my parents are going away for the day they will be leaving in an hour or so and we can have the whole house to ourselves. Pat told him that she wasn't interested in the whole house she was only interested in his bed room and looking up at the ceiling from being on my back for as long as we can.

William thought this girl speaks her mind and there is never a doubt as to how she feels. William introduced Pat to his parents and they were friendly but not that friendly, that's just the way they are. Pat truly understood and didn't take any offence to it. They sat with his parents at the kitchen table over some ice tea and talked about current events. Finally, Mrs. Smith said they must get a move on and asked William if he will be ok and she told them to have a pizza on them, there was plenty of sodas in the refrigerator. They thanked them for being so thoughtful and watched his parents leave and they told him again that they won't be back until just before 9: o'clock, that gives them plenty of time to screw all day and I know what Pat wants to do and I want to do the same.

I'll bet money that when that door closed Pat was making a bee line for William's bedroom with him leading the way. William locked his bedroom door and he started undressing Pat until she was down to her undies. In the meantime, she was undressing him, all the way down, he was unusually harder and big and she wanted him badly. She pulled back the blankets and laid there with her legs wide apart and asked William to take her forbidden fruit. He didn't need any cream or oil she was wet enough. He took it easy and she held back a little until it stopped hurting and that was when they got into a rhythm and she told him that she can feel every bit of him inside of her. William didn't even want to get close and after she came about three times, he pulled it out and he asked her how it felt to lose her cherry. She cried hugging him and he washed himself and she did more things to him that I would have a hard time describing of how much she loved him. He knew it and he had no problem with her showing him how much she wanted to show her love for him.

They both laid there fondling each other and Pat was hoping that William will rise to the occasion again; she had one climax after another until she fell asleep. They both did for a few hours and William wanted to put it back in Pat again and let her have another orgasm with him inside her. It was around 4: o'clock when they ordered a large pizza with extra cheese with mushrooms and peperoni and had it delivered Pat found some paper dishes and poured some soda and waited for the doorbell to ring. It wasn't long and with the tip and all it was still only $14.00 dollars. Pat couldn't stop holding William's hand and told William that she wants to marry him someday.

William told her if they go to different colleges, they won't be seeing each other that much. Pat said that they will have to go to the same college then and William told her that it won't be that easy. He told her that he will probably go to a top-notch computer science school and that she will have to cram a lot of computer knowledge in the next three years. She asked William if he would help her and he said he is looking forward to it, he told her that she would have to eat and sleep computers. She told him that she is screwing the teacher now and that is a big help. William told her that he has a lot of confidence in her that she can pull this off with a lot of hard work and you won't have much of a social life being on the computer most all of her free time, that will be the biggest draw back in getting ready for a computer science test that will get them a scholarship.

William told her to pay extra attention to her hygiene's because she is using her vagina for more than she had been using it before because of all the activity she is getting down there it could easily cause her to get a rash that any doctor would be easy to see that she was screwing her brains out. She told him that she will make sure that she uses all the feminine things that will keep her healthy down there. He explained that he didn't want her to see a doctor because she was having sex and she would have all the telltale signs to prove it. They both decided to call it quits for the day and William would walk her home.

They kissed goodnight and as soon as Pat got in her mother wanted to know how her day went, that was when she told her mother that she wanted to take computer science and go to the same school as William does. The mother said that was a long way off and Pat told her that this is something she is going to do no matter how far way it might be. I will do whatever it takes to go to the same school William goes to and he feels the same as I do.

The mother knew that when Pat talks like that she will put her head down and do it. She dropped the school conversation and asked Pat how were his parents and that's when she told her mother that they bought them pizza for dinner and not telling her that they screwed the whole afternoon because his parents went out for the day. She did say that they were as nice as two intelligential can be, they love their son but they don't make a fuss over him like you do me. They are not touchy people, Pats mother said that she gets the picture; he must have spent a lot of time by himself with no one to talk too.

I can see now why he is so good on the computer, being by himself and using his computer all day. Pat told her that he has her now to talk too, he won't be alone anymore. Her mother said boy are you hooked on him and Pats reply was she isn't any different than any other woman in love you were in love with dad like I am William.

Well that knocked he mother back on her heels she knows now that the pill is the best thing that she can do for her daughter. She doesn't have the nerve to ask her if she is having sex because she knows that any woman in love doesn't have a reason not to and from the way she is talking she is doing it all it shows in her conversation and in her facial expressions.

Well its back to school Monday and she knows now if she is going to school with William, she will have to improve her grades to a higher level. When she got home from school that week her mother told her that she has a doctor's appointment Wednesday after school for a checkup. Pat knew what that was all about and wondered if she was going to have to take her clothes off and what is the doctor going to say to her. She knew that her mother was going to be there with her so he knows that he is talking to a fifteen year old young lady that her mother doesn't want her to get pregnant and he knows that and he will be a professional about that.

They got to the doctor's office and they were ushered right in. The doctor looked at his clip board and he gave Pat a very non personal checkup and gave her mother a prescription and said it was nice to see them again. Pat thought that was easy, her mother was very solemn about the whole office visit and her daughter of fifteen having to go on the pill. All though this sounds bad it really isn't because it's for her own good. There are a lot of girls that should be on the pill and aren't and they are screwing their asses off. On their ride home Pats mother said to read the instructions because she doesn't know a single thing about it, she never had to take the pill. Pat just sat there and she waited in the car when her mother went in the drug store to fill the prescription.

She was gone about fifteen minutes and when she got back in the car, she gave Pat the prescription bag and told her to read it over a few times so as not to misunderstand it. She never spoke another word to Pat all the way home. They went their separate ways when they got to the house and Pat sat on the bed and read the instructions over a few times. Pats mother isn't upset with William because she knows that it takes two to have sex and she also knows that her daughter if anything like her mother is, she is some hot woman and

William has been selected by Pat to put her fire out. Her daughter fell in love with a very smart guy that can enhance her life tenfold.

She has decided to take a pill every morning after she brushes her teeth and she will keep them in her toothpaste draw out of the eyes of a nosy person, she would rather her mother not knowing what she is doing with the pill. She knows that she should wait at least a week before having sex with William, he will understand and it's worth it to wait rather than get the news that she's pregnant. William didn't care how long they had to reframe he was ok with it. They could still have sex except he would have to pull out before he ejaculates. Nothing is going to stop them from having sex, nothing.

They got through their freshman year and spent the summer mixing up taking pictures and Pat working on her computer. William had her reading all the books he can find on computer language, he knew she would need to know any term or saying that can help her in getting higher grades. She will need to pass some stringent tests to go to the same school as William. The first time she felt William have a climax in her she cried and said nothing has ever felt better and she understands why they want to keep young couples away from each other because once a woman feels that climax in her she is hooked and she will never be the same again.

They are now in their senior year and they are joined at the hip they are the talk of the school they are always together. Pat is still cheerleading and people are taking her picture all the time, she draws a crowd where ever she is especially when she is cheering for her team and kicking her legs high in the air and opening them wider for her main man William. Never have two people been so in love, it was nice to see it. Pats mother was happy for them and really relaxed that the pill is working just fine and it seems to them that Pat is a lot happier having William in her life.

William and Pat applied for a scholar ship at Michigan State and they also had to be tested before they are approved. A month had gone by and William and Pat received their letters that they have been approved for a scholar ship and William's being a full scholarship and Pats being a half scholarship. Pat was disappointed in that but she knew that if it wasn't for William's tutoring over the last three years, she would have never received anything. So, she was happy that they could still be together and Pats parents were very happy for her that all that hard work paid off. They did have a while to go before they had to report to school the last week in August, needless to say they were planning on a full summer together and go and do everything like going to the beach and some camping in the mountains. Just to be alone with William and what could happen was enough to make them happy as two love birds could ever be.

They went some where every weekend from the Poconos to hiking on the Appalachian Trail they were well traveled and Pats parents bought her a car to drive out to school in and to use around the town where the school is. They decided to leave a few days early and get their dorm assignments. They didn't need anything but their computers some clothes and William wanted to take his digital camera. They decided to buy some clothes out there. The car was packed to the rafters and William being a computer buff rigged his and Pats computers so that if anyone would steal their computers and try to use them, they would catch fire, so if there is a fire on campus it will probably be there computers causing it and the thief will be in for a big surprise especially when he becomes homeless from the fire.

Pat was saying her goodbyes to her parents and was going to pick up William at his house, pack some of his things and head for Michigan. Because of a late start after they packed William's things they decided to stay overnight in Erie. It was a good idea they talked a lot about what it was going to be like away from home and it was getting on to be about 6: o'clock when they decided to stay at the new Holiday Inn. It was beautiful and they had a great view of the river but that didn't prevent them getting it on for the longest time. They found a nice restaurant and had a great time. They were looking forward to getting back to the room for round two.

William parked the car under the light near their room and went to their room. They wanted to start early again and get on campus before sundown; they wanted to go to East Lansing Michigan. They got there and the admittance office was still open. They identified themselves and they received their room assignments and now they will be separated from now on, to meet where they could and study and meet their scholarship requirements. They were starting to meet for breakfast in the morning and this one morning Pat never showed up. William stopped by her dorm and they said she was taken sick during the night and she was rushed to the hospital we didn't see her. There was quite a scene here with all the emergency people here and campus police looking all around her room and outside the dorm looking if there was any foul play.

Her roommate told him where she was taken and when William got there, they told him that she passed away a few hours ago. William lost it and he had to be taken to a recovery room and try to get him settled down, nothing worked so a doctor came and gave him a sedative that put him right asleep. In the meantime, the hospital notified Pats parents what had happened. Well needless to say that they both screamed so loud you could hear them all the way to Michigan. They chartered a private plane and left immediately and found William in the hospital emergency recovery room. They were trying to talk to him but he was out cold. They found out that Pats body was in the hospital morgue. They wanted to see her and no one could ever not want that moment but they wanted to see her again for the last time know that they will always see her from then on in their minds eye, it usually the last thing you remember of how she looked to you. They didn't take the time to think of that they just wanted to see her before they take her back home and it was not a very nice thing for them to see she wasn't that nice looking young girl that went off to college instead they saw this young lady that had turned purple because of the heart trauma and the lack of blood not being pumped through out her body.

This was not a good idea and one that they would regret after seeing her in that state was something no parent should ever want to see their child in, it was bad enough she was dead and now this on top of that. They left that morgue far worse off than they were before they came. They were so happy that William didn't see her that way. It was bad enough for him to lose his first love than to see her in such a state.

They had the hospital put her body in a casket after they saw her for the transportation home in their chartered plane. In the mean time they came back to William to see how he was doing, they found him awake now but in complete shock as how this could happen to this very young girl. They read the hospital report and it said that Pat caught a virus and it spread to her heart and took her life immediately, it's rare but it happens and of course he felt why me. They have lost a daughter and they have a very hurting young man to take home to his family which made their loss even harder. They were hoping that William could spread some light on what had happened.

He told them that they would meet for breakfast in the morning and this one morning she never showed up and when he ran to her dorm that's when he found out that she had taken ill and was taken to the hospital. He tried to get to the hospital as fast as he could and when he got there, they told him that she had passed away a few hours earlier. He told them that he doesn't remember anything after that until I saw you just now. He told them that she worked so hard to get here and be with me and it ended before it started and he was left with this horrible night mare that he will take a long time to get over, if he ever will. We were always in each other's company and we never got tired of each other which only proved how much we loved each other.

William knew she was their only child and that really hurts even more. It was impossible to measure who was hurting more, them or him. William found it very hard to collect Pats things from her room and his things and get them in boxes on the plane. Mr. Weber was a big help and it took hours before they could leave for home to Delaware. William's family met them at the Wilmington airport and they could see that he was in shock. They thanked the Weber's and they were truly sorry for their loss. William was out of it and he would have to get over it soon or he will not be any good to anyone or himself. They got him home in in bed very quickly. The funeral was horrible and William had to be helped by two of his school friends just to stand with him and not let him walk alone because he had no balance and he would fall down.

All of their school friends came to the viewing; it was a very emotional sight to see, all those young people in shock that this happened to their friend. Not one never held back there was a rain storm of tears and a continuous outburst of crying that lasted through the whole viewing, it didn't make her loss any easier witnessing all that emotion. William thought this was going to be the worst day of his life, the viewing and the funeral.

William eventually will not remember any of these past few days, it will erase itself from his mind which will allow him to function enough to get by and he will be in shock on and off having a good day and a bad day but he will get better and come around to the way things are in time. To lose a love one as close as pat was to him is a shock that will take a long time to heal. He will have a hollow spot in his life no matter how much he looks like he has gotten over his loss of the only girl that captured his heart and he felt her love every moment of the day. She can never be replaced and he isn't going to try. Pats parents want him to come by for dinner if and when he can on Sundays, they will always have a plate set for him every Sunday weather he shows up or not, he was quite taken back with that and he wanted to be with them as well. They knew how close they were and now that they have lost her, they were hoping that he might fill in the gap whenever he can. Just to hug him and shake his hand is the closest they can get to their daughter, it's sad but it just might work and he will do all he can to be with them on Sunday, just to feel her kiss him would almost turn his legs to jelly.

They were very pleasant to William and they were very concerned for his health, William didn't look the picture of health and his skin colors were a little washed out they knew how close they were to each other and it gave them a peaceful feeling to have him around. You might say that with him being there with them it was like having Pat around. They didn't want to give that up if it was at all possible. Whenever William looks at Pats mother, he saw Pat and he loved looking at her because of the feeling it gave him it was indescribable and it warmed his heart. She doesn't know how much she reminds him of Pat and it might be better that she doesn't. They were prepared to help him in anything he was going to do; all he had to do was just tell them. Pats mother would hug him very tightly and kiss him on his cheek and hold his hand all the way to the front door whenever he visited and by the time she let go of his hand this time he was drained of all his energy and he could barely walk home, she didn't know that she was having that effect on him and he didn't know what to do about it, if anything.

William knew that Mrs. Weber would be the only woman that he would ever let kiss him, it was great and it made him feel good inside. He was afraid to hold her close to him and kiss her back because he was so attached to Pat and she looked just like her and he was afraid of what he might do and he knows that her feelings for him would let him get away with anything. Mourning is one thing but cutting yourself off from the rest of the world is a little over done and that seems to be what William has done. The person that shuts themselves off from the rest of the world usually lives an uneventful life and never accomplishes anything. William wasn't doing much hanging around the house when his parents are at work; they had no idea the pain he was in or how to console him. All you have to do is be around him and know something was wrong, his parents couldn't be bothered with anything like that, they have eyes but they couldn't see. It was something they didn't know how to show him their love but he knew they were there for him but he would have to ask them for help before they would offer it, that's just the way they were.

He was messing around with his camera and he wanted to take some good clear pictures with his telescopic lens. There was a technique that he had practiced for a long time and the weather played a big part in it, he would go out every day weather permitting and he tried to avoid the humid days they tend to not give him the best clarity of the picture. He knows from taking pictures in different places at different times and different overcast skies would make for a better picture.

His parents came home and told William that they were moving to Washington D. C. his father has taken on a teaching assignment at the Georgetown University. William didn't care he would go anywhere at this point in his life. He knows that Pats family will be in shock to hear the news that he was moving to D. C. with his parents, he always looked forward to having Sunday dinner with them. It wasn't easy saying good bye with her mother crying rivers of tears and the father wiping away a lot of water, they agreed to write as much as they could. Pats father gave him a big hug and he had tears running down his cheeks while Pats mother said they would miss him very much and he gave them a lot of comfort knowing how close he was to their daughter, Mrs. Weber made it hard for him to leave that evening.

William's parents hired a mover and they had everything packed and on their way to D. C. by early afternoon. William rode with his mother who needed the company for the ride down to D. C. They beat the moving van by over an hour and by the time they were all moved in it was after 8: o'clock. He found a set of sheets and made his own bed and went to bed. It was after 11: o'clock and he just laid there thinking of Pat and how much he still misses her and he can close his eyes and still see her, no one can ever fall asleep under those circumstances. There were a lot of nights he cried himself to sleep, his parents had no idea about his feelings he had for this girl that ran so deep and if they did, they wouldn't understand it. He misses her so much and nothing will replace her, so he will have to find something that will keep him busy and lose the sorrow that is in his heart and comes out when he is in bed by himself.

There were a lot of things that William could take pictures of; this place is a photographer's dream. His parents were always at work or going to parties meeting the faculty. William knew that you didn't have to attend parties to meet your coworkers but by doing that they didn't have to be home with him. He preferred to be on his own and they didn't mind him staying away from them or vice versie. William bought a very expensive digital camera computer system that will allow him to turn any picture he takes in any dimension he wants to view it in. Believe it or not it took his attention off of Pat and he seemed to be on the mend but it won't be over night, he put a lot of her in his life and he wasn't in any hurry to get her out, he took a lot of comfort in thinking of her and some of the things they use to do.

William received a letter from Mrs. Smith and she told William that she misses him and it will be nice to see him again one of these days, you know I was missing her to and she must have had some relief in writing him this letter. William replied that they will meet again; we are not that far away and he misses them too and he promises to visit them soon he loves their company and he feels close to Pat being there with them.

He walks to most of his places that he hangs around to get that perfect picture. He really liked sitting in the park where he has a variety of people to observe and he gets to hearing the water trickle over the rocks and watch the different birds come there for a drink of water or for a splash where it wasn't that deep, he was surprised in seeing how often that like taking a bath. He knew he was getting some great shots; one day he got a squirrel grooming himself that he had never seen before he even got in some water and rinsed off, and they were crystal clear and that squirrel was taking a drink of water and taking a small bath were the best he has taken for a while. He is starting to get some of his color back and he feels like he has a little more energy than he was having so things are looking up.

The park seemed to have the most variety of things to choose from for a good picture. He liked watching the different people sitting on the park benches and doing a variety of different things trying to look normal they almost acted like they knew that someone was watching them. A lot of people came to this park for lunch or to meet with someone or just sit around and have a good smoke. He saw this fellow dressed in a suit sit on one of the benches and take a piece of chalk and mark a line on the left side of the bench, not a long line but one that was barely visible, with my telescopic lens I could see the white mark clearly now this was different and he will have to watch this guy more closely.

He would do all the close ups that someone could do of a person sitting by himself trying to look normal. He had a strong suspicion about this guy and he quickly made a judgement that this guy is hiding something and he plans on coming back every day and piece the puzzle together and if it's nothing then he feels there is nothing lost. William knew that this guy failed at looking normal and he was up to something because he looked far from normal. This guy left as fast as he came and never looked back. William thought that he looked very suspicious and He went back every day and he never showed up again but he was determined to come back every day and maybe see him again, you don't mark a bench with a piece of chalk if you're not sending a message to someone.

William had nothing better to do so he kept coming back to his spot that he used for taking pictures until finally, after nine days he was back and he reached under the bench this time and pulled out from underneath something shiny and it seemed like that through his telescopic lens that he twisted this object apart and took something out, so he is getting messages from someone and why all the cloak and dagger. He put the shiny thing in his suit pocket, he sat there looking out of place and left after a few minutes thinking that no one saw what he was up to, he didn't count on someone watching him and photographing him.

After he left William went to the bench to snoop around and he couldn't help but to look under the bench and he found a half round piece of metal that was big enough to hold a fifty-cent piece if you wanted to slip it in the slot and someone was doing just that. William thought this was going to be fun for him and he liked being busy with something and he went back to the park every day until this guy showed up again, He reached under the bench and took his shiny thing out of his pocket and reached under the seat and when he pulled his hand out from underneath it was empty. He had taken pictures of all these moves. He was compiling a photo collection of this out of place gentleman giving messages to someone the guy waited about five minutes and left but not after he put his little chalk mark on the side of the bench. Without thinking too much about what he has come across, he thinks that this guy is talking to someone and marks the bench that he was there and has a message for them.

William wanted to look under the bench and see what the shiny thing was, he sat there for a few minutes and reached under and felt a large coin and slipped it out of its holder and walked to the next bench. It felt light and it twisted apart and when it opened there was a microchip inside. Now what is he going to do about this, he placed the two pieces on his knee and he took a picture of them. This was something that really interested him to the point that he was going to see this through to the end so He decided to put the coin back and leave for another spot to see if someone was going to pick up the coin. Later in the afternoon a fellow in a grey jacket came and sat on the bench and he didn't look like someone that would visit a park and eventually he reached under for the coin, he put it in his pocket and left but not after William taking a lot of pictures of him. William knew there was something strange going on here and he has a lot of pictures of everything he did and everyone that was around him. This is something big and he was going to get to the bottom of it and he has a lot of pictures to back him up, good clear ones all on his camera chip.

He went back every day and finally that guy came back and reached under the bench and pulled the coin out and he put something in it. He seemed very nervous and he left so William wanted to follow him after he took some more pictures putting something in the coin. He stayed about a hundred feet behind him until he stopped at this building entrance and when he looked up it said in stone the Federal Bureau of Investigation. He decided to go in the lobby and asked to see the fellow in charge because he thought they might want to see what this person working here is doing leaving messages in a coin under a bench. The girl looked up and asked William to have a seat. He wasn't there that long when this well-dressed gentleman came out and told William that he hoped that he didn't have to wait long when he knew that he did.

William told him that if he wasn't the man in charge, he couldn't help him because he wanted to talk to the person in charge. He told William that he wasn't the man in charge but the man in charge will listen to everything you have to say about this encounter in the park. William told him that he was sorry about so demanding he is getting over his girlfriend dyeing prematurely so he took up photography as a good way to keep busy and it is working. He told him about this fellow that was interesting enough for him to photograph and how he started reaching under the seat and marking the seat with a white chalk mark and leave and then in time some other man would come and sit on the bench and retrieve the object from under the bench.

The only reason I saw all this is because it was my hobby photographing the different people and how they act in the park only this guy acted out of place that started me photographing him and all of his moves. I took pictures of everything and I have him nice and clear in all my shots. I have pictures of everything I went to the bench and I took the object out from underneath the bench and this is what it was. I opened it up and it is a microchip and the person that put it there works in this building, because I followed him here. He just sat there amazed at what he just heard William tell him and now William is showing him the hollow coin and the microchip that he took from underneath the white marked bench.

William handed the Agent the coin and he excused himself and he said he would return as soon as he looks at what is on the chip. He never returned but two other guys in suits did and they asked William if he would follow them, they looked very serious. William thought here we go now the bull shit starts maybe even try the good cop bad cop on me. They went in a room and the fellow he first met was sitting at a meeting room desk and he asked William to be seated. He was real quiet and he finally asked William if he had the pictures, he took of all this park bench exchanges on him. William told him that they were on his camera chip and I can down load them for you. They asked him what does he need to do this and William said a good computer for starters and a good copy machine to make some clear pictures from my chip, I assume you have one here at the FBI offices.

William took the camera chip and the chip adapter and put it in one of the internal ports and lord and behold here comes the pictures. They asked William to point out the person that you followed here to this building and watched him put the coin under the bench. He pointed to the fellow in the suit and said it was him and you can see all of the pictures I took of him even him walking beck here to this building. It got real quiet and they said that he has just picked not just anyone he picked an FBI agent he must be mistaken he's one of our top agents here at our headquarters and he has been with us for over twenty years, if you didn't have those pictures it would be too hard to believe.

"I can assure you I am not mistaken; I don't make mistakes and I don't appreciate it by you inferring that I do, I got you everything you need so don't be disrespectful to me or I will leave and take my pictures with me they are mine you know. I am the good guy here so treat me like one."

"That's quite a statement you have just made to me and maybe you are still being remorseful and easy to jump to conclusions."

"Look don't even begin to show me any disrespect or bull shit or I will walk out of here and you can harass somebody else you're not going to harass me because quite frankly I won't put up with it so show a little respect or I will walk out of here."

"We did a fast check on you and you won a full scholarship at Michigan State and you had to drop out for medical reasons, like the death of your girlfriend Miss Pat Weber that you are still getting over her loss."

"That's correct."

"You took the coin before it was supposed to be picked up. Can we run back to the park and put the coin back and maybe see who is picking this coin up."

"Sure, I can recognize anywhere so let's go, he usually comes later in the day and we will be able to spot him I have taken his picture before on another pickup and these people are on a schedule and once I spotted them and wise to their game that aren't that

secretive and if I spotted them they need a little sprucing up because someone else might put the puzzle together like I did."

They walked rather quickly to the park and William put the coin back in the holder and picked a good place to wait and they looked through some high-powered binoculars while William had his camera set up to take some very incriminating pictures. They waited till dusk and finally that guy that came the time before showed up and reached under for the coin. William took some great pictures. The FBI let him walk away and the next time they told William they will arrest everyone involved. They had plenty of time to investigate this spy before he would go to the park again. William had discovered a spy ring right under their noses not even a thousand feet from their building and the FBI were going to get this rogue agent and put him behind bars for the rest of his life.

William told them that he goes every day but there is usually an eight to ten day waiting period. They told him that he will have an Agent with him all the time. On the twelfth day this agent came back to the bench and placed the coin back under the bench in its holder. The FBI swung into action and caught up to him while he was still in the park. They came up from behind him and grabbed his arm and pulled him to a stop. They told him that he was under arrest and he knows why so please don't cause a scene because there are a lot of agents that would like to kick the shit out of him. One of the other agents went and retrieved the coin and were not going to open it until they got back to the office. William figures that they will be pushing him out of the picture now and use him when it suits them, he didn't know what to expect he would let things develop on their own and see if he was right about them. It's them that have the reputation for being cold towards people that are helping them not him like they are holier than thou. I guess that are the victims of their jobs. They are America finest and I am glad they aren't after me

3

They took the agent in question to the meeting room and opened the coin up in front of him, there was a piece of micro film in it and there was a list of our CIA agents operating in Europe. The agents were thinking that it was one thing to rob a bank but to sell your country out is non forgivable. They asked him why would he sell his country out to people that want to enslave us and ruin our way of life. Surely you are mad at someone or you were passed over on a promotion please if you can tell us what you could have gotten out of this. He Just sat and he was quiet and his head was down the whole time,

I guess he couldn't answer their question. They showed him all the pictures that William took of him walking on the foot path walking to his bench sitting on the bench, reaching underneath with the coin that had the microchip in it and then stand and start walking back to the FBI building and go inside. He reminded him that our country is at war with Iraq and spying during a war brings a death penalty sentence. You have a wife and a son that you have just destroyed their lives. If you say you did it for the money you have more than you need to retire on so it must be more than just the money it sounds like to me that you have developed a hatred for your country, what other reason could it be.

The lead agent told agent Gaulman (the spy) that it wasn't for the money because you had more than you could spend and right now, we have a team of agents going through your home looking for anything that proves their point. Your wife and son are being detained to see what their part was in this and I hope for their sake they are innocent. Now he wants to talk after he heard that, he told them that his wife had no part in this. They told him that they will decide on that not him. They reminded him that he was caught by a very smart person that liked watching people and you were someone to watch, you easily gave yourself away and he started photograph you and all your moves until you made that fatal mistake reaching under the bench seat. He had you on film dead to rights, the camera doesn't lie but you do and the camera will put you away for the rest of your life. That's if the jury are tolerant of you selling out your country and not give you the death sentence. He told them that he wants the death sentence and no sentence of life in prison.

They did tell William that they will need him for the pickup and to take as many pictures as he can to get this spy. He went back to the park and waited for hours with agents everywhere waiting to pounce on that bastard until finally the guy showed up and reached for the coin under the seat and when he pulled it out from underneath the seat, they arrested him with the coin right in his hand. This spy got caught with his pants down by a person that made it fun to watch the human nature of people sitting in the park. He had learned that every face tells a story and he enjoyed watching them, he never said a word.

When the spy came to the bench for the pickup and there was a van at the curb waiting for him to take to the office. He was taken into custody by at least a half dozen agents and he was put in the van they had waiting at the curb to take him back to the office. They went through his belongings and found all kinds of identification cards saying that he was an employee of the Russian Government at the UN as a secretary. I am sure he or someone will declare that he has diplomatic immunity down the line until we have to set him free and for them to get him out of the country.

They have forty-eight hours to tell the Russian Embassy that they have one of their employees in custody for spying and they will say that he has diplomatic immunity and they have to let him go.

The FBI agent told them not until after the trial. They sent over some lawyers to talk to him and he was told not to cooperate in any fashion with them. His name was Ivan Blaski he was a Russian citizen and when not living in Manhattan or D.C. his home was in Moscow, he was single and no children. That is usually the makeup of their spies, no past and no one to go home to. They thanked William for all that he had done for them and from time to time he will be called on for his assistance in preparing him for the trial. In the meantime, Ivan's wife was devastated by her husband spying for the Russians. It wasn't that big in the news they were waiting for the trial to begin. You might say that they were helping the wife and the daughter to get through this awful disgrace that he put on them.

William had made a copy of the recording chip where all the pictures were on and gave it to the FBI. William knew this Russian spy was going to get off because he was assigned to the UN as a diplomat, but one thing for sure our FBI agent wasn't going to get off. He had a while to think about the sentencing of a spy during war times and I am sure that he's not eating much chow having this sick feeling in his stomach. This was something that he never gave a thought about and when he was approached again, he said he would talk to them but he wanted the death sentence to be lifted in his case. The lead agent Mike Todd told the agent that if he should lie or cover up anything that would alter or attempt to get to the truth in this case, he would recommend the death sentence to the court. Now if that doesn't alert him on what the FBI expects than nothing is registering with him. He told him not to agree to anything he isn't going to back up. We want the whole truth and nothing but the truth from you. We caught you dead to rights and you can be put to your death for spying for the Russians when our country is at war.

He told the agent he didn't know where to start. The agent said that he is being recorded both audio and video of the entire meeting so please don't go back on your word your life is involved here. He said he understood. He told the agent Mike that he was only just getting by on his salary and his wife had to work to take up the slack, their mortgage and two car payments were killing them. Mike reminded him that this kind of struggle is happening all over the country, there are a lot of two workers in a family now, as long as you know that none of these working families are spying for the Russians.

He said one day after work he decided to stop at the local watering hole for a drink when he met this nice couple and they bought him a drink and that was the end of that, until the next time he went in for a drink again and it was just her there this time. She said her name was Anna Surence and she said she was hoping that she would get to meet him again, that he left this great impression on her that she could only think of him 24/7. She told him that she needed a ride home she was dropped off here by a friend and luckily for me you came along and give me a ride home otherwise she would have to catch a cab.

He said he didn't think that there was anything wrong with that, he had no idea that she had other plans for him and when he got to her house, she quickly invited him in for a night cap. She seemed very nice and she was very pretty and she would often touch him when she spoke to him, for some reason that made him feel better towards her. When they got in, she left him alone in the living room and came back in just her under ware and said she was hot, the bells were starting to go off in his head about her. She got real close to him and she told him that she has to have him now and he can't remember when any pretty woman ever said anything like that to him and he just sat there in shock and she pulled down his fly and she laid on the sofa and told him to come and screw her, she wanted him inside her now. He said they had sex for hours and she wanted him as often as she could have him. He told them that at this point it was only the sex the kept him interested in her and she never asked anything from him up to that point.

Needless to say, I would see her two or three times a week so I wouldn't make my wife suspicious and have sex with this young lady as much as I could. After a while she was asking me about my job and how important I was for her to hear all of the stories that he must have about top secret information that he handles every day and only a few people know about. She told him that she would pay dearly for any information that he would give her whether it be about the troops in Germany or how many CIA agents are there in Europe. She would give him oral sex just to speed up his reply to her. He never gave it any thought that she only wanted the top secret information from him, she was using the sex to keep him interested in her mission. She would give him sex anyway he wanted it every time they met and finally one time, she told him if he could leave a microchip in a designated area when he has some good information for her, he would mark the side of the bench when he had a chip to give them.

She told him that she loved him and was going to have his baby and she would really need his help now she said they would give him $50,000 dollars every time he gives them a chip. They had sex again that night and she asked him if he liked it and he said very much. That's when she told him that there was more of this if he wants it. He told them he was out of his mind for this woman and he was glad his wife wouldn't suspect anything about his affair with this very young woman. He said he would ask his wife for oral sex and she reluctantly gave it to him but never once asked him what has gotten into him, she never knew what he was doing. Mike the good agent asked Alex the bad agent how far back does this thing go and he said around five years. Mike asked him did she have his baby and he said that it turned out that she had a miscarriage and that was the end of that scare. He said that he didn't dare take her out in public for fear of being seen by someone and she didn't have a problem with that. Mike said to Alex what kind of things were you *giving her and he said anything he could get his hands on. Now with all this money that you have it was becoming clear that you were doing it for the sex the money was just another way he was being paid for his service is that about right.*

He said that one time he asked her if he could move in with her and get married and she said no to that request almost right away because she needed better information then he was giving her, he didn't have enough money to give her the life style she was used to. He said so I got her more highly top-secret information and sex for hours at a time. He told Mike he couldn't help it she had complete control of him the whole time they were together. She knew how to manipulate him into giving her his secrets that he saw in his office from time to time he said he just wanted to get back to her every chance he could get and his wife never suspected what he was doing with this girl and coming home drained of every bit of energy that he had. I guess the marriage was getting stale and sliding into a rut that happens a lot when one of the couple is having an extra fling outside the house.

Mike couldn't believe that his wife didn't see any difference in him with you wanting her to give you some oral sex and all that. He said she thought that it was just a phase I was going through and little did she know how true it was. The truth of the matter was that it was just that was brought on by your nightly visits with Anna. He agreed with that and told Mike that he didn't like losing control of his life, like she had taken away from him. He knew he was hooked on this girl but like all addictions you chase after them for as long as you can and always with the same ending they drain you dry and come up with a way of dumping him usually the partner finds out about the affair and the marriage breaks up, you might say a perfect ending of a spy tale.

Mike asked him how he found some of the things that he was giving her and he said some things he would read in reports and some things he would copy and he would put them on microfilm in his basement some evenings when there wasn't anyone around, I felt better when no one was around like the sneak that I was. I know it was wrong or I wouldn't have to sneak around, it didn't stop me and I got better as I went along with it. My wife never asked me what was I doing in the basement she had enough on her hands keeping the house and working full time.

Mike wanted to know whose idea was it to have the hollow half dollar, he said it was her idea and even the park bench was her idea, I went along with everything she asked me too. In exchange for sex, I guess that's the size of it. Give us her address where you would meet her at and he wrote it down and gave it to one of the agents sitting with them at the conference table. He left the room and Mike knew that she has had sex with her for the last time but he never threw it in his face. They did go to her house and they knocked on her door gently with a search warrant, there was a slight delay and finally the door opened and the agent asked her if she was Anna Surence and she said she was. Alex was right she was beautiful and sexy looking.

They told her that they have a warrant for her arrest and a search warrant to search her home. You could have knocked her over with a feather, she was so shocked to hear that and to look at her face, it showed.

"What am I under arrest for?

"Well we can start off with stealing State Secrets which is punishable by death when the country you're stealing the secrets from is at war. That is one offence, how about debriefing a federal officer of top-secret information like you have been doing for years."

"How was I debriefing a federal officer?"

"With all the oral sex that you were giving him so he would get hooked on you because you made the sex good and you probably had to screw a lot of people to get in the position, you're in now."

"I have never heard of such lies in all my life."

"Are you saying that you weren't giving Alex Gaulman oral sex three or four times a week and that is a lie, how would we know that if it weren't true?"

"If a girl wants to do that for her man what's wrong with that."

"Nothing but in your case, you were doing it to get our country top secrets and you made arrangements for him to put some microchips in a hollowed out half dollar and place them under a park bench seat we know that because we have plenty of pictures."

"You will have a hard time proving that."

"Not really we will have at least two people that will swear on a bible in a court of law to exactly that. Now listen young lady from my experience this attitude that you have just presented to me will get you hung by your neck and when its snaps after the trap door that your standing on drops you to a very horrible death. In most cases your eyes will pop out of your head and you will lose all control of your facilities and look a mess. If you don't cooperate this is what you can look forward to and I will be the one pushing the jury for that verdict."

"If I am found guilty, I am better off dying rather than rotting away in prison, although the American prisons are a lot different than the Russian prisons."

"I feel better when I offer an option and if it is turned down then I know that I at least tried to make it easy on someone and I agree with you on what you said at the beginning."

The agent stood and told her good luck she will need it and as he turned to walk away, she asked him to come back and sit down. She told him that he didn't paint a very nice picture of what might happen to her and she asked him what can she do to get out of this mess. The agent looked her square in her eyes and told her that a blow job wouldn't help and she has used up all of her sex rewards to help her out of this situation, not only did you ruin Alex you destroyed his wife and daughter and you might feel sorry now that you caught but you didn't care about them while you were screwing this weak and pitiful agent out of his countries secrets. That's all you wanted was the secrets and you didn't care about anything else.

"You have to tell us everything that you know and don't leave anything out or we will tell the court that you didn't cooperate. There are a lot of things that we already know so don't think you can fool us so please don't lie to us and we will tell the court that you cooperated with us."

She starts off by telling him that she was a dancer in a strip club and this guy asked me if she would like to make a thousand plus a week for hardly doing anything, they will also pay for all of her expenses all in cash. She said this was too good to be true so what's the catch; she said that he told her that she would have to get some guy to like her enough that he would give her some information so she could hand it over to his friends. She wanted to know what kind of secrets, he told her any kind from rockets to top secret reports and for this you want to give me $2,000 a week, of course he said $1,ooo. a week was his reply and that's about it in a nut shell.

"Sorry I can't do that; you need to find someone else to spy for you."

"You want $2,000 a week and that is your final answer."

"Yes, and not a penny less."

"We will have to train you to be submissive and the aggressor in getting the selected person to cooperate with you. It won't take long for us to show you what men fancy that will break down all the barriers for you to get what you want. You are a beautiful woman and you will be trained how to get a man to open up after you perform certain favors on them in the bed room where they will be the weakest."

"It was a class on sex and how it works on men for you to get your way with them and when I screwed all my teachers and gave them oral sex, I graduated from finishing school to the real thing. They set me up in a house and paid for everything and all I had to

do was to extract secret information from the candidate which they assured me I wouldn't have any trouble doing with my looks. I did have to screw all of the teachers as well as blow jobs almost daily."

"It must have been pretty bad to have to give them all that sex."

"It wasn't that bad the money was good and that was the price I had to pay for that lifestyle."

"How did you meet Alex Gaulman?"

"He came into the bar one evening for a drink and my teacher and I bought him a drink and I did everything but seduce him in the bar. Now the test will be if he will ever come back and he did about a week later and I was able to get a ride home from him on the pretense that I had lost my ride. I got him in the house and I screwed him silly and it was enough to make him want to come back for more and he did, he couldn't stay away. I told him what I needed and where to put it and I gave him all the sex he wanted and he was starved for sex the way I gave it to him. It's the oldest trick in the world and that is you can always trade sex for favors. He was very easy to get him to spy for us; you would have to feel sorry for this guy being so vulnerable that he would sell out his country for some oral sex and whatever sexual adventure he wanted to go on. I let him do anything to me and it would remain a secret between us and no one would ever find out about them.

"I can assure that we don't feel sorry for him, we feel sorry for the widows who lost their husbands working as undercover agents for the American interest overseas that some of the secrets that Alex turned over were murdered by their Russian counterparts, that is what motivates us to get to all the facts in this case and we will work day and night to prosecute you and your cohorts."

"In the end I had no idea what was going on. My job was to make this guy so dependent on me sexually that he couldn't help himself. After a while he was led around by me to do a job that had

sex as a pay-off, that is the weakness of most men and he was the most vulnerable of all the people she had ever met."

"What you call a job we call spying and that is a very dangerous job to be involved in. It's rare that spies get caught some times and in this case it happened."

"What's going to happen to me? I didn't know that any spying was going on to me it was just another job that paid good."

"Well it's my guess that you will go on trial for your life and anyone that can read a newspaper will know how low you stooped to get information for the Russians to use against us, even if it meant killing us. You didn't have any restriction on how far you would go as long as you can get the secret information for the Russians."

The agent got up and left the room feeling a little sick to how low people will go just to steal information that they can be used against them. Mike the good agent would interview Alex as much as he could and wanted to know how he could get so much information over the last five years. Mike asked where he got it from and Alex said from the computer and letters that came across his desk and the list of CIA agents that were left on someone's computer because they didn't sign off. Mike told him that three of those agents were murdered soon after you turned over their names. His head went down when he heard that and said how dumb he was to do this horrible thing and he was sorry for the shame he brought on his wife and daughter. Mike told him that he put a lot of shame on the FBI that one of their agents would be a spy for Russia, that is the worst part for us to live with, we trusted you and you abused that trust and caused some good men to be murdered because this beautiful looking girl would give you all the sex favors you wanted and as often as you were screwing you could never wear it out.

William was asked to come in one morning for an interview and in that interview, he was asked if he wanted a job working with their computer systems and photo department of the FBI. He went on and *told him that he had a very high-test score when he wanted to go to Michigan State and you had a full scholarship and if he didn't want to go back to school, they would like to hire him to work on their computer systems and find ways to make it safer. He said he didn't know and Mike said that he could offer him a starting salary of $65,000 dollars a year with hospitalization and retirement benefits and vacation. William asked him are you sure you want to do this I am only twenty years old. Mike told him he has a lot of promise working with us working for the department. We will have to get you a top-secret clearance first and you will have to be squeaky clean in order for you to get that clearance, do you have a problem with working for us.*

Mike asked him if he could start Monday and spend 90 days in their boot camp at Quantico, it won't be a picnic but if you graduate, we will welcome you back to start here at the FBI building. Monday morning you would come here at 5: am and catch the bus for Quantico. Whatever your wearing you can store until you come home. We will supply you all of your clothes for the entire 90 days. This is a big time in your life so please do good. They will teach you everything you will need to know to be a good field agent. You single handed caught the biggest spy in the history of this country. The full story hasn't been released yet and when it is you will be a national hero; you have what it takes to be a good agent. You have already proved to us that you have the ability to excel at this new position.

William spent the weekend getting himself ready for a hectic 90 days, he told his parents what has happened and they seemed like they were happy for him, he figured that because they didn't say they weren't. He called Pat's parents and told them about what he's been doing and how he caught the biggest spy in the history of our country and now that he is caught and behind bars they offered him a job to work for the FBI but first he has to go to Quantico for ninety days and return being a full-fledged agent. He apologized that he will miss their dinner meetings for three months or more. He could tell that was devastating for them and the mother was all choked up. They told him good luck and they would miss him and to please be careful and come home.

He packed all the things that he will need to shave brush his teeth and shower. He went to bed early and he set his alarm for 3: 45 and he got a ride to the FBI building from his mother and when he stepped out of the car, she sped off not one good luck or see you soon or even be careful. He knew some day they will need him and he will do unto them as they have done unto him, turnabout is fair play. He knew he was ready and he could take a lot of abuse. He knows that it will be tough but not as tough as the military boot camp would be, so it was time to go and he was ready both physically and mentally.

He stood outside headquarters with some other recruits that were older than him which would be to his advantage when a blue bus pulled up and a guy in black fatigues stepped off with his clip board in his hand and he asked them to form a line. He called out the list of names he had and with everyone present he told them to board the bus for their hour and a half ride to the base for their FBI boot camp. William was happy that he had some cereal this morning or he would have been starving. The ride was quiet and their leader told them they will be assigned a living quarter and then they will get a full supply of clothes and they will take them to their living quarters to drop off their clothes and come back outside righty away, when that was finished, they will be grouped outside and they will be marched to the chow hall a mile away. They didn't march that good but they will get better, you would be surprised how good they could get in a mile. William thought this was easy so far, he was only twenty and that would be a big help for him to get through this boot camp.

William could smell the food a long way out from the chow hall and he was starting to get hungry. They took their food trays out of the rack and started to enter the line. There was some SOS and some scrambled eggs. There were some muffins and some assortment of beagles and toppings. William loved everything and they were told that lunch will be light today because of some testing that will run through lunch time.

William thought that it isn't a good time to test anyone on their first day in boot camp after being up since 3:30 this morning. He knew he would be ok but he didn't know about the others, he made friends with a recruit name William Riordan he said he was from Wilmington Delaware and they were roommates, two to a room. There was nothing there but their beds a shower and two desks with a computers on each one. He was hoping that this Reardon guy will be ok because they were going to be roommates for the next ninety days.

They had to meet outside the living quarters rain or shine, ice or snow at 5:30 and stand for roll call and then they will go back in and get ready for the day and meet back outside at 7: 30 and march to the chow hall. It was the first bit of food they had since the day before at 5:30 fourteen hours ago. The next week was very physical and the second week simmered down a little then they had to spend the week at the gun range as well as getting a dose of tear gas. William did very well with his target shooting and he was able to field strip his guns and put them back together faster than anyone in the class. He was starting to make a name for himself as someone to keep up with and someone to beat.

They had personal interviews about their test and over all adaptation to the boot camp process. The person doing the interviewing had a folder of papers that he took out and started looking at them and congratulated William for his high-test scores and all of the testing with the guns they were using. You did very well in all of your physical testing. He told William that a lot of time now was going to be on crime investigation how to charge someone for arrest and all the duties that an FBI agent can expect to come in contact in. Over all he said that William will have a very successful career with the Bureau if he keeps this up, you're a natural and you have all it takes to be a good agent. You are very well rounded and that we don't see that much of that here at the school. He sticks out as someone to watch.

William felt real good after that interview and when they were all finished it was chow time and they marched all the way, in fact they marched everywhere they went. They had to be in bed at 8: o'clock so there is no excuse saying you're tired after nine hours sleep. One morning they were rustled out of bed at 5: o'clock and a truck pulled up and they were told to hop on and they were driven out in the woods twelve miles away and let off and they were given a knap sack that weighed forty pounds and they were told to hike back to the barracks as fast as they can, they were being timed and time is very important. You will be observed and you won't see us but we will see you. You must complete this test or you will fail your boot camp requirement. They couldn't make it any plainer than that and I can assure you that I wasn't going to fail anything. I was to determine to make something of myself and the FBI were willing to give me a chance. I was only twenty and I should be able to complete this test faster than they do and even break a few records in this march back to the barracks.

Before the truck left William had started a very brisk walk and he figured he could get back in less than three hours. He could hear the recruits behind him and he could hear the remarks they were making about him. Like is this guy superman and William had gotten himself into a tempo and he has pulled far away from the other recruits until he couldn't even hear them anymore. He reckoned he was doing better than a mile in twelve minutes. He feels real good and he wants to pick it up just a little more and finish soon then he thought. He recognized the barracks area and stepped off to give it a strong finish and he did there was someone there with a stop watch and they told him that he was fast. They said his time was 144 minutes and he did it with a forty-pound sack on his back. He was told that it could only be done by someone that is determined to do good in this session and make a name for himself. His folder was getting bigger by the day.

They gave him a cold bottle of gator aid and they told him he can go to his barracks or wait for his classmates to finish and go to·chow. William told them that he would wait with them, they will be along soon. It must have been almost an hour when they started coming in. They were in a mixed group and minutes apart from each other. William came to them and said he was glad to see them finish. They said that his time was so good superman couldn't even catch him. A lot of fellows in his group were good but William was the exception that stood out just like he is standing out in everything that he commits to in boot camp. With a month to go, class work was an important priority that will catch all the law breakers that want to harm this country. This is what it's all about and he was going to learn all they can show him and put that together with his common sense and solve anything he can come across.

When the boot camp was ending the twelve men were asked to vote on who stood out in their minds as being a leader that could be relied on, no matter what. It was announced on graduation day just before they handed out the diplomas. The asst. director came down from Washington for the ceremony and said that they have the name of the person that was selected by his class mates as being a leader and he can be counted on to come to anyone's aid, he unfolded the paper and said you have voted William Smith as that person. They sent an escort to where he was sitting and told him to come with him. William walked onto the stage and received his award. It was a gold FBI badge that very few agents will ever get and it will tell a lot of agents who you are when they see it. William knew that when you set your mind to do something you should be able to do it well and he proved it here in this boot camp tour that the FBI sends all its recruits to in order to be a FBI agent.

They applauded him with high whistles and cat calls with their approval of the award that they had unanimous voted for him. They came down on a bus and they will go back on a bus. No fanfare or kisses and hugs goodbyes It was Wednesday and they were given off till Monday to get caught up on some things that had to get handled before they report to work Monday.

William was going to get caught up on some lost sleep and relieve some of the tension that was always around them. He was definitely curious as to what he would be doing when he comes in Monday. He knew there was no use trying to figure out anything because he didn't have all their facts. His parents were the same and they were right back to treating him the way they always treated him, a lot of times treating his parents like the way they treat him might just wake them up but if it didn't at least he got some satisfaction in giving it back to them. They couldn't be bothered with William showing them how they are towards him, they have been unaffected by him to long to start taking an interest in him now, it's been going on too long to change their ways.

William being away for ninety days didn't change them one bit, they are cold blooded and they don't know how to be a loving touching parent. He doesn't know where this is going, he will wait and see. There doesn't seem to be any love in his parent's life, he knows that things with them won't improve. They really don't know that their son uncovered the largest spy ring that there has ever been in this country, single handed. He won't receive and recognition until after the trial and then they will be shocked to read about it when he was living with them and they never asked him what he does during the day when they are at work.

William had dinner with Pats parents Sunday and they treated him like a long-lost son. He told them how he caught this spy and how the FBI wanted him to become an agent and they sent him away for ninety days to learn how to be an agent. They asked him if it was hard and he replied that he passed, he was too modest to tell them everything else. He stayed as long as he could and he told them that he is expected to carry a gun at all times now. It was time to say goodbye now and holding and kissing Pats mother is very hard to do for William because holding her and kissing her was no different than how he felt about kissing Pat. When he held her and kissed her, she had a very strong body and he was hoping that she didn't suspect how he felt about her.

As soon as he gets some money together, he is going to move out of the asylum where he lives now before he turns into what they are. He figured he could do it in a year and he will stay away from his parents like they do him when he moves out, they haven't given any incentive to be any different. He is already making plans to move out when they are at work and they will probably not even know that he is missing, he is just there taking up space who they occasionally talk too. They couldn't imagine how his parents aren't all over him with all the love and affection that a parent could give their child. He knew that pats parents wish that Pat were alive and she could feel their love they had for her even now. Now that is the difference between two parents she is gone and deeply missed by anyone that knew her and if I can add I loved her so much that it hurts me every day and mostly at night.

He was given orders to report to Mike Todd's office Monday morning at 9: o'clock. He was a little nervous what he was going to say or ask of him. He walked up to his secretary's desk and said William Smith is here to see Mr. Todd. He must have heard his voice because he came running out of his office to see him. He shook his hand and told him to come in and take a seat. He said he spent Friday looking at his boot camp report and they loved you there. They even want you to be an instructor, but I put an end to that, you can do better working in the field with us. You are destoned to go far with the bureau. He asked me to work with a profilers and try to profile some real bad killers that are running lose around our country and I know if you put your mind to it you can catch them, I have all the faith in the world in you and after you showed us what you can do we will sit back and give you all the help that you ask for to succeed in this mission and solve some of these unsolved cases.

He told him to work with Miss York and see what you two can come up with. She is expecting you sometime this morning and she will go over all of her cases that are outstanding. He left for her office and he found it on a higher floor out of the way. When he got to her office and the sign read Ann York senior case studies. He walked in and there was this absolutely beautiful young lady not much older than him looking through some folders. He cleared his throat and she looked up at him and said you must be William. He smiled and said yes, I see by your wall plaque your Ann York, she held out her hand and said she was pleased to meet him, she has heard nothing but good stories about him and she is tickled that he is going to assist her in profiling some of these murderers. She told him by profiling they will close in a little on who these murderers are and maybe even catch them soon before they can murder someone else. We are not under a deal line but us two could speed up a conclusion in some of these cases.

William told her that he was looking forward to reviewing these case files and finding the makeup of these murderers. He told her that if it's us two against them, they don't have a chance, she thought that was funny and she will soon find out what he meant by that. This is only their first meeting and she will see him in action soon and how he will uncover clues to solve some of these crimes. He asked her if there was one case that interest her the most and she said it was the strangle cases in Boston. She told him that all of the victims were women. He asked her where all the files were and she asked him to follow her to the meeting room where she has them spread out on the large meeting room table. On the wall was a six-foot square cork board that can be used as a visual post board for quick comparison and it will come in handy for them to post all of their notes for them to see in a glance rather to look through the boxes all the time.

William asked her where was she at with this case and she said she just started a week or so ago. There were eight boxes stacked on the floor, he started going through the top box that he would call x1 and he asked Ann to sit with him and review every single thing that was in the box and to compile a composite of the room she was killed in. They made up 5x7 cards that they would write down points of interest, it took about a week and then they reviewed what facts there were to review.

Ann was excited to be working with such a knowledgeable person like William and she looked forward coming to work every day and being with him and like most women she covered it up for some stupid reason instead of just doing what's natural its easier that way, I guess she didn't feel right just now about showing her feelings just like girls do sometimes but sooner or later it will come out and she won't be able to cover it up any more and it will be harder for her to explain how she feels about him.

Now it time to go over their work that they agreed were points of interest. William pointed out to Ann that the victim was always a female in her thirties, murdered in her home, in their bedroom with no signs of struggle almost like she wanted him there, but not for sex either, for some other reason. He told her that he thinks that it was a man because women don't strangle people by choking them to death with a scarf. They might shoot them or stab them or even poison them but not choking them.

She was strangled with a silk scarf and then she was made comfortable like he cared for her. There was no note and the apartment door was locked when the door was pulled shut. She had the day off and she gave the reason to her employer that she had to get some things fixed at the apartment. The report shows that the maintenance people in that building had accounted for every moment of their day, they were squeaky clean so that is one thing out of the way. So, if they are clean then there must someone else that can go there and no one would give a second look at. It would be almost like he is expect to be there.

He told Ann lets post them up on the bulletin board. So, we can look at them fast and get what we're looking for fast. Speed is of the essence we want to catch this guy before he decides to come off break and start up. He is a male because women don't kill like that and usually women don't kill women. William didn't know it but Ann was called in and she was asked how was it going with William, she sat quietly for a second and she said that when he gets done reviewing this case, he will be able to give her the murderers name. Mike asked if that was possible and she said anything is possible with him, he is a genius. Mike asked her how was it working with a genius and she said she loved every moment of it, he doesn't miss anything. He asked her if she is falling for this guy and she said it would be hard not to. He is very considerate of my feelings and my opinions and he shows me all the respect that any good and kind hatred man could give a woman and she isn't surprised that he caught our agent selling secrets to the Russians, they never had a chance not with him looking over the scene.

Mike told her that he was happy that they get along so well and that you two will solve this case he was very confident of that. He told her that they have the entire bureau at their disposal. She felt good leaving his office and headed back to William that was heavy into box three. It had the same findings with no variations at all. He was very precise in these murders of always being a women and always choked to death and always in an apartment. He asked Ann why an apartment and why are they out of work that day of their deaths. Ann said that it sounds like they were expecting someone to call on them, he said that is very possible but these are not sex crimes and it looks like they stayed home waiting for him like she knew when he was coming and there no defensive marks or bruises on any of them, nothing could be so calm before they were murdered then they appear there lying on the bed with a scarf around their throats.

William took box seven and made sure that it was not boring and he took his time knowing that there is a clue here and that every case had its differences and it was William's job to spot them. He saw that this murder victim was different in that she was strangled by a telephone wire and he left it around her neck, this was going to be a fatal mistake that William knew he would final do. He told Ann we got him he finally made a huge mistake, that got her attention that finally we are getting somewhere, He showed her that all of his murders were by some form of light but strong materials such as a scarf and this one was by a telephone wire. He said that this guy is a repair man going to the residence probably on an appointment to repair their phones or something in their house, he went there on an appointment that why they took off from work and all we have to do is to take it from there and with a few phone calls we should be able to arrest him and put this file to rest.

He asked Ann what would a person need repairing that they would have to take off the day to meet them. Ann said the telephone or the tv cable or washing machine or maybe a computer but it would have to be inside and they had to be there to let him in. It could have been anyone of them and William said that he wants to contact the phone company and go over the dates that these girls were murdered that he had on a 3x5 card. They had to go through all of the telephone company service call logs to see if they could find something. It took a while but they did find some service calls to those addresses on those days those women were murdered, they were all the same repair man whose name is name Carmine Alexander and he lived in the city of Boston. He told Ann that they will have to turn this over to Mike and see what he has to say. It doesn't hurt to have another set of eyes for an opinion.

He was amazed how they pieced all of this together and came up with a name who in all likelihood is the murderer. He always left his home for work by 7: o'clock that gave them time to search his residence. They didn't find anything but a few scarfs but they were in his underwear draw, that was really not evidence. He told Ann that they weren't gone to find anything in his home that he would use to murder someone in all likely hood it would be in his service van. William wanted the phone wire that was used to kill X6 and it took a few days and they met with Mike and said that if they follow this guy around until he kills another woman it would be sad. He recommended to Mike that they bring him in for questioning and show him the wire that he used to kill X6

Mike thought they didn't have anything to lose and said that he wanted him and Ann to go up there and arrest him first thing in the morning They caught the Bureau Jet and was in Boston by 7: o'clock and they arrested him just as he had pulled into his parking spot just before he went in for work at the service building. They didn't expect any struggle because they profiled him to be very dainty and soft spoken and at first impression, he was all that.

They put him on the Bureau plane and they were in Washington by lunch. They took him to an interview room cuffed and asked him to take a seat. He was left there for the longest time and then William and Ann came in the room and they had a brown envelope with some things in it. William pulled out the pictures of the murdered girls with the telephone wire and scarfs still around their necks and see if he had any response to these pictures or play dumb. They think it will shock him into admitting to them that he was the murderer

William held it for him to see for a long time and he asked Carmine if he ever saw her before. He was visually shaken when William told him that she was someone's daughter and her parents were never going to see her again. That worked and now William was going to show him the cord that was used and when he did, he said he had seen enough. He said he was sorry for causing people so much pain. Ann asked him how many of these girls did he murder and he said eight.

Mike was behind the glass partition and was in shock how William and Ann solved this case and now have this guy behind bars and not killing anyone else again. He knew William was good but not that good; this will make every newspaper in the country by night time that the FBI caught the Boston murderer and the women in Boston can relax he is behind bars.

He would have to be extradited back to Boston for him to go on trial, the news about his capture was all over the news 24/7 for weeks. Mike called William and Ann in and he told them that they did a great job and that William has to attend the trial of Alex Gaulman even though he has already pled guilty and he was going to be sentenced tomorrow by the judge because he waived a jury trial to spare his wife and daughter from anymore smearing of them by the news media. Mike told them that when this is all over William and Ann will be honored properly so by the Bureau for solving the strangler murder cases. They went back to the meeting room and they had all the case boxes put in the basement for safe keeping. They sealed them so to keep out any moisture that could age the papers prematurely.

Ann was so in love with William that she couldn't be away from him without thinking of him, even when she was home, she would think of him and she would often fantasize about him and yet she didn't tell him or even give him a hint of how she felt about him. She was hoping that he might ask her out soon so he can get the vibes of how she feels about him. She had a lot to offer him and she wondered why he wasn't making any advancements towards her and she would fold like a table napkin.

4

Ann asked William if he felt like celebrating this arrest and he asked what did she had in mind and she thought dinner out somewhere and he said he was game. She said let's go to the restaurant in the Ritz hotel for a seafood and steak dinner. He told her that was a perfect choice and asked her what time does she want him to meet her there. Well She was knocked for a loop on that one but didn't let on visually that it bothered her, but it did. She asked him if seven was alright with him and he said he would be there.

They worked that whole day looking over a long list of serial type killings and they couldn't make up their minds where to start. They both went thought the real old one's that would be hard to solve and Ann agreed, so they started back to the ones that were less than five years old and they spent the rest of the day reviewing some of those files. Ann wants any way she could touch him like when they might be exchanging folders something like that, just to feel how warm he is.

Ann wasn't too happy about meeting William at the Ritz for dinner, he wasn't going to pick her up at her apartment he was going to meet her at the restaurant. This was a first for her going out on a date that she had to meet the person at the place they agreed on. She didn't form any opinions because she knows him from working with him, so there must be a good reason why he wants to meet her at the restaurant and that in time it will surface.

She liked him enough and she decided to play the hand and see where it goes. She wore the best dress she had and she wore nylons and a little Shaw to throw over her shoulders if it were too cold in the restaurant with her bare shoulders exposed. You know when you're having dinner in these restaurants all the women have on something over their shoulders to keep the chill off. He got there before her and he waited in the lobby and she was running a few minutes late that told William that she maybe she wanted to send him a message. William thought she was trained never be late for anything. She said she was sorry for being late and he told her that they gave their table to someone else and she said they couldn't have and William said they did and they have to go somewhere else because they won't have a table ready for two for two hours. Now little did she know that William wanted to teach Ann a lesson one she might never forget. She just stood there dumbfounded how this could be happening especially on their first date and she ruined what might have been a great evening and celebrate solving this very big unsolved murder case. She could have cried but that would have sent the wrong picture of maybe a sign of weakness that she knows she will lose him that easy.

She asked him where can they go and he said he would leave it up to her. She said harshly, hell I don't know you left this dinner up to me and look what I did and he told her to slow down and what happened is in the past lets solve where to eat and what she would fancy to eat. William said let's get a pizza to go and she was so worked up she said, "go where." He said he would leave it up to her and there you go again leaving it up to me again I would think by now that you might be leaving it up to you and she said ok let's go to my place, he told her that he was glad about her choice because he was still living with his parents until he can save enough to move out. She started laughing about how the evening was progressing and how their big fancy meal was going to be a pizza at her place. She said that they make a great pizza near her apartment and he said let's go there and he would follow her. It was about a ten-minute drive and William ran in to Pizzeria and place the order for a medium pizza and was back out in ten minutes. He followed her to her apartment and parked underground and they took the elevator to the tenth floor and she ran to open the door because she knew the pizza was very hot. She wasn't expecting company so she hopes it looks clean or he might think that she lives in a dirty apartment.

William put the pizza on the table and she got some dishes and she said she felt funny wearing a dress like she had on that was fit for the Ritz and not eating pizza in. He told her to take it off and she started laughing again how innocent some of the things that come out of his mouth and she was howling all the way back to her bedroom to change, she said she would be right back and she came back in a bathrobe and William had a big laugh about her changing into a bathrobe and now he is in a suit.

Now she laughed and she told him to take it off like he told her, well they both were howling with laughter and it made the rest of the night a good date night. He took it off and he sat right there in his shorts. She was howling about also what they have just done and she could see the comedy in it. She got the glasses and put some ice in them and now the celebration has begun. She said she would never be late again for any reservations meeting or anything else that they are together in, look at the trouble I have caused us on our first date he smiled and told her it was to funny not to enjoy and he got as big a laugh out of it as she did.

William said he was happy to be with her other than at work and she asked him if he really meant that and he said he was looking forward to this night for a long time. He told her you are sitting with me in your bath robe eating pizza and I am in my shorts, that's one for the books. They laughed a lot and William said he should be going now tomorrow is another day and tonight was a date gone wrong but we did hit it off real well. She said she was sorry again and little did she know that William wanted to teach her a lesson and this first date was perfect; she will never know what happened and she will never be late again.

She walked him to the door and he said goodnight and left, if she was expecting something to happen, it didn't and now she will have to spend some time wondering if they are right for each other. She was wondering why he didn't to see what was under her robe and all he had to do was to undue the belt and see that she was willing and able to make his night. She thought that she would either want to do it again or they will just be good working buddies, he was going to leave it up to her like he always does only this she was going to make the fatal move on him where he will have to be a man of walk away. She loves him too much to let him get away from her.

At the office Ann tried to act like nothing was wrong but she wasn't doing a very good job of it. She fumbled over everything and she looked lost, Finally, William asked her what is wrong and she told him that she expected something different from eating pizza in my bathrobe and you never even kissed me goodnight am I that such a turn off don't I have any appeal to you, you had me that night and you left me barely saying goodnight. He said that he didn't feel the vibes coming from her, a man likes to know where he stands on a date and you made it very clear that you couldn't even show up early and give a good impression of how you felt, he told her that being late is no excuse. She apologized again and said she would make it up to him someday. He wanted her to squirm a little before he would ever go out with her again. She broke the code, never to be late for anything but boy did she have the hots for him and he kinda knew it and he is putting her through the ringer and see how she would hang in there through over troubled waters.

There were quite a few cases to pick from but they picked the one that the victims were shot in their car parked along the curb on a dark street, usually through the car window on the street in Manhattan and Brooklyn. The victims were always young couples making out in their cars. I guess if you live in the city a dark street is just as good as lovers lane. The killer would come up to the window and tap on the glass with his revolver and when they looked at the window, they were shot through the window in the face neck or heart.

The police were clueless and it always ran into a dead end with no bullet casements because he used a revolver. By the time the police came on the scene thirty minutes had elapsed and the killer was far away. There was no motive and so far, there have been five murders. One of the victims survived and couldn't recall much or even seeing anything except the flash from the nozzle that blinder her from seeing the person with the gun. Once he startled them and they looked up he shot them, this one victim a young lady survived and she is lucky to be alive, she knows it and is willing to help all she can. Even surviving she won't be any help to them, there wasn't enough light to see anything.

It took a couple of days before they received the case boxes; and again, they labeled each case as X1 and so on. The first victim didn't have anywhere to go so they parked on a dark street four blocks from their house in Brooklyn. The car was parked at the curb on the right-hand side of a one-way street, if he walked the same way the cars were parked, he would never have been seen, that would be he would have to be walking from the rear of their car to the front.

They would have had to be on the lookout for people walking on the sidewalk and they were too busy for that, like someone taking their dog for a walk, something like that. The shootings were always between 10: and 11: o'clock. None of the five murders were committed on a Saturday, mostly a week night and one on a Sunday. The weather was good and not raining the shooter picked the time and day to kill these poor people.

William said he was in his early thirties and he lived by himself in an apartment and he didn't have to answer to anyone. He was somewhat religious and more likely he was Jewish no taller than 5ft -5in and slightly stocky build and wants recognition from someone, probably someone close to him. How he figured he was

Jewish was just a hunch. Usually Jewish people don't have a record of being a serial killer, so why that call.

They went through X1 looking for the slightest clue and they didn't find one. They went on to X2 and spent days on that one and they were single and also making out in their car on a dark street that was one way and they were shot from the sidewalk part of the street and he shot them both in the face and heart right through the car window. Someone did report some shot fired but that was all there was. It happened on a week day at the same time between 10 and 11 o'clock. The killer left the scene and in fifteen seconds he was gone. It was the same 38 revolver and at least four shots were fired. There was another shooting on another one-way street, now these murders were starting to be predictable and that is going to make it easy to catch him.

It was time to look at X3 and the first thing that they noticed was that these shootings took place within ten blocks of each other, there was a wittiness that said they saw a person walking quickly away from the scene not your typical walk but one where they were in a hurry. William looked up the person who said he saw someone walking quickly away and placed a call to him and he asked him if they can talk to him about what he saw that night about the couple that was shot in their car. He said he was open to a meeting and William asked him if he would mind coming to the station for a chat, he said he would be glad to. William knew who he was and what he did for a living and where he lived and how come he was out that night, which was nice to have that information when you are making an interview on someone that might be a wittiness. They met in a Brooklyn police station and Ann as well was with him and the wittiness came right on time and they went back to an out of a way meeting room and William introduced Ann first and then himself, they told him that they were with the profiling department of the FBI out of Washington and they just want to stimulate his brain for more information if he didn't mind. He has had some time to go over what he saw that night and maybe he can add something to what he told the police.

He wasn't nervous because he didn't have anything to be nervous about. William asked him what was he doing out that late at night on a dark one-way street. He said he was walking his dog Puddles he was a Scottie dog and he has a routine like we have and I enjoyed walking with him there was never a dull moment with Puddles.

"Is he smart and does he do whatever you tell him to do?"

"In most cases he does and to answer your question I think he is very smart and I see it every day."

"Did you see the person fire the two shots in the car?"

"No, I didn't but I did see a person walking rather quickly away from what I know now to be the murder scene and he definitely didn't walk normally, he was acting very strange and very suspicious."

"Was he smoking a cigarette?"

"No, he wasn't smoking, but he was definitely trying to get away from something and he was looking over his shoulder a lot."

"What did he do that would make you believe that he might be the killer?"

"It was the way he kept looking over his shoulder, it just didn't look normal. You can tell when a person is just walking fast or trying to get away from somewhere fast, that was him to the tee. I could tell by the way he was moving his legs when he walked that he wasn't athletic, you can tell an athlete the way they walk or run."

"So, you positively believe that he is the murderer."

"I have no doubt in my mind about it at all and you would too if you saw what I saw."

"Ann told him that he is very confident about this."

"Yes, I am and I hope you can catch him before he does it again."

This wittiness was very sure that he saw the murderer and how did the police not see that in him when they were questioning him William told him if they are successful checking this thing out, they will catch him. William told him because his dog was with him that night, he would like to meet him and let his Scottie dog have a sniff around, it can't hurt. Sal said it been around six months and there were a lot of rain storms that have come and gone, there wouldn't be much hope in finding a scent of him. Again, Ann said it was a long shot but one worth taking. They met that night and walked to where the car was parked from the opposite end of the street. That morning William had a couple of parking spaces blocked off so there could be no doubt about the right space the car was parked in. William had Sal sit his dog right where the shooting took place and he had him sniff around and he just sat there and out of nowhere he started walking down the street where Sal saw the suspect walking. Puddles the Scottie finally stopped about five blocks away in front of an apartment house and sat at the front door. He looked at Ann and said can you believe this dog sitting at the door of this high rise apartment building, for what and the owner of the dog said that puddles smells something and you can bet on it now. William told Ann that he thinks that maybe the murderer lives there and he wants to find that out or not so let's put our heads together and see what we come up with.

They decided to speak to the fire chief spoke to the fire chief and he told him that they are looking for someone that has made a very serious crime and asked him if they could have a fire drill, they might just be able to spot him. The fire chief went along with and thought that was a good idea so they sent out a couple of fire security vehicles and went inside the apartment building and rang the fire alarm. It took a couple of minutes and they started flowing out of the building and Sal was looking at everyone that came out of the building when he spotted the guy, he saw walking quickly down the street. Now

William asked the fire security people to ask everyone returning for their names and what apartment they live in. this information will be a big help in finding out who this guy is and they can be very discreet about it and look a little deeper into his life for sure it will be very enlightening.

They photographed everyone that came out of the building including our friend and now they know his name and what apartment he lived in and a picture, all this from a little Scottie dog that has the greatest nose for sniffing anything even six months old and he can still smell it. They carefully went through the list of names and they concluded his name is Samuel Schreiber a pharmacy assistant at a local pharmacy. Now it is time to check him out and unfortunately there was another murder so William asked the wittiness with the Scottie dog if he could use him again. Sal asked where could they meet and William said at his place, he told them he would be outside waiting. The shooting scene is a good ten blocks away and William drove to Sal's place and picked him up They drove to the murder scene and they stood there in the spot the shooting took place only a few days ago.

Sal let Puddles snoop around and finally he started walking down the street for the longest time until he came to the same apartment house that he stopped at before. Ann and William were in complete shock and said they will have to get to the bottom of this. It was a long walk to the car but William thought it was good exercise. Now they have the murderer and they can't prove it so they started an around the clock stake out and try and catch him at something. If they don't get him doing anything soon, they were going to have to get a search warrant and go through his entire apartment and storage area and find something no matter how small it is. He is too calculated to be caught; he will have to slip up. Ann couldn't get over how Sal's Scottie dog traced him all the way back from the murder scene to his apartment building twice and to them that is a lot of proof but not enough to convict him of murder.

The manager at the pharmacy was interviewed and when he was asked about Samuel and said he was kind and has nothing but some good reviews. William asked him if he could read his last six review, the manager hesitated for a second and said he would have to put it to the human resources manager. William told him he would wait if he can contact him right away. His reply was you want me to call him now and William said, right now if you don't mind. This is not an Easter egg hunt this is for the real thing. He spoke to the Human Resources manager and he handed the phone to William and William told him that they were investigating a case in which they want to know more about one of their employees named Samuel Schreiber so I asked to read his last six reviews there might be something there that can help them.

He told William what will happen if I should deny you this, William told him that he would go to the district attorney and get a warrant to make you show us these reviews while we close down all your pharmacies until we get the reviews and go over them which could take a month. He asked William to put the store manager back on the line and he told William that he would have to get them out of the filing cabinet and it will take a few minutes. He left the room and Ann asked him what did he hope to learn from these employee reviews. He told her that they might reveal something in his remarks when he has to sign off after he read them, or his manager might have something to say or add that we would pick up on right away either way we need to see them and we can evaluate the review from our stand point and see if the real Samuel is hiding in some folder in a steel filing cabinet.

The manager dropped them on the table and started to walk out of the room when William lost it and he was pissed off at this son of a bitch was acting like we did something wrong. William told him that he would have done more harm if he would have refused to hand over these files and you can't justify the attitude you are showing us and if there is any way they can file a federal charge against him for not cooperating in a federal crime investigation.

They started looking at them from when they started giving the employee reviews. His manager wrote that Samuel didn't like to make a mistake and he would go to any means to rectify it. They always said he was a good worker and when he was asked if he would ever get married, he said that he hasn't met the right woman yet. Now the next to the last report Samuel said that his life was boring and when asked how is that possible he said that he just goes out for a walk at night for something to do, it's makes him feel good and it is good for his mind.

Now the last report that was a few months ago he said he was happy to be working for the pharmacy and not out there looking for something to do. Ann said that it wasn't like reading the history of one's life because his reviews were job related and you could detect a bit of unhappiness in his reports. They gave them back to the manager Michael and told him that he ought to be ashamed of himself for acting like an ass and you make me sick and they walked out before he really cursed him out but not before they warned the manager not to say anything to Samuel about this.

Ann asked what's next and William said we have to search his apartment and plant a mini camera in a couple of places and see what this guy is doing. It wasn't hard to get permission to break in his apartment and plant a few cameras. It took some tall talking but they did get permission to enter his apartment just after he left for work and they searched everywhere and they found a letter that he was going to post to the editor of daily Mirror and he was taunting them that he is the guy they were looking for and number five will be coming soon, son of a gun. William was convinced that he is the murderer and they will arrest him the next night he starts off on one of his walks. They had 24/7 police stake outs and they knew that it was a matter of time before the urge to shoot someone was stronger than to stay at home.

Ann and William took some rooms in an apartment on Lexington ave. just to be ready when they will need to be close and ready to go. Ann was staying by herself at night while William was out riding with some of the stake out guys. Ann wasn't getting any of William's attention so she started dressing different and she had her hair cut short, now that really made her look a lot better, it didn't take long for the guys to start looking at her, all except William the one that she wanted to notice her. He was letting on that she was just another girl. They ate lunch out together almost every day and he was working very hard looking for an apartment in DC rather than buy a house and get transferred at a moment's notice at least that was a plan and probably a good one for his position that he has with the FBI.

Finally, Samuel went out one evening and William and Ann followed him as he turned down this very dark street and that's when William said he had enough and walked up to him and told him that they weren't going to let him commit number five. He was very quiet and when they searched him, he said that they don't have any proof that he was the shooter and William said that he just gave them the proof by what he just said that he was the shooter.

We never called him a shooter. You can't pin that stuff on him, he doesn't own a gun and Ann said they never said he did. You are certainly being very defensive in your remarks to us They took him down to the station and William and Ann sat with him in a room used for questioning prisoners. William asked Samuel if he could explain this letter satisfactorily, and if he can he would let him go and that would be the end of it, is that sound fair to you, it does to us.

He took the letter from the folder and laid it in front of him and he asked him to read it out loud, he said that wasn't his letter and Ann said we never said it was. William said that if he doesn't read the letter out loud, he would. He still refused by asking where could you have found such a letter and William said in your apartment a few days ago when we had a search warrant to go through his apartment. Then he showed him the pictures of his dead victims with the bullet holes in their faces with their mouths open sucking the last bit of air they could suck in before they died from your gun shots wounds, that you took it on your own to murder innocent people who were only just getting started in life and you took all that away from them and in the most painful way you could.

He just sat there quiet and William told him that he can lift that terrible weight from his shoulders because we Gotcha and you can't hide anymore we have you without a doubt. William told him he has been dragging this guilt around for a few years now and it's about time that you get it off of your shoulders. Tell us that you did these murders and free yourself from carrying this awful burden of what you did you will feel a hundred percent better after you confess. He said he was only trying to please his father who looked down on him for only being a Pharmacist assistant.

Ann wanted to know how killing eight innocent people would have your father give you the respect that you dearly needed from him. He said he knows now that it was wrong and he wanted to set a good example at work. They took video's and taped every word and he would be arraigned before a judge in two days but now he is under arrest for the murders of eight people and the shame you have brought on your family will never go away. I don't think your father will be happy with you going on a killing spree just to please him. One thing for sure you picked the wrong way to please someone, murdering innocent people is not the right way and if you don't get the death sentence you will live a lot of sleepless nights over and over until you start to lose your mind.

He told William that he doesn't want to go on trial and be a public spectacle he will plead guilty be sentenced by a judge, no jury and no over blown news coverage. William told him that it will be up to the judge to decide that. He stood and told them that it's hard to believe that a little old Scottie dog found me out and William said it was true and you folded like a cheap suit when he identified you. You fooled a lot of people but you never fooled us, we were determined to catch you and the Scottie dog made it easy. He turned and walked away with his jailer that he will be spending a lot of time with. They checked out of their apartments and headed back to Washington and clean up some of the boxes they left behind.

The trial didn't come up for months but when it did, he was found guilty of all eight murders and was sentenced to eight life sentences. They had another award ceremony in which Ann and William were given the highest recognition that an FBI agent could ever receive and that was Federal Bureau Medal of Honor. That was quite an honor and they had a gala reception for all of the agents that worked in the headquarters building. Ann told William that she would like him to have their own ceremony that might be more intimate if you get my drift. He told her that he got her drift but is she sure she wants this and she said with all her heart.

She asked him to bring a pizza over to her apartment tomorrow evening and they have their own party. It was Saturday and William went for a walk in the park and he started running and he ran for an hour, he was sweating but he felt good. He got back to his apartment and took a shower and put on some casual clothes that included shorts and watched a little golf and walked to Ann's apartment that wasn't that far away. He got there about fifteen minutes early and Ann had on a nice outfit and she too was also wearing shorts. Her legs looked divine and so did the rest of her; he didn't know what he wanted more, her or the pizza. William knew that she was turning down a lot of requests for dinner, ballgames, movies and things like that; she turned every one of them down unbeknownst to William.

William asked her why him, he is probably nothing but a bore ass and she said she liked bore asses. The pizza was still nice and hot and they each had two slices. The radio was playing some nice music and she reached for his hand and they slow danced to the summer of 42. She was pressing against him so tightly he thought she was going to pass right through him. She was giving all the signs that she was in heat so William reached down her shorts and felt her all over and she said, "I guess this is it," I've been waiting to be alone with you for months. This was as good as time as any; you are a hard person to catch alone. He told her she got him alone; it wasn't that hard was it? "Her reply was not right now but I plan on it getting hard."

There wasn't any doubt in his mind she was ready for him, she put it in for him like any nice girl would and she told him she loved him and this is what she wanted to do with him for the longest time. He told her that they didn't take that much time off and he said that we should try and get together as much as they can. She said that is what she wanted to hear. They went at it again only this time they went at it a lot longer. She had some great moves and she enjoyed it and him, and does he think her to be crazy because she told him she loved him. He said no because that was how she felt and she wanted to tell him from her heart. She asked him if he could ever love her and he said it will be easy to love her and he missed her as much as she missed him, he said I felt you the whole time you were near me. I am very happy that you were the aggressor and came after me because you loved me and you couldn't control your feelings, love is a very hard thing to hide and thank God you weren't good at it.

She asked him if he could do it to her one more time and he said he might need a little coaxing she asked him to go and wash and come right back to her. She heard the water running and when William got back in bed, she was all over him kissing him until she asked him if she had coaxed him enough. He rolled over on top of her and she was howling like a wolf. They finished and she asked him to stay the night so he can bang her in the morning. He said that was perfect and they slept till 9: o'clock and she had his Johnson in her hand stroking him to get hard and give her a good morning wake up. She loved it and didn't want it to stop, they both saw the clock and it was near lunch time.

They both showered and Ann made some sausage and eggs and they ate out on her little balcony and it was perfect. William took her hand and he told her that he loved her as well. That really chocked her up and she took a couple of gulps and shook it off, she couldn't believe that he just told her he loved her. She asked him would it be better living in separate apartments or move in and save all that unnecessary spending when we can be together all the time. He told her by living together they will find out how much they really love each other. She asked him does he want to move in with her or her move in with him. He told her she had the better address, how about I move in with you; I don't have that much furniture and nowhere as nice as yours.

Ann told him she has the one piece of furniture that they would need the most and I know what that is. William got some guys from work and they moved him the following Saturday morning. They had pizzas delivered and some beer and they sat around talking about the two big cases they solved. William told them it comes down to reviewing the evidence and try to put the pieces together, the ones you see and don't see. He told them that both cases were solved easily when they got close to the end. They left before 3: o'clock and William had Ann in the sack in no time, he gave her a good screwing and she told him how much she loved him the whole time. And he didn't have any doubt about whether she meant it or not. William asked her if she was on the pill and she said she went on it the first time he touched her hand, she also said that she knew he would eventually be touching her everywhere else that she would want him to take her to bed, it took you a while but we finally got there.

They packed up all the case boxes and put on every one of them solved and the date, this was when they went back to work Monday and they started right back in reviewing some unsolved serial murders, there was one that was going to be difficult and would require some help from the newspapers. There were about a half dozen cases where there were girls traveling out of Canada going to school in America and never reached their destination, nor did their cars, either of which their cars and bodies were never discovered. It took a while but Ann and I got the VIN# from the parent's records and in some cases their insurance companies. It took almost a month but now that they have them, they contacted shipping companies and asked to see their manifest as far back as three years ago. They picked up about two boxes of manifests and sat day after day looking for these cars on a shipping list.

They found some records of these Canadian cars they were being sold out of the country to a receiving company in South America. There was no way they weren't going to let that go unchecked. Ann and William signed out for the company jet and flew into Rio de Janeiro and they checked into a nice ocean front high-rise hotel and got a beautiful view of the ocean and miles of small mountains that were all over the ocean that you could see for miles. They found the name of the person that received the cars from the shipping manifest over a period of time and got a cab ride to the used car lot. It was customary to tell the country that you would be working there in and ask for their support if they would need any. They gave the dates when they would be coming and leaving and who you might be seeing. Mr. Bandarez was the person they wanted to talk to and luckily enough he was in when they got to his car lot. They introduced themselves and they told him that they were tracking down some cars that he bought from someone in the States. He asked them what state are you talking about I buy from a lot of people in a lot of states, do you know what state you want me to look up.

They told him that they weren't sure; they were hoping he could tell them. He looked for the longest time and said that all four of the cars they have records of were picked up in Dayton Ohio. They asked him if he knew who sold him the cars and he said it was from a person that called his business the Dayton Motor Works. Who did you make your check out to and he said the Dayton Motor Works? They pressed him for a name and he said the person was always avoiding giving his name. He was very cagey and hard to deal with, he was strictly business, He would sell the cars cheap to me and that was good enough for him. I could over look his lousy attitude, only for the money. I never dreamt that there would be something wrong with buying those cars, I can assure you he is contemptable and a very bad business man to boot.

Ann thanked him for his help and all the information he gave them on where the cars came from that will be a great place to start our investigation. William was ecstatic in getting all this information about the missing cars and now comes the hardest part in finding the bodies that go with the cars, something that they weren't anxious to find. It appears that Dayton would be the next stop but first they wanted to spend the day on their famous beaches and taste the local food and watch the bathers and get a little sun. They deserve that the way they work with endless hours and chasing after leads that don't always pan out. They rented a cabana and had a ball and they strolled along the beach and right through the topless beach and there were some very fine sets of boobs to see as far as the eye could see and there were some boobs that needed some tops on them. They got a little sun and had dinner out on the hotel veranda and watched the sun go down and they had the best surf and turf they had to offer. They sat there and were happy that they didn't come to any dead ends and they will now devote their attention to Dayton Ohio. When they got back to the room Ann took her clothes off and tantalized William until he carried her to bed and gave her what she wanted and for as long as she wanted it for. William could see that he and Ann were getting very attached just like he did with Pat and they will in time become inseparable.

They put themselves on a 7: o'clock wakeup call and Ann asked William if he could do her one more time before they left. She didn't have to talk him unto it not with that body standing naked in front of him. He gave her what some girls want most and she shook for the longest time and then he put it inside her and she shook some more. She told him that turnabout is fair play and commenced to do it all to him. She asked him if he liked it and he said what was there not to like. He asked her how did she like it and she said it was the best. They checked out and they were both very contented with each other and the ways they had in satisfying each other it was turning out to be a picture book relationship and they will notice them at work and never have any doubt about how they feel about each other and everyone will know it because that is how the work place is.

Their jet was running when they got to the hanger where it was under guard 24/7 the captain came out to greet them and they told him that they would like to go to Dayton Ohio; he said he would have to file a flight plan and for them to board he would be right back and when he is through with that we can get out of here. Ann was noticeably hanging on to William there was no doubt they were having sex because no one can be that cozy if they weren't getting laid. Mind you William and Ann were searching for information the other investigators never dreamt to look at. The bureau gave them all the help they would need to catch these murderers, including the use of the bureau's airplane and they were getting closer to catching this murderer.

The flight to Dayton was a little long but they threw a blanket over each other and put their faces together and slept for five straight hours. They woke refreshed and talked about what they were going to do to find out where these cars came from. They knew they had to find the Dayton Motor Works first and go from there. They had a great landing and they were dropped off at the charter arrival lounge and their plane was taken to a safe hanger for safe keeping. It was late in the afternoon, too late to get started so they got a room in the Hyatt and they ate in the dining room and prepared for the next day's work. William told Ann that they will have to be really on the ball to catch this murderer and if they are willing to put out the effort, they will get another case resolved.

The first thing in the morning after breakfast they went looking for a used car dealer that goes by the name of Dayton Motor Works. It took two hours to find out that no such car dealer ship exists. William said that couldn't be so, they contacted every bank and identified themselves and told them that they were looking for an account under the name Dayton Motor Works. There were twenty-six on the list and twenty of them said there were none and with six to go things were looking slim. Finally, the Dayton trust co said they have an account under that name but it hasn't had any activity for over a year now. William told them that they would need all the information on that account and he was told he would have to have a court order. He called Washington and it was faxed to them in less than twenty-four hours.

This time they went to the bank and asked to see the branch manager and they were taken to his office right away. The manager greeted them and asked them how can he help them and they gave him a copy of the court order to release any and all information to them about Dayton Motor Works. He asked his secretary to come in to his office and when she did, he told her to bring to him all of the file papers we have on this account. They chatted for a while and in walked the secretary and handed the branch manager the folder he asked her to get. He asked William if he could make him a copy of the papers in the folder. William said it would be alright with them and did he mind if Ann goes with the person to the copy machine and give her a hand, he would feel better overseeing the copying this way there can be no doubt of the authenticity, I think the branch manager knew that this is something serious without asking what was this all about and he told William to feel free to go with his secretary to the copy machine, that he completely understands the procedure.

The branch manager said the person doing the copying is capable of doing the copying. William told him that was probably true and you just told me few minutes ago that you completely understood and he was sorry if he has given the wrong impression to us. Never the less Ann would still go along and if he knew how serious this is he might decide to get off of his high horse, unless you wish to make an issue out of it like your bank seems to want do, he told the manager that he doesn't need to be on the wrong side of the law because they will do whatever it takes to get all the information about Dayton Motor Works that they can get their hands on, his response was no please go ahead. It took only a few minutes and when Ann returned William was asking how much money was deposited in this account or withdrawn. He went on his computer and said his deposits were done in person at the bank and his withdraws were also done the same way, in person. He asked him is there any way you have any surveillance tapes of the day of the deposit or the withdraws. He picked up his phone and asked the security chief to come to his office right away. Now this guy is starting to get on the stick and help out a little.

He must have ran because he was out of breath and asked the branch manager how he could help. He asked him could he produce the surveillance film on these dates and he held the list of dates for a few seconds and said if we give him a few minutes he would go look. When he came back, he gave them a half dozen pictures of the guy making the deposits and withdraws. William thanked them for being helpful and they left for the Hyatt and sat in the room and looked over the folder and the papers that Ann made copies of. His name is George White and they have his address and phone number and they wanted to stake the place out so they rented a car and sat slightly down the street and waited to see what could happen next. William didn't like these stake outs because you drink too much coffee and eat to many donuts.

There weren't any house lights on for five days when there was finally an inside light was on the sixth day and they could see through the window. Now they know someone is home, but whom. So, they called to see who would answer and it was a woman's voice and William said to her that they were hoping that George was in. She said George is the owner but she rents from him. Finally, William told her who he was and could he come by and speak to her as well as his female partner. She said she would put an outside light on. They were there in minutes and she let them in. they showed her their badges and ID papers. She walked to the kitchen table and offered them a drink. They are not allowed to accept and liquid from anyone, so they politely said they were fine, thank you for inviting them here and talk with them.

They told her that they were trying to locate George White and maybe she could give them the address to where she mails her rental payment. She told them a lot of time he comes by where I work or by the house and one time, he had me meet him on one of the down town streets He is a very cagey person and he doesn't trust anyone, he very hard to figure out. Ann pulled his picture out of the folder and asked her is this person that was her landlord. She said no, he's not the person I pay. Ann told her that the person in the picture is George

White, she said maybe it is but this person says he's George White when he calls her. We are going to stay here and when he phones you were to meet him with the rent money you are to call us immediately.

William asked her if she understood what they just asked her to do. They gave her their cards and the Hyatt room phone # and left her, it was starting to get late and they headed back to the Hyatt for some relaxing time and maybe a good dinner on the Bureau. William told Ann that this guy is shaky and usually shaky people are unpredictable and very hard to catch or pin down because they don't trust anybody and that comes from doing a lot of shaky deals

They checked in with Washington and they told them to stick it out and catch him. They spent days reviewing the file and were surprised that none of the bodies were found and concluded that he must have a way of getting rid of them. On the last day of the month they got a call from the tenant that he wants her to meet him at the mall at 5: o'clock in front of the theater. They told her they would be there ahead of her so don't worry you won't see us but she is to sit on a bench outside the theater and when she stands, they will assume that he is the one that is stopped in front of her then they will close in. William had about twenty-four agents everywhere and this guy wasn't going to get away. William met the agents out back and he told them what to expect, he described him as possibly armed and dangerous and he probably has something planned if he suspects anything is wrong with his meeting, he is shaky and has the jitters and that makes him unpredictable.

5

It was only about 4: o'clock and they had an hour before this guy will show up, he must suspect something or he wouldn't act this cautious about coming to his house instead of meeting the tenant in different places. William spotted the Tenant coming towards the theater and sat on the bench out front of the ticket booth. All of a sudden, she stood as this person approached her and he was converged on like bees on a hive.

The Tenant was visually shook up and Ann thanked her for cooperating with them and they will make a note of it in their report. Then William asked the suspect is your name George White and he said hell no where do you get my name is George white and I want you to tell me what the hell is going on. Here and why am I in handcuffs and drug down here for questioning, I didn't do anything wrong and you will have to answer to someone for falsely arresting him. This is not allowed and you haven't even told me what I have supposedly done.

"Then why do you act as George White to this Tenant of his and lead her to believe your George White on the phone and in person why are you misleading this woman into believing that you are George White?"

"I do it for the money; this guy pays me $50.00 to collect the rent with no questions asked so I do it to get a little pocket money, you can't blame a guy for that. Hell, that is easy money and I couldn't pass it up."

"What is your name?"

"My name is Jon Riley."

"Well Jon we are going to take you down to the police station and find out if you're telling us the truth or not and for your sake, I hope you are because if you're not you are going to be in a world of hurting's and spend some time with us for a while."

"This is preposterous."

"Never the less you're going down to the police station for some questioning and for us to verify who you are and if you're telling us the truth or not, we have to get to the bottom of this before the day is out."

They drove to the police station who were expecting them and they had a room ready for them. William gave some detectives the information they had on this Jon and he asked them to see if he is telling them the truth, dig as deep as you can on him, he is an important link in this case. They escorted this Jon into the room and he was still handcuffed and he was sat at the table in front of the two-way mirror. He just sat there for a few minutes when Ann and William came in and took a seat on the other end of the table and looked at him for the longest time think this would scare him into telling them the whole story about this George White.

"Ok you're not George White then who is George White and how do you know him, we need to know everything no matter how small it is, please be assured we mean to get to the bottom of this so please cooperate with us or be arrested for interfering in an federal investigation which is a felony which means you will be going away for some prison time. Not cooperating is another word for interfering and the court doesn't look ton favorably on that charge"

"Now he's scared out of his mind and said he's just a guy I met at a truck stop restaurant and we struck up a conversation and that was when he made the offer to me about picking up his rent payment from the tenant every month and he will pay me fifty dollars just to do that for him, the last I checked that not illegal."

"What were you doing at a truck stop restaurant, are you a trucker?"

"No, I like the food so I come out to get a good home cooked meal now and then. Being single I looked forward to that once and a while."

"Do you have a pickup truck?"

"Yes, I do it's just a small Mazda two door it gets me around and its inexpensive to run. It only has an engine under the hood so nothing can go wrong, just some spark plugs and a carburetor and a battery"

"Did you by chance see what he was driving?"

"Yes, I did he had a faded red tow truck with a lot of lights on a bar on the top which was higher than his roof top."

"Did you notice the tags; I know that is asking a lot for you to remember?"

"Yes, I did they were Ohio tags and the first number was 8."

"How did you remember that from such a casual meeting?"

"That was easy to remember, that was the month I was born, I showed him a picture of George White and asked him if he knows who this guy is just to see his reaction.

"That's him, that's the guy that pays me to pick up his rent money and if my memory serves me correctly, he said his name was George and that is him in that picture, wow where did you get that picture I wouldn't thing there would be any pictures of him anywhere that's how shaky he is, he's a mess and I don't think he would let anyone take his picture he's just to paranoid to ever let that happen."

Little did he know that he got the picture from the bank security cameras. That confirms the name they have and with this guy identifying him as George White they are getting close. so, Ann asked him how does he get his money meaning the rent money, he laughed and said that he has me mail it to him at a P. O. box and that is the last I see of it less my fifty dollars. You don't mail cash, then *how do you mail it to him William said that isn't true, you left out one important thing in your story and that was how you got your $50.00. He said that he mails me a money order from the post office.*

"Can you remember if it said what post office it came from?"

"Yes, it always came from the post office in Beaver Creek"

"That's probably the post office that he has his mail coming to his P. O. Box they know that it will be harder to trace him using that P.O Box. Then a home address the P.O. Box is at the post office that are usually used for getting some mail"

A month is a long time to wait for this murderer to pick up his mail maybe he gets other mail there so they posted a team around the clock waiting for someone to open the P.O. box # 83 at the Beaver Creek post office. They would use all the resources they can find to get to him sooner. They went to the Motor vehicle department and asked them to find them a red tow truck with the first number on the tag being 8. The manager came and told them to follow him he would find a computer open and see if they can find more. He found around 150 tow trucks and three that had a license plate with the first number being 8. Ann asked him if they can have a copy of the three tow trucks registration cards that will be a big help for them in getting closer to this person and maybe the color might be on it, she was trying to focus in on the color that would eliminate the other two trucks.

They handed them to Ann and she told William that one of them is registered to a George White who lives in Beaver Creek. It was a trailer park and they were so excited being so close to catching this murderer, they made plans on watching him around the clock. He wasn't home for a few days and he pulled up to his parking place and got out. When he got to his front door William was right behind him and told him to stop and he swung around and he had a gun in his hand so William shot him in the shoulder a few times and he laid on the ground screaming, "Just take my money, don't kill me." William wanted to ask him if any of those young girls said that to him when they begged him not to rape them or hurt them. He didn't want to tip his hand but he knew that they final caught him, so they called for an ambulance and got him to the hospital as fast as they can. William made sure that his shots weren't going to kill him.

"You didn't have to shoot me I was just letting myself in my home, I am not a burglar."

"You had a gun in your hand and you were going to shoot me, weren't you we clearly saw it in your hand?"

"I didn't have a gun; I don't own a gun your mistaken."

"We have the gun with your finger prints all over it so why are you saying that you didn't have a gun when we have it here that you dropped on your step."

"If my finger prints are on it you put them on it. You're not going to put those finger prints on me."

"We are going to have an around the clock security at your hospital room and we are going to search your trailer that will tell us what you have been up to. That is all I am going to tell you for now, just hurry up and get better because I want you healthy enough to walk to the gallows and hear your neck snap when that trap door drops you down to your very violent and messy death and I want to stand there and watch it. You can't hide anymore because we have tracked you down after months of following the trail you left even to South America where you sold those girls cars to Mr. Bandarez who didn't have anything nice to say about you because you not very nice but you are cagey but bot cagey enough to fool us all we did was to follow the trail that led us to you and you didn't cover up enough not to get caught. You made it easy for people to remember you with your sneaky and paranoid ways."

"What are you charging me with? I 'am going to get my lawyer on you two and you will have to deal with him and I can see a lot of things that you broke the law to arrest me."

"Right now, it will be an attempted shooting of a police officer for now that resulted in me defending myself and shooting you and not with any intention of killing you."

"What do you mean for now?

"We will tell you when the time comes, right now we want you to reflect on your life in the past couple of years and you can answer your own question why you are under arrest."

"I have a right to know now, you have to tell me or I am not going to cooperate with you about this arrest."

"I will tell you when the time comes and right now this is not the time."

"Well that's not good enough for me I want to know now."

"It will have to be good enough for now. Please tell me why you were going to shoot me when I walked up behind you at your door if you are so innocent, my partner saw everything and we have you with a gun in your hand and you had every intention of shooting me without any doubt or you wouldn't have to have a gun in your hand to open your door."

"I wasn't going to shoot anyone that is my only protection I have from all the crime that is out there."

"I guess the gun you had in your hand when you swung around was just a water pistol and you were going to spray some water on me just like a joke."

"No, I don't own a gun."

"Well then let that be your defense when your finger prints are all over it."

William and Ann left the room and they called Washington to give them the news about the capture of the guy that they feel who is responsible for killing those missing women coming from Canada.

William told them he had to shoot him twice in the shoulder area, not wanting to kill him and not being able to find out more of what he could tell us, he did try to shoot me I didn't have much of a choice, they were very happy for both of them.

He said he was going to search his trailer and see what more they can find about this guy. They had his keys and they had a forensic teck. To come out with them and look the tow truck over for anything that could aid them in these murders investigation. The trailer was dingy and dirty so they wore mask so as not to breathe in any of that damp dirty musty air that could take a toll on their lungs later on in their life. Ann is very cautious and will never take any chances like breathing dirty air like what was in that trailer that they will be inside looking around, they even wore latex gloves so as not to touch any evidence or get anything harmful on their skin.

It took them a couple of days; they took everything apart and any place he could store something. They did find some ladies underwear and a couple of Canadian driver's licenses of two of the missing girls. Then they found a road atlas with a back road marked with a yellow marker and some black dots of the possible grave sites. They took a team out there in the morning and they tried to understand what the map was saying.

The road on the map was showing five black dots and Ann said that was probably where they might be buried. If it was the place that he used for burring the bodies they might not be a deep grave they would be a shallow grave because of the time it would take anyone to bury a person deep in the ground and next to an access road that anyone could drive down. So, for this killer time was very important, one that he had to get these girls buried and two he had to work fast before anyone came so he must have been digging like a wild man not wanting to get caught with a dead woman lying on the ground ready to dump in the hole.

The word came back to William and Ann that they found a body from the location on the atlas map that they found in his trailer; they would put as much of the body as they could in the body bag. They will probably use the dental records of each victim to identify them. This kind of work was the worst anyone could do. It took a few days but they did find five grave sites. They did this from the Atlas map what they found in his trailer.

Other than a confession they thought things were looking up for them and their nonstop relentless investigation for a month or so. They called Washington again and told them about the bodies and there were praises from everywhere. They told him to start in on the prisoner and make this lock tight and no chance of him getting off and spoil everything that him and Ann had worked hard for. He knew that they weren't going to cause that to happen not all they had gone through; they were going to continue until they get a confession out of this murderer.

The hospital called and said that George White will be discharged in three days. They were there when the doctor signed the discharge papers and turned him over to William and Ann. He was shackled and there were two other police officers that will transport him to the jail where he will be questioned some more. William got there a few minutes ahead of them and held the door open when he walked through the police station door. They took him back to the interrogation room and cuffed him to the bar that was in the center of the table. He sat there quietly and William was shuffling through his file folder when this murderer who couldn't stand the quietness and said,

"You have no right to hold him like this."

"Well let's see if that is true or not, are you George White."

"You know I am why are you asking me what you already know who I am. Did they teach you that in police training and now you want to try it out on me?"

"We plan to be very thorough with you because you have a selected amnesia memory and we have to record our entire interview with you just so there won't be any denial of the facts later on that we lay out in our interview with you if you want to look over from time to time just to jar your memory."

"What is that supposed to mean."

"It means that you pick and choose what you want to remember, what we call selected amnesia and so far you have been denying everything we ask you about and to boot you are very combative like you were to those innocent young girls when you were raping and killing them."

"Do you know Jon Riley?"

"No am I supposed to or is this a name you picked out of the phone book."

"You will when we go a little further in to our questioning with you and then you will see the puzzle a little more clearly."

"Well then show me, because I don't believe you have any missing pieces of this puzzle your talking about. You're just trying to mix me up to say something that you can use as evidence against me."

"Jon Riley is the person that you pay $50.00 a month to pick up your tenants monthly rent money. Now do you still don't know who he is surely he is a very important person in your life at this time."

"What tenant are you talking about?"

"The one that rents your house from you for the past year, please don't tell me you don't own a house in beaver Creek because we can prove that you do."

"That's my business what I own and don't own."

"Right now, everything you say or do and have done is our business and being a wise ass doesn't help your case, in fact you are making us dig as deep as we can to get you. You have a piss poor attitude towards us and we don't like it . Jon Riley will miss not

picking up the rent for the $50.00 dollars that you were paying him from the deal that you agreed on the night you two met at the truck stop restaurant. I am guessing that you don't know him either, I am not impressed with your selected memory and denial of every question that I ask you, it's not working and I hope that you can see that"

"There is no law against me meeting someone at a truck stop restaurant and having a cup of coffee with."

"I'll have to agree with you on this one, there is no law against that. But we do have laws that will punish anyone who commits murder of five innocent young girls that were just wanting to get to their colleges, where they were going to start their first year of college and along comes you and you murdered and raped them over and over until you murdered all five of them and buried them out on Pond rd. Thanks to you we found their bodies and some of their panties and driver's licenses in your trailer. I can't even imagine what you put those girls through and how they begged you for their lives and what sexual acts you made them do to you hoping that it would save their lives and end this torture you were putting them through it must have been horrifying for them and how you were stopping them from fulfilling what they planned for years."

"They weren't that innocent."

"How would you know; they didn't have a chance with you. They didn't pick you to murder them, you picked them to murder and you were clever enough to cover your trail that wouldn't lead back to you because you didn't think of everything in covering up this nasty murdering of innocent girls. When you say they weren't that innocent, who could be innocent when you were demanding these girls to preform sex acts on you with the fear that you were going to kill them"

"You seem to know a lot about me and I don't know anything about you."

"I know you sold their cars to a Mr. Bandarez the owner of the South American car dealership in Rio. I have so much proof against you that twelve kindergarten kids would convict you. I guess you thought you would never get caught. We'll let me just say, Gotcha and we really gotcha and you can't hide anymore."

"What do you Know about me that you can arrest me and shoot me?"

"I'll tell you what I know, if you don't cooperate like you have not been doing, I am going to charge you with first degree murder, one for each girl you killed and I will strongly recommend the death sentence. Either you admit to these murders and tell us how you caught these innocent girls off guard or I swear I will see you hang by the neck and see your eyes pop out when the hangman's noose snaps from your fall through the trap door and you shit and piss your pants while you dying which was probable more civilized then what you did to those girls who couldn't fight back probably because you had them all tied up so you could do your dirty deeds without them resisting your demands of sex and god only knows how nobody could hear the screams that these girls were doing that might attract someone, anyone to come to their aid ."

William wanted this guy to know what it was going to be like hanging to death. George started crying real tears that were rolling down his cheeks and the slobber was coming out of his mouth all over the table begging William not to hang him. Ann had to step out of the room so as not to throw up in their presence. William told him that he wanted every detail of how he got these girls to go away with him and what he did to them in detail if he is going to show him any mercy. So please start at the beginning and we are all ears and the cameras are running.

He started by saying that he would sit in a diner or truck stop parking lot and watch the cars pull in and he would choose the cars that only had a girl by themselves that had a Canadian license plate seeing as how they weren't that far away from Canada. He watched them pull in and go in the diner or truck stop for something to eat. He said he liked the fact that they were from Canada better because they would be harder to trace there wear a bouts. He would puncture the two front tires and when they came out, they could see their car low to the ground and I would drive up in my tow truck and offer to take them and their car and have their tires fixed right away and get them back on the road without losing any time. They were more than willing for him to help them and they couldn't thank him enough for helping them out of this situation.

That wasn't a hard decision to make and they were real quiet sitting in my tow truck while we drove to my garage I would back their car into my garage and lower it down on the garage floor where I had backed their car in to work on and I drove the tow truck outside so it would give me more room. I spread plastic all over the floor so as not make a mess. I threatened them so badly that they were almost paralyzed with fright and they did everything that I asked them to do and then when I was finished having sex and they were in complete shock of what I did to them with them, I took my machete to them and hacked them to death.

Ann left the room again and William asked him to go on and he said he found that guy from South America from an ad in a car magazine and he bought my cars through me getting touch with him and sending him pictures of the cars that I wanted him to buy. How did you clean up all that mess on your garage floor, he told William he had plastic laying on the ground like I told you earlier and it was contained on that and it was very easy to clean up.?

Was it hard to hack a human body into pieces, it's not that easy of a thing to do especially if your machete isn't that sharp, so how were you able to do that five times? How did you find the place to bury them and he said he was very familiar with Pond rd. and he knew it was a perfect place to bury someone? I told him that we found the world atlas where you marked the burial plots on the map. I told him that we have it all and he also told me how he did it like you asked him to do.

William could question him all day but he wanted to avoid any repetition. He asked him why would he keep these girls panties and drivers licenses in his draw for someone like me to find them and Georges reply was they were things that he could go to and get off on just to think of what those girls did to him to save their lives gave him such a sexual relief that he would go back to when he thought about them.

William asked George to read over the statement he made to him and sign it on the bottom line. He was looking at it for the longest time and picked up the pen and signed it. William signaled for some assistance and a couple of security officers came in and undid George from the bar on the table and started out the door with him when he looked at William and said you promised me you would get me out of the death sentence and I kept my word now you have to keep your word. William didn't think that it would be a problem in getting him five life sentences back to back.

He was gone in a matter of seconds and William was drained from all that conversation with this mad man for almost five hours and Ann said let's go home you need some relief, so they left for the Hyatt and a nice shower and grab a sandwich on the way home, rather than room service that would take forty-five minutes. Ann was hugging William all the way to the hotel she said you were excellent the way you handled that son of a bitch. You had this guy begging for his life and spilling his guts out. They got into bed and Ann put her naked body next to his and the rest is history they both needed that release. They made sure they had all of the paperwork from the police station and called the hanger and told the flight service to notify the pilot that they will want to go back to Washington as soon as possible.

His chief agent Mike Todd was waiting for their return, they solved a case that everyone had given up on and he wanted to give them the recognition for solving such a case. The plane was going to take another two hours so they went back to the police station to thank them for all their help and that he will see to it that the right people will know about it. He prepared a letter to the bureau chief recommending because the killer helped them in finding the bodies of the women he murdered and confessed to all five murders in the detail he asked for, he was recommending that George White be spared from the death penalty. He had the letter finished and it was ready to be handed to Mike Todd the next time he sees him.

Ann couldn't believe the success they had in developing these brutal murders and going where no one ever thought of looking for clues and dug deeply into the outskirts of the evidence in this case. William would tell Ann, "If you can't find it where you're looking then look somewhere else. That was exactly what they did and it paid off."

The plane landed at Andrews AFB and there was a ride waiting to take them back to the bureau and they went to their office and started filing all of their papers and write the case report that the bureau chief wanted to read in its entirety. It would take a while for the two of them to write it but they allowed themselves a week to get it finished. In the meantime, Mike Todd, their supervisor wanted to see them right away. William had the letter he wrote on the plane in his suit coat pocket to give to Mike his supervisor when he sees him. They were escorted into his office and he jumped out from behind his desk and said you two did it, how did you manage to find this murderer when everyone else have given up on it. You never get tired of looking under the rocks to try and find something no matter how small it might b, it would fit the puzzle.

This case that William and Ann finally solved is on the news every day and the bureau is getting all the credit Paul said it was you two that deserve the credit and we are going to release a statement to all of the news media saying that you two solved this case single handed and spent endless days and nights tracking down the slightest hint of a clue. You two have reached a level of investigation that is mind boggling. William handed Mike the letter he wrote asking for the death penalty be lifted because of a promise that he made to George White in trade for the graves and how he murdered all five of the girls.

Mike said it will be shown to the court and he hopes that the judge and jury will honor his promise that he had no right to offer him. Well that knocked William back on his heels and he felt let down hearing that from Mike and he was standing too far away to understand the problem they were having of getting this very combative murderer to admit to anything. It took all he had not to walk out of the room and say fuck it. So, he did the next best thing and made a deal with him that broke the case wide open.

About a week had gone by and William was called into Mike's office and he was told that the bureau was going to overrule his request for leniency and recommend the death penalty.

"Are you sure about that and you want to ignore how I got this guy to admit to murdering these five girls?"

"The decision was just handed to him just a few minutes ago and it was someone higher up then he was that over turned your decision for leniency."

"If that is your final decision then I resign right now."

He put his badge and gun on his desk and walked out of the room and found Ann and told her what he did and she said if he goes, she will resign as well. She left her badge and gun on her desk and walked out of the building and got in their car and drove home. They were very quiet and the ride felt like it took forever. William fixed the phone that you couldn't tell it was ringing and he switched off the answering machine. There was no way he was going to talk to them after that refusing my request for leniency rather than just letting it go through the legal system and let that determine a life or death sentence, no someone wanted to flex their muscles and go against their top investigators.

The bureau was a wreck and this will hurt them for years to come, they couldn't get up with William and Ann and William thought that with no job they will have to come up a way to make some money. Ann said let's write a book about how you caught that agent passing secrets to the Russians. He thought for a second and he told Ann let's go to a book publisher and tell them what we are planning. They actually went to three publishers and two of them had no foresight and they decided to sign with Universal Books and they gave them an advancement of $500,000 with a contract to have a completed manuscript in four months, they knew they can do that in less than ninety days. When they got back to their apartment there was Mike sitting on their front step and he asked William and Ann if he could speak with them.

William told him that he has already spoke and you didn't tell your people that they should let the legal system give the sentence and pass on my letter of recommendation and let the chips fall and that would have been the fair thing to do. Ann and I can't work for you any longer when you showed you hand in being politically correct and not satisfied in what this murderer gave us who was very combative and we assured him that if he told us everything, we would not recommend the death penalty. He would die in jail, what was so bad about that. Mike was shocked and stood up and said it looks like we lost you and Ann, and you lost all those unsolved murder cases that will still be unsolved because of a bad decision that you made. Those people still have a job and Ann and I were forced to leave our jobs and we made a good decision when we resigned.

Mike asked them to reconsider and what are they were going to do and they said they didn't know right now. He asked them *again, you still won't come back and William said no, never. He left never saying goodbye with his head down. William and Ann went to the apartment and made up a list of things they will need to get started on the book. First, they went and deposited the check in an interest-bearing checking account until they can look to see if there were any good investments. Ann had a great idea and said let's buy a $100,000 dollars' worth of stock in Universal publishing because with the three books we are going to write the stock will go through the roof and we could be lucky enough to make millions on the stock alone, not counting the book sales. They knew that had to look at everything if they are to succeed in this new world that they just entered in that it was fair to say that they were very unfamiliar with.*

They bought two lap tops computers and a twelve-box case of printing paper and boxes of everything they would need to write this book. They were pleased about the half million-dollar advancement. Ann told William that most everyone in our shoes would have kept their job and went on like nothing happened. It was considered by them two as a slap in the face and they had no choice but to resign and it was a matter of principals that they resign or they would get worse over time.

William called a security company and had the apartment swept for listening devices everywhere an inventive person would put one. It took over six hours and $400.00 to tell us that the apartment was clean of listening devices. That made them relaxed but they will do it again in ninety days, now when they leave the apartment together, they would set little things around if anyone came in the apartment the devices would be on the floor and that would be a dead giveaway that someone had entered their apartment or those little things wouldn't be on the floor.

It sounds paranoid but it was just a precaution they had to make to feel secure. Let us not forget what a person would do to get something on another person, no one is exonerated, there isn't anything that can't happen to them and they have to be on the look-out for unauthorized trespassing in to their apartment and anything else that might be thrown at them.

William started writing down notes on how his life was before he started watching and photographing people and tell all about Pat and her passing away one day short of her starting her classes at MSU. William talked about his dropping out of MSU and not taking much of an interest in anything after Pat passed away. He was still living with his parents and generally speaking not giving a shit about anything. They spent 24/7 until they have all the notes in the order they will be typed in the form of a book. William went into detail about his surveillance and picture taking and keyed in on how he singlehandedly caught this spy. Ann loved it and she said she could have it typed in three or four days and presented to the publisher, soon after they both proof read it more than once.

They made an appointment with the publisher to come to his office and turn over their manuscript and sign the contracts to William's and Ann's first book called (You Can't Hide.) The publisher wanted to read it first and have them come back for the price setting. Two days later they were back again and they sat at a conference table and they were told how great of a story this is and how popular it will be. They put a sale price of $28.00 for a hard-back copy. They will pay William and Ann $15.00 a copy as Royalties to be paid each month until the sales stop. They were told about their advancement and how they would keep $5.00 of the $15.00 dollars they are paying in royalties as a payback for the advancement they are still getting a clear $10.00 until the debt is paid.

They were starting to see a lot of advertising about the book and when it will be available. This went on for weeks and each day there was more advertisements then the day before. Some stores were given thousands of copies to sell. The cover showed a person sitting on a *park bench reaching under and doing something. The book clearly spells it all out. The total of books sold the first week was mind boggling the total was 240 thousand copies or William's and Ann's total was $3,100,000 dollars after paying back the $500,000 advance. They can't wait to see how the second week goes. It was a whooper that went to 280,000 copies and they got now $15.00 a copy or a grand total of $4,200,000 they are richer than they could ever believe. The book was the talk of the news and literary world, they are trying to keep a low profile with all this going on around them.*

Before the sales petered out, they had sold another 500,000 copies. The royalties were great and they put all of it in the bank $7,500,000. They never dreamt that they could be so rich and William was only 24 years old. Ann said that she read an article in the newspaper asking is there anyone out there that can solve any of these serial killings. Why isn't William Smith working for the FBI anymore, they were demanding a congressional hearing looking into his resigning his position at the bureau. They knew it would all fall on death ears and make William out to be the bad guy.

It didn't matter anymore they have found a new life and William asked Ann to marry him and her parents wanted her to have the wedding they always planned for her. William thought that was a good idea and when William told them that he could pay for everything they said they could also. She was from Vero Beach Florida and she wanted to be married there. They went down a couple of weeks before the wedding and stayed at the Vero hotel on the ocean. Her parents said they were going to have the reception at the Grand Harbor Reception complex on the ocean. They took us up to see the reception hall and it was out of this world. They were going to do it all from this five-star DJ to their five-star food display.

They didn't chinch on anything; the church was the Roman Catholic Church on A1A St. Josephs. Now they were spending almost every evening meeting Ann's relatives it was a lot of fun, she didn't come from middle class she came from upper middle class and they can afford anything they wanted. The morning of the wedding we all met for Sunday Brunch at the Disney hotel on the ocean. Ann and her mother stayed home and anyone that wanted to come came for a great breakfast. My best man was Ann's brother Allen and we dressed at the hotel he was staying at rather than anywhere else.

They were picked up by a limo and driven up the road for a few miles to the church. They were instructed to come in the side door of the church thirty minutes early. They went to the sacristy and waited for the priest to tell them to go out in front of the alter and wait. Ann's father walked her down the center isle that had some very nice white carpet down all the way to the alter. William was looking at them walking down towards him and he saw this beautiful girl holding on to her father coming towards him and he couldn't believe his eyes how beautiful she looked. Her father put her hand in his and sat with Ann's mother to console her as best he could.

The wedding ceremony was the short version and when they were pronounced man and wife they turned around and the place erupted in applause and the organ started playing Halleluiah and the went down the aisle to the church entrance where Ann's parents were chasing after them and when they caught up, they had a big hug. The picture taking was a big pain in the ass but we wanted a record of the whole day. Ann was telling William all day how she was going to get him in bed and never let him out. That was music to his ears and he knew there would be some time before that could happen. He knows that she will want to do everything to him on her honeymoon and knowing William he will want to do the same to her. Ann's parents wanted everything to be nice for their daughter; the dinner was surf and turf.

The disk jockey had a group of girls that went into the crowd of guest and brought some of the men out on the dance floor, they all *had on skimpy skirts the showed their underwear every move they made. It was hard for the dirty old men to eat their meals. They were the loosest girls that he has ever seen. They were there to help the disk jockey get the party in a high pitch for the rest of the evening. They did everything that one does at their reception and then some. They cut the cake and they did the last dance; Ann had this large silver looking pocketbook holding all the cash wedding gifts. With the $15 million they have in the bank from their book the wedding gifts was the icing on the cake.*

They planned a honeymoon in Bermuda for ten days and they expect that ten days will be the best they will ever spend together. They don't have to be at the airport until 9: o'clock. They were back at their hotel by 9: o'clock. The reception went for five hours and Ann's parents gave them a ride to the hotel and Ann gave the pouch holding the envelopes to her mother for safe keeping as well as the gifts that were there on the table. They were excited about their honeymoon in Bermuda and they booked a suite at the South Hampton Princess on the ocean. This hotel has the reputation for making their gest feel like royalty right down to their room service.

Their wedding night was one for the books and they decided to stop by 11: o'clock and pick up where they quit tonight, they had plenty of time to enjoy their honeymoon and the privacy they were going to have out on the ocean on the third floor overlooking that beautiful pink sandy beach They had heard so much about this place and they were excited to see it first hand for themselves. They had a small limo to the Orlando airport and checked in quickly and went all the way through to the lounge and gate area that was assigned for their flight to Bermuda. They didn't know anyone and no one knew them and that was ok by them. They always are looking for the same faces where ever they go because if they see the same faces then they are being followed.

They landed and their shuttle was waiting for them and their ride to the hotel took over an hour. Ann told William that they had all the time in the world so let us not get mad at anything and enjoy the scenery. Finally, they saw their hotel off in the distance, it was pink and it looked like a palace, not quite but to them it did. They went up to the desk to sign in and they were welcomed like they were family. They were told that there were some complimentary gifts in their room, compliments of the hotel manager and that they were honored to have them stay here as their VIP guest and we will be treated as such.

That didn't upset Ann and himself to know that they were going to be treated like royalty and being under British domain they know about treating people like royalty.

6

They planned on making this the best this honeymoon the best it can be, the hotel manager got wind that that Michael and Ann were guest and he invited them to his table for dinner, to be honest with you it was a banquet. He had invited anyone that was somebody including the Governor. The Governor praised them for their long hard work in piecing the puzzle together, when it wasn't easy to find the pieces. The banquet turned into a celebration and the last time that Michael looked at his watch it was past 2: o'clock It broke up soon after that and they finally got to their room and crashed and slept like a couple of new born's until the sun was shining brightly through the windows and woke them up and the clock was showing 10:30. They got up and showered and because of the time they decided to catch the public bus into Hamilton for the day.

Everyone uses the bus system in Bermuda because the roads are too narrow to handle a lot of traffic, so there is a limit to one car per family they visited all the stores and they had a great lunch in the Princess hotel on the canal. We did buy some Waterford Crystal and they had it shipped home rather then lug it around and carry it on the airplane and of course not have to declare it for duty taxes. They didn't get back to the hotel until after 9: o'clock. They took a shower together and they continued on with the honeymoon

They decided to take a tour of some underground caves that were accidently founded by some school kids kicking their soccer ball around their soccer field. The ball suddenly disappeared and they stood there dumb founded as to what happened. They approached the spot where they thought the ball disappeared and they found a hole big enough for the soccer ball to fall through. One of the boys went and got a flash light and when they shined it in the hole, they saw the most beautiful cave they had ever seen. The field was closed for any more soccer playing and after some careful investigation and digging after a couple of years it was open to the public and has a large number of daily visitors, all because of a soccer ball disappearing in the ground.

They were looking forward to this kind of attraction and the wooden paths they walked on so as not to come in contact with the boiling water that was crystal clear. They must have walked a couple hundred yards before they were finished. They did see from the tour bus window the man that stands out in the intersection waiving to everyone, come to find out he is a national hero. I asked our tour driver how it felt to live in paradise and he said, "He didn't know." Now that was a shock to hear him say that and we left it alone because he must have had some not to nice of a reason to say that.

They went back and spent the afternoon on the beach, the sum was bright but not dangerously hot, it was perfect for lying out. He went back to our room after a couple of hours and Ann took off her bathing suit in front of him so he did it to her. Needless to say, they were honeymooning again and they took so long that they had to run down to the dining room before they stopped serving for the evening.

There meal would be something to remember sitting in those high back chairs and watching the boats out on the ocean through this very large window that was at the end of the dining room. They are having a great time and they wanted to do something every day, from boat tours out on the ocean to a round of golf and their time in Bermuda was coming to an end and with one full day left to go, they were going to rent a cabana and spend their last day on the beach, it turned out to be a great idea.

They didn't watch any tv while they were there and looking back, they never missed it. They planned to catch a shuttle when they land

and go to Ann's parents house in Vero and stay one night and catch a flight back to Dallas. Ann's parents were happy to see them and they wanted to take them out to dinner at P.V. Martins, it was right on the ocean just off of A1A south of Vero. They went back to the house and Ann's father gave them their money pouch and they opened their wedding gifts right there. They were beautiful and they decided to take them to Fed-x and ship them home. They had breakfast in the morning and Ann's parents drove them to the airport for their flight home.

They said their goodbyes at the curb and walked in to the departure room. After their security check in they had two hours to kill. They had a nice ice tea and before they knew it, they were boarding. The flight was short of three hours and the landing was perfect. They caught the airport shuttle and they were home in no time. Ann reminded William to be sure and look for any of their security things that they had sitting around and see if any of them had been moved. They were both glad that they had their small motion cameras around that would pick up any movement in their apartment.

They entered the apartment and all of their little pieces weren't where they belong and their security cameras showed a lot of activity going on. When they viewed them closely, it showed as many as six people planting devices through their apartment and their faces were crystal clear and identifiable as co workers that they know and work with at the bureau. Michael told Ann that it was time for another security sweep and Ann said like tomorrow. Not knowing where their cameras were, they changed in to their pajamas in the bathroom just to be safe from their candid camera shots.

Michael asked his security guy if he could come right away and he said he could come right away. This sweep took a little longer because he was finding devices everywhere like sixteen of them that included their phone and a video camera in their bedroom. He thanked his friend and gave him a large fee for coming right over right away. They decided to get in touch with the newspaper and ask for an interview with the senior editor to see if he wanted another Watergate story.

The editor knew who Michael and Ann were and after talking to Michael he knew he had a big story ; it was big as Watergate. He showed him his bag of listening devices and the camera and he told the editor that when he would need these devices, he would let him show them. He reminded the editor that they were X FBI agents and they broke in to our apartment when they were away on their honeymoon. The editor thanked them both for their service to their country and he promised them this will be on the front page of their paper in the morning with names.

The next morning the newspaper had their front page story like they said they would and the headline read, "Is anyone safe from ease dropping anymore?" It was on every news station locally and nationally. I showed those FBI agents running around their apartment planting their listening devices. It didn't take long for Michael and Ann to come into the office for a chat with their old supervisor. They talked it over and decided that it wouldn't hurt so they went just to see what they had to say. There x supervisor Mike asked them to come in his office and talk this thing out.

"You didn't waste any time in coming after us and you picked a good time when we were on our honeymoon. How do you have the balls to come after us we didn't try and hurt you or the Bureau, we didn't draw first blood, you did and you botched it up real bad and when the press gets done with you and the bureau you will be downsized to being park guards."

"Are you planning on suing us over all this misunderstanding."

"We would be a fool not to and you know that it's going to happen and it will be all over the news."

"Would you consider an out of court settlement that would have gag order strings attached to the settlement."

"I guess it would all depends what number you throw at us."

"I am authorized to offer you $20 million dollars if you settle now."

"Michael said that if they make it $50 million with the taxes paid, they might talk it over, other wise we'll have to let the chips fall as they wish and we think that is a bargain even though you don't."

"I don't have the authority for that amount of money and he would have to go up the ladder to get approval on that number but he would get back to us right away."

"Our phone is ringing right off the wall so out of doing the fair thing we can give you twenty four hours to make a decision; you might say that we are giving you the first opportunity of settling this case."

"I can try and meet your deadline, but I will call you weather they will settle with that number or not."

Mike knows that I am no one to play around with and he will play a big part in getting us the money. They stood and left him sitting there and what a difference these two people are having to go against them and he knows that the Bureau will lose going up against Michael and Ann.

Michael told Ann that he has a couple more stories to tell, Ann told him whenever he's ready she can start taking notes. They were having breakfast when mike called them if they could come back in again. They didn't get there until a little after noon. When they went into his office Michael noticed that Mike had a folder on his desk and he told them that the Bureau agrees to their settlement terms. There was a lot of papers to sign and there was a gag order like the knew there would be and it was for five years.

Michael couldn't hold back anymore and reminded him how he let some stuffed shirt over rule his and Ann's hard work in getting this serial killer to spill his guts only after I would recommend that the death p[penalty we withdrawn. Those five hours of interrogation Ann had to excuse herself from not throwing up in the room that how awful it was with all of those murders explained in detail to us. You people have a very small memory of all we did for the Bureau and we only asked for one request and we were turned down flatly and coldly and not even a lets talk about it request I caught that Agent that was stealing secrets for the Russians right under your nose not to mention all of those five Canadian girls who families have some closure now when Ann and I caught the murderer.

You people showed that you are capable of making some very bad decisions when you ignore the information that your getting from your field agents. The part that takes the cake when you put a camera in our bedroom, that tells us how low down you are and we are glad not to be associated with the bureau anymore. They stood and left not shaking his hand and nothing but disgust for him.

They didn't waste any time in putting that money into their account. Ann couldn't believe how easy it went and how much money they can get their hands on. She couldn't believe how much money we have in the bank. I said to Ann on the way home, "Now what?" and her reply was not to worry we have all the time in the world. She told Michael again that she loved her new name and how wonderful their honeymoon was, he told her that is the best way to start a marriage. He laughed and said that they won't be having any more listening devices planted in their apartment anymore, that was an expensive lesson for them to learn.

It was a couple of days later that the press was reporting of a massive shake up at the FBI headquarters, they reported that it was a clean sweep of all the department heads and this came about that after their top two profilers resigned. Michael thought that all of this should have ever happened, you might say that the serial killer got them as well.

The paper was critical about the handling of some recent cases that will never be solved, they went on to say that they don't have any one that is even assigned to them. Michael told Ann that he has never seen the bureau get so much bad press in all of the years they were credited in saving America. It wasn't long after that bad press that their publisher called them to ask if they have started on there new book yet, he told him that they are talking about it but they haven't made up their minds yet. She reminded Michael of their success in their first book and now that they know who you two are and your second book will sell more copies.

Ann thought they should move out of Washington for a new life in a warmer climate like Florida who id known to have beautiful weather. She thought that they would like the Vero Beach area that has a lot to offer them and we should go down and have a look around and see if would like to live there. Ann doesn't want to say anything to her parents in case they decide not to live there. It was in the paper today that they replaced the bureau chief and that makes the shake up complete. Ann told Michael that his resigning started this whole thing, even Mike Todd was finally let go. There isn't anyone there that you know ort knows you. When someone say that they paid a net $50 million dollars to an X Agent for a cover up somebody has to go.

It looks like there serious about moving to Florida but they want to wait until they write another book, this one will be about this guy killing all these couples in their parked cars. Ann sat with Michael every day until they had their story complete, it took them almost ninety days but it was worth it. They both reviewed it twice and they got up with the publisher and he asked them to bring it in right away. They sat with him when he sped read about ten pages when he put the manuscript down and he told them how much he liked it and how good their other books did and he is recommending that we go with a soft back and charge $24.00 of which they will net out

$20.00 and he will charge $4.00 a copy' He said that he wants to start an advertising campaign for three weeks and put a million copies on opening day on all of the shelves all over America and at least eighty countries. Michael was taken back that they could only a million copies and his publisher reminded him that it was for the first day.

The publisher told them that this story will hit home to all the murderers or even future murderers that they aren't safe from a good investigator While they were waiting for the book to go on sale, they decided to go to Vero Beach and have a good look around. They love the architecture of some of the homes especially the big houses on the ocean. They stopped at a realtor's office that was owned by Donna Livingston, she was every thing a realtor should be like and she had the looks to back it up. Ann told her that we wanted a house on the ocean with at least seven bedrooms and a second master bedroom on the first floor as well as the second. It will have to have two floors that we can live on. We want electric hurricane shutters and a four car garage, with a large pool and deck and a private beach access.

Donna looked up at them and told them there isn't anything for sale around her for what you just subscribed. She recommended that we build one on an ocean lot because what you want doesn't exist. She told them that she can get them an architect that can design them their dream house and she can find them a reliable builder to finish the job. She asked them if they have some time to look at some ocean front lots, they were anxious to see some. She showed them an acre and a half that was between two $15, million dollar homes that were on a slight curve of the beach. Either way they could see up the beach from either side left or right for five miles. They both said they would love it and does she know who the neighbors are and she told them that one neighbor on the left owned three automobile dealer ships in New England and the one on the right is a retired meat packer from the Chicago stock yards.

Ann finally got around to asking Donna what does this lot sell for and her reply was that it all depends on how you were going to pay for it. The best price would be if you settle in a week or less and if you pay cash. Michael asked her how does she find people like that, "I am already talking to one." And now they wanted to know what the lot would cost and she said with out hesitation a Million five for a fast sale. Then Michael turned to Ann and asked her if this is what she wanted? and her reply was God yes. Donna asked them in the most sensitive way she could if they could have the money tomorrow and they said they could and with that she told them that they have just saved a million dollars, she showed them that the asking price was for two million five, a savings of one million dollars.

Donnas aid that when they come to her office tomorrow, I will have an architect there for you to meet who is the most proclaimed architect in Florida and then she said she has read our book on how I single handed caught that spy that was working for the Russians, in the park. She told them how she loved the story of how you were observant to do that. Ann asked her if she has seen any advertisement on their second book that will be released in about two weeks. They were told that the campaign will be building up momentum until it is released for sale. She said she would be one of those people standing outside the Vero book store for her copy that she hopes that they will sign for her.

They called their bank from Donnas office and instructed his banker to have a million five hundred thousand dollars available in the morning to be routed in a short notice in a day or so. They assured Michael that they will do whatever he tells them to do. Donna heard the whole thing and she felt they made a good deal. They left her office starving so they decided to have dinner at the hotel where they are staying now. The interest they are making on their money would be enough to buy almost four parcels. There dinner was perfect and so was the rest of the evening, the close encounter they had in their room would be one to remember. They were reflecting on what they did today and they were as giddy as two school kids.

They got to Donnas office after that great breakfast a little early and they found Donna sitting with this very successful looking young man, they stood to greet them and donna introduced them as Mr. Michael and Mrs. Ann Smith. He said that he looked over the notes that Donna made for him and he said that this looks like a lot of fun to build. He asked them if they were interested in an in-law suite and a guest room and they said they were, he thought that was a good choice. He asked them when do they want to move in and they said in about a year if that is possible and that suited him perfectly and he said he would try and put an elevator in his design, he also said that he would put in a security camera and screen for viewing. He told them that the first living floor would bed about ten feet above the shore.

Michael noticed that the other two houses have a high sea wall and they would like the same. He told them that the ground floor would not be wasted, he wants the elevator to start on the ground floor. Michael was curious to know what the square footage would be? And he quickly replied 12,500 Sq. Ft. give or take a few feet. He said that he will get back to his office and get to work on some exterior sketches and do some work on some interior drawings I will call you and ask you if you could come down and give you the cost of such a house to build. I could mail them over night to you if you prefer. They both said that they would like to come down and see everything first hand, he told them he was hoping that was what they wanted to do because if we had to, we could always stop by the lot.

A few days later they settled on the lot and they decided to wait for a phone call from Bill Feeley to come back down and see the drawings. The book was finally publisher in the US and a few days *later overseas. This was going to tell them a lot about the number of book sales to expect. It was only a few days later the publisher called and said they were a big hit and the last count is that the sales in the US after five days were 500,000 copies and overseas it was a touch higher with sales of 890,000 copies and your total at this point was $33,800,000 not bad for an opening week.*

Michael told Ann that they will have to get one of those private Swiss savings accounts with a private number and all that stuff, Ann liked that a lot and they will have to pay taxes on some of that money, it has to be and there is no getting around it. Their architect called back and asked them to come back and review all the plans for the interior and exterior. They have already paid for their first class tickets in advance and that kept the cost down a little. They caught an early flight into Melbourne that would arrive at 10: o'clock and they can be at the architect office around 1: o'clock. They rented a Bentley for there stay and booked a room at the Vero Hotel for three nights.

They arrived at the architect's office and he was ready for them, he offered them a cold drink and they both settled on some ice tea. We sat at a large conference table and he rolled out this real thick roll of drawings and the first three were artist designs of three different houses, they were all great looking homes and there was one that really turned them on and that was the contemporary one with the cement roof that they thought would be hard to blow off in a hurricane that had a twelve foot stairs that led to their double front doors that were stained in a dark mahogany with a mixture of walnut in it, now that with the cement railings was a perfect touch and would look like their dream home. They knew that they would be very happy there.

He put their favorite house design over to one side of the table and now it was time for him to start in on the floor plans there were about three different floor plans that had a multiple of coinciding floor plans in the three. They were spending so much time on the floor plans that they ran through lunch but he had lunch brought in for them and they could continue looking at the plans until they were definitely sure of what they wanted. They finally finished around 4:30 and decided to meet again in the morning for another fresh start and do a final pick of all the rooms and colors. They all agreed on a 9: o'clock start they left the office and ran back to the hotel and put on their swim suits and jumped into the pool that was very relaxing to them. There was a famous restaurant down the street called the Black Pearl that was suppose to be great. We decided to walk down to get some exercise in that couldn't hurt.

The walk felt good and they were seated right away, Michael doesn't drink so they so they settled on the water this time. I don't know what they put in it but we both got refills before we ordered their meals. They decided to share their sliced salmon appetizer that was so soft and tasty they could have eaten it all night. Settled in on the menu and Ann ordered the cream linguini for the bed and the seafood would lay on the top. Now I had their famous seafood platter with brown rice. Michael held on to Ann hand and told her how lucky they were to be together and are living the good life that most people only fantasize about.

They had a night cap at the hotels outside bar when they spotted Donna and she waived them over to join her, she said that she heard about the meeting and how much they loved the house that you picked. Ann was happy to tell her that tomorrow they would finish picking the entire house interior, from floor to the ceiling and he hired the interior decorator that he called Liz, she was from Melbourne. He told them she would be with them the whole time. Ann said she can't wait for tomorrow to come she hopes she can sleep tonight. Donna asked them how the book was doing and Michael said it was through the roof just like the publisher expected, he told them including the overseas sales it totaled over a million five hundred thousand copies. Donna said that is high for such a short time, little did she know how high it was.

When they got there, Liz was sitting there with all of her color charts and swatches and samples of all the molding and trim and the crown molding and anything else they could use to spice up the home. There wasn't anything that they missed including the garage doors even the interior of the elevator walls. They had to initial every page and every selection of anything that was going in to that house. It took till 5:o'clock before we could rap it up which included picking all the shrubbery that would be on the property, he did ask them to come back in the morning for the pricing and the deposit. They said they can do that and at the same time they came today 9:o'clock and he said he had an appointment later on that day.

They got in their Bentley and drove to the chart house in Melbourne and dined in their exquisite dining room overlooking the marina, they had a special way of making you feel welcome. They were told that there were two drinks that are called bloody Mary's but, in your case, they will be alcohol free and no spice, in other words they are called Virgin Mary's. That sounded ok to them and the waiter handed them the menu's and he told them he would give them a chance to look over their menu's and walked away.

Ann told Michael that she has never been so contented in all of her life and as well with him, with the life that they have made for themselves. The restaurant served them a five star meal and with the view they couldn't beat it except for an ocean view. They drove home by the way of A1A along the ocean. There was still time to celebrate this wonderful day they did it and lasted for two hours. They were up early and had a light breakfast at they were at Bill Feeley's office at 9: o'clock sharp. He has the artist conception and water color prints. He opened up his folder and he presented the entire run down of what it was going to cost them for him to build thid one of a kind home on the4 ocean. His price was $9 million 500,000 dollar, *payable in five equal payments of a million 900,000 and the first payment is due at the signing of the contracts. Michael gave Ann all the papers that he read and she gave him all of the papers she read.*

They were not under any pressure to sign these contracts right now and Mr. Feeley excused himself and he told them he would be back in a few minutes. They called their bank and told their banker that they had hired a contractor to build their home and they will have to pay five equal payments of $1 million 900,000 dollars of which one of them will be due now and they will tell them when the next four payments will be due. Mr. Feeley left the room, and came back quickly asking for their routing number so they can send him the first payment. He wrote it on a scratch pad and told Michael for them to send it to his account. Michael called the bank back and gave the manager the routing number and he said that it would take ten minutes, Michael thanked him and hung up. I told him that it would take a few minutes.

Mr. Feeley gave them all of the house plans and all of the artist color drawings of the exterior of the house. Lis came in the room and told them that they lumped the decorating of the house in with the house constructions so it would be easier to keep track of where their money is going. She showed them how their home will look and a list of furniture and pictures and the sit arounds. The drapes were beautiful and the shutters were in all of the right places and they would be more appreciated. She did a great job and she told them she would be keeping an eye on everything and after their final walk through she would bring all the furniture that same day and get everything set up so they could sleep there the first night if they wanted to.

Michael told Mr. Feeley that they can come down even it was a short notice and not to check up on him but to see how the house is going. He assured them to feel free to came anytime un announced and he will have their home ready for them to move in about a year, weather permitting, they were happy to hear that news and Ann wanted to go somewhere special and Michael said lets try and find that Italian restaurant out on Rt1 on the way to Sebastian, the story out there about this restaurant is that this little old Italian lady prepares and cooks their entire meal for everyone to see if they choose to. It is very popular and quite a treat for any Italian food lover. They left for the hunt for Mama Mia's and they never dreamt that it was in an old white stucco faded church that she converted into her old Italian restaurant, it was a hundred feet off the road and hard to find.

Every now and then she might come out to see how the patrons liked her cooking, if she did while you were there would be a treat to have met her. It turned out to be a night of easting Italian food to remember. They were happy to have found it and they couldn't stop[talking about the meal they had all the way back to the hotel. They started to talk about when they should visit or call her parents about what they did and Ann wanted to call them tonight and see if they can see them tomorrow. Ann tried to get up with them for over an hour so she said she would try again in the morning.

The next morning Michael called their publisher for the latest count of book sales he told them that it 512,000 for the US sales and 628,000 for the overseas sales market that totaled 1 million 140 thousand copies and it is still going strong. Michael told Ann that if this keeps up it could grow like the harry Potter book sales went that reached about a billion copies. They were going to wait before they start on their next book about the guy that killed all those college girls, they know that would be a great story. They want to go to a Swiss bank and see what they can do with their money, he told Ann that he wanted to pay their taxes and he would feel better when that is finished. Ann said that she knows of such a bank in Washington and we'll have to go there when they get home.

Ann tried to get up with her parents again and there was no answer and thought they must have gone out. They went down to the pool and laid out and relax on this there final day and finally it was around 3: o'clock when Michael said he knew where they can go, how about P.V. Martins on A1A for there scrumptious oysters Rockefellers and their inch and a half prime rib. Ann said she was game they jumped in the shower and they were on their way by 4: 30. The salt air will be alright on the car ; it was a rental and the three days they will spend here it wouldn't hurt the car.

The place was just starting to fill up just as there were being seated, they tried those Virgin Mary's. they looked over the menu and decided on the buffau. There was more of a selection, maybe the prime rib will be a little thinner but it will still be thick. Michael told Ann that it was a shame that she couldn't get up with her parents, he told her that they will be back in a couple of months and try again. They got back to the hotel and sat out on the veranda and sipped on some ice tea and they felt the warm breeze that was coming ofc the ocean and the waves breaking on the surf. They were definitely going to miss Florida and Vero Beach when they leave tomorrow. They knew that they invested in living here only because they loved it. They knew that they can get in touch with anyone through the computer and they can live anywhere and get in touch with anyone in the world in seconds. They put themselves on the wake up and there was plenty of time to have their last shot before they left for the airport.

The guys in valet parking gave the Bentley a good washing compliments of the hotel for being a valued guest. The drive to the air port was short and the car rental was right there where the check in place was and we were out of there in minutes. We just walked across the street to the check in counter. They had a few hours to wait so they shared a cold drink and watched the airplanes come and go until it was there turn. They booked in first class again it was only a two and a half flight and they landed in Dulles and caught the shuttle back to their apartment and they just sat in the chair and enjoyed the peace and quiet after a hectic three days in Vero.

Ann asked what he wanted to do about dinner lets order a pizza that would free us up to unpack and put our clothes away and put some in the washing machine. They ordered a medium with mushrooms and it was there in twenty minutes. It was so good that they both had two slices and the other two they put in the refrigerator for safe keeping. Michael doesn't like reheated food like pizza he told Ann that it loses its taste. It looks like they aren't going to work anymore and they want to enjoy what they worked hard for and if you think about it who could afford them. Maybe they can speak to groups like some famous people do and they make a very good living from that. If they do that will they have to have an agent to book their speeches and give them advanced notices of what they will be discussing and to who.

7

Ann said that she wasn't sure that she wanted to travel around the country on speaking engagements, her point was that they didn't need the money and besides their next book after its release they will be worth a fortune. Michael called the publisher ten days later and said that the sales are going through again, he told Michael that after that they talked last, they have sold here and overseas a million 500,000 copies. They both were speechless and the first thing that Michael would realize that they would have a lot of taxes to pay.

They looked up where the bank of Switzerland is and called and made an appointment to speak to a financial officer. They were waiting for them when they came in, they notified Roy to come out and meet the Smiths. He took them back to his office and asked them to be seated and for privacy he closed the door and put on some music. Michael knew that he was going to make it very hard to be eased dropped on and he liked that and after all it is Washington.

He asked them how can he help them, and Michael told him that they heard some stories about their private banking accounts and the high interest rate that they pay to its depositors and they would like to become a depositor. Michael asked Roy what are their interest rates at the moment. Roy told them that it varies on how much you have to deposit into our very private savings account. Michael told him about $150,000,000 dollars so he opened a chart and said with that deposit they qualify for an 11% interest rate for that deposit. He went on to tell them that we will issue a charge card that they can use anywhere and for as little they want with no ceiling on a higher amount. You will be assigned a very secret number that you will have *to memorize and not write it down on anything I think you know that this is the safest thing that you can do*

Michael asked him how can they pay such a high interest rate and he replied that they lend large sums of money to countries that want to fix or repair or even build their interscructure and they are willing to pay us a high interest rate to do it. We provide a service to these countries that might implode by not having the funds to fix or repair new hospitals or bridges. They thought that was a good idea and they never gave it a thought that things like this went on around the world. And you are lending them money to stay afloat and now by depositing our money with you we are now lending them money as well. Roy told Michael that they pay their interest every quarter and you only have to log into our computer system and put in your account number as of the day before.

Michael told Ann that they would earn approximately $4,million 500,000 dollars every quarter. Ann asked Michael why didn't he put it all in if they can buy a cup of coffee or a house and still earn the 11% in interest she said that she can appreciate how he feels but he will be missing out on $810.000 dollars a quarter and the money that you keep out won't earn anything like he will lose for not putting it all in.

She wanted him to know that she wasn't criticizing him on the decision he made but she reminded him how they always put their heads together an make the best decision there is. She went on to say that our money will be growing rapidly and paying cash for our new home is a good idea as well but we might want to consider in putting all of our money with the Swiss private account. The bank rep Roy congratulated then as being a member of this unique club of investors that have accounts with them, their cards were being printed and they spoke and for them to call him day or night home or away if we have a problem or we want to ask him a question, Michael told him that they don't require much attention.

The builder called them whenever he could and kept them up to date on how the house was going, he told them he would have it under roof in a few weeks and he invited us down for the next draw payment if we could. Ann called her parents and finally got up with them and they told her that they would be playing golf when she was there so Ann got off the phone by telling her Mother that she would be in touch soon and hung up.

Ann told Michael that they were acting very strange not to call them anymore and see what they call her. They flew into Melbourne again and rented the Bentley again and checked into the Vero Suits and they drove over to the lot and they could see from a distance their home that was nowhere near finished. They were putting the roof on with the cement shingles that they agreed on. They could see that their home could clearly hold its own in a hurricane.

The windows weren't in yet and the front steps weren't finished either. Mr. Feeley drove up a couple of minutes later and he walked them around the house both inside and outside, they both knew that he had a long way to go before they could move in. They couldn't ask for a better location and Mr. Feeley told them they can see the shuttle launch from their back patio they couldn't wait to see that. They gave him a check for the next draw payment, they told him to call again when he wants them to come down. They planned to stay down for a few more days. They want to visit the cape and spend the day. They did everything including the shuttle ride and walk past the rocket that took the men to the moon. They had their pictures taken in a room that looked like the shuttle and they made them look like they were floating. They finished off at the I- Max theater and watched the take off to the moon on a screen that had to be hundreds of feet big. Going to the movies will never be the same after that.

The next day they drove to Orlando and booked a show called Circus Olay was one of the best carnival type shows that they have ever seen. You name it and it happened, they finished the show and they decided to have dinner at the Wolf Gang Puck restaurant on the lake and it turned out to be the best way to end the evening, it ends up being one of the finest restaurants in all of Orlando. Now they have a two hour drive back to Vero and in there Bentley it was like being on a cloud. They got back to the hotel around 9: o'clock, they decided to have a night cap in the bar lounge. Donna our realtor came up behind us and said, "High strangers." Michael thought to him self that he few times they have come there for a night cap she is always there and maybe she has a drinking problem; it was just a thought.

She said she drove out to see our home today and it is really starting to take shape and how did we like it so far, they told her that it looked great and they can't wait to becoming a permanent resident She had a drink with them and she said that she had a big day tomorrow and she said she was going home and crash. They left to and took a shower together and jumped in the sack for some good lovin. They had breakfast in the dining room and they were interested in how their book was doing. They got to the airport and checked in and waited to be called to board they flew first class that's why they were called to board, they were hooked on first class and they will never fly any other way.

They were home in no time and there was still time to get up with the publisher to see how the book was going. He told them that their overseas sales were down a little down to 320,000 copies, believe it or not the US sales went up a little to 680,000 Ann said that they were still growing and they know like all good book sales they will slowly trickle away. Those two books have shaped their lives forever and they will never need or want for anything. Their home on the ocean is the icing on the cake and Liz told them their home will be a show place like before and crashed they were in bed early but not to sleep but they both would fall asleep very fast. Michael mentioned to Ann if they should be doing something and she asked him what should they want to do she was thinking about an agent that could keep them busy and Michael butted in and said that he would bleed us for 15% for every penny they made. His suggestion was to have a thousand letters printed up and send them out to the companies that have a lot of security and security problems that could use there help through seminars and speeches. It took a while but they got the address labels from the printer that the labels peel off that they can stick to the envelopes. They mailed them in increments of 200 and waited if anyone would be interested in what they had to offer.

They put a business card in with each letter and they called themselves, secure interventions with their names on the bottom of the card. They made it very clear in the letter that they would give seminars and speeches. The price for a seminar was $100,000 dollars a day or a two hour speech or a two hour speech w2as $25,000 dollars. The price was left of the letter it made good business to do that. Two weeks had gone by when they received a call from the LA pd to call them about their letter. Michael called them and they told him that they were interested in his skills in solving some of there outstanding murder cases out there, Michael told them the price for a seminar or a speech he was still on the line and he didn't hang up on him so that is a good start.

Michael asked him what services was he interested in, he told Michael if they have a seminar, they can get a lot of officers and detectives to come to the classes that would give them the extra training they would need. Michael wanted to know how much time are we talking about and his reply was at least two four hour days sessions. Michael told him that they require five star lodgings, that is what we are accustomed to. The phone conversation went well and they planned to meet in a week at the police auditorium for two four hour sessions, they booked them a suite at the Beverly Hills Hilton for at least three days. Michael asked Ann how is that in keeping ourselves busy. Ann applauded Michael that she knew he wouldn't waste any time in landing them their first job.

They left for the coast early Sunday morning and checked into the Hilton by 2: o'clock, they were told that they were expected. They had all of their books and a lot of handouts that will answer a lot of questions and help the seminar go very smoothly. They weren't that nervous because they had the confidence and experience to back it up. They were very young and in their case, age was not a problem. We were there very early and we stood on the stage and waited for the policemen to start coming in. Everyone that comes today will know that Michael caught that Russian spy singlehanded with nothing to go on but his but this guy's telltale behavior signs and if a person can identify those signs or signals, they will be more successful in arresting the bad guys.

The doors opened and the policemen started coming in and sitting as close to the stage they could sit. There were about fifty of them and these were the ones that were off duty. When they got settled down Michael introduced him and Ann and Ann as his wife, he told them if they are not the inquisitive type now, they will be at the end of the seminar. The secret of good crime solving is that you don't take anything for granted and to look for any lose threads in all of the places you wouldn't expect to find one. He went on to tell them how he caught the FBI agent that was stealing secrets for the Russians and Ann and were a couple of cases where the cases were put away as unsolvable because there weren't any clues.

Ann and I found clues and we had to look hard for them, it wasn't easy but when we look back on it, we could say it was. You will take lots of pictures and interview lots of wittiness's and reinterview them asking them to think hard about what they saw. Follow our simple guide lines and you will start to settle some cases that other people have given up on. Tomorrow we will tell you how we caught that guy that killed five girls all from Canada and there wasn't any clues and n o bodies were found never the less we knew they were murdered. I also couldn't find any of their cars I told them to have a nice evening and I will see them tomorrow and tell them how to look for a murderer. They applauded them for a long time when they finished and filed out of the auditorium, they were happy that the first day went so well. They went back to the hotel and showered and went down to the casual dress dining room for dinner.

They were seated when out of no where Robert Wagner came up to them and congratulated them on their great book, they thanked him and he walked away, he knew how it felt to get bugged by fans. Ann liked what they did on the first day and she said she can't wait till tomorrow. They got a good nights sleep and they were in the auditorium early and they started filing in rearing to go. Michael told them that Ann was going to start them off and her extensive details on how they looked for things that made sense to them in how could all of these girls cars be missing that is too much of a cover up and this murderer never knew that someone would be looking for them a few years later when the trail would be cold. He never dreamt that someone would take so much time on such a small detail like that and something so little as that eventually led us to him but with a lot of dead end clues and a lot of people not willing to cooperated with them.

Ann went on to say if they were in London when Jack the Ripper was killing all those girls, I can assure you that Michael would have caught him. Michael stood and thank Ann for saying every thing the way she practiced it and the place started laughing for the longest time and Michael gave Ann a big hug. He went on to tell them that the cars were put on a ship and taken out of the country to South America, it made sense that if the cars weren't around then they are somewhere else.

The question we pondered was if they weren't here then the only logical conclusion was, they were shipped out of the country. Michael went on for hours and when he finished, he told them that there isn't any thought that you have that you should pass up or any situation that if you were the murderer what would do not to get caught, if you can do that you will catch the murderer.

He told them how this little Scottie terroir caught that lovers lane murderer of five couples. Ann and I made things happen, we even staged a fake fire drill to see if the dog would recognize anyone when they filed out of the building, we will show you to take the initiative and solve the case you're on, he told them we'll do that tomorrow. They appreciated all that Michael and Ann had to say and applauded them for the longest time. They left with their books and handouts. The next morning Michael wanted to start off by telling the officers that none of these murderers ever wanted to get caught you have to search hard for them and drag them out kicking and screaming that they are innocent and they were going to get their lawyer on them. He spent a lot of time on the lovers lane murders and they thought that was the best detective work in solving this clueless crime.

Michael and Ann decided to spend the last day with questioning the accused. It went great and everyone wanted to ask them questions, when it was over everyone rushed the stage to shake their hands. They were the last to leave and they had dinner in the hotels casual dining room again, they went up to their room and the first thing they did was to start the fire place that they had in their bedroom and it was their first experience in going to bed with a fireplace on. They loved it enough that they had two put into both of their master bedrooms in Florida. They loved their seminars and they are looking forward to there next one Monday. They kept the room at the Ritz because it was easier then checking back in. This new seminar they wanted to put on some skits they showed them how they got these murderers to admit their guilt. It was amazing how you can question someone and make them squirm in their seat.

The skits showed them a lot and finally the day was done and the colonel came on stage and gave them a plaque and he thanked them whole heartedly. There were a couple officers that wanted us to sign their books that we were glad to, one officer really wanted to know if they were really x-FBI agents' Ann assured him they were. They both felt the class was a success and they couldn't wait to make the next one even better. Ann told Michael that this was only the beginning of a very long career. They hade the weekend to do something so they decided to go to Mexico in the morning and spend the day site seeing, they had a knapsack full of food because the Mexican food would give them the screaming shits all day.

They entered Mexico through Tijuana the border agent prewarned them not to buy any Mexican silver because it was fake. They wanted to take a bus ride out in the country and they saw things that they never realized ever existed. Their mountains weren't that high but they were beautiful, they didn't get back to Tijuana until after 5: o'clock they decided to leave for Los Angles and they stopped in San Diego and get a restart in the morning. They left at9:o'clock and they didn't get to their hotel at the Ritz until 4:o'clock they took a shower and had a salad for dinner, when they got back to their room Michael lite the fireplace and sat up in bed and watched the news, they set the timer to turn everything off at 11; o'clock

They never woke up until 8: o'clock the next morning and after their breakfast they booked a tour for the redwood forest, they knew that vit was going to be a long day and they were ready for it. They were in awe the whole time walking amongst the large trees, it was definitely a great idea. The week went by pretty fast and that didn't hurt. The second week was like the first week except they did more skits that were a big hit and it made the officers feel better about investigating a crime, they could see themselves being acted out in their jobs. They could see for the first time how to do a successful investigation. It was easy for Michael and Ann to do because they lived it. They received rave reviews and the word went out to law enforcement to hire these two x-FBI agents and improve their murder investigation skills.

They decided to stay overnight and leave in the morning around 11:o'clock and get home by 7:o'clock which includes the time change. They flew first class and took a nap for a few hours and they liked the dinner they served in first class; it wasn't their favorite but never the less they enjoyed it. Ann seemed a little tired but she said she was alright, their plane landed at 7:07 in the evening and caught the shuttle to take them home. They checked for intruders and their hidden camera and everything was ok, that was a relief knowing they were being left alone.

There wasn't any good on the tellie so they decided on a early night. There taxes were coming due in a few months. They planned to check in with the publisher on Monday for an update on the book sales. Ann was thinking that they might have peaked . The publisher hadn't spoken to them for two weeks, he told Michael that their book was still going strong, he told them to expect a slowdown but so far it hadn't.

The publisher wanted to keep the sales up so he came up with a marketing strategy that they would give a free CD to anyone that would but a book in the next thirty days, Ann liked that idea and the advertisements were everywhere, they were both anxious to see if they worked and make the book swales grow a little higher. So, when they checked in, he told them that the book sales in the US the number reached 3,880,000 in sales and they were still climbing. Their accountant told them that they owed $38, million in taxes for the year, sob they wrote a check and got rid of it.

The only good thing that they knew was that they would make more than that in interest next year and having everything be downloaded to their Swiss bank they escaped the taxes. They were getting a lot of speaking request all over the world. Michael would make them pay in advance before they took one step out on that stage, the money had to be routed to their bank and confirmed that the money was received and in their account. They had three speeches in England, one in Switzerland and one in Scotland, one in California, one in Manhattan and one in Dallas Texas, it took almost a month but it was worth it.

They received another call from the builder asking them to come down for another look see. They flew into Melbourne and rented their Bentley again and started out for Vero beach, and they checked into their favorite hotel and went out to their lot and see how things were going. The first thing they noticed was that they stucco over the cement blocks and framed cement molding around all the windows and doors and the front steps and entrance as well. Most all of the drywall was up but not finished or painted. All of the fireplaces were in but not finished, they weren't paint the stucco until it was the end of the job. All of the interior doors were in the garage waiting to be painted or stained.

Mr. Feeley apologized for running late and asked them how did they like it so far and they told him they did. He walked with them all through the house with them and Michael gave him his next draw check for where they are now. He knows that he has two more check of $1,million 900,000 to pay and the house will be all theirs. Their home was not going to be the thorn between two roses, in fact it will hold its own the contractor and the decorator will see to that. They haven't started on the pool yet. They know what there doing and I wasn't going to ask them anything about it. They decided to stay out and drive down to P V Martins for their famous seafood dinner on the ocean, it was still early so they stopped at the hotel lounge for a cold night cap for their favorite ice teas.

They signed up for a tour of the Airplane assembly plant at the airport. Michael was looking forward to see how they put these babies together. They saw everything and concluded that their plane isn't for everyone especially if they were over six foot tall and overweight. The tour lasted around three hours and they heard about this Italian restaurant in the Vero Beach shopping center called Vincent's as soon as they walked in, they knew they were in for a treat and Michael loved their Posta Fagioli and he would come back just to have it again. After that they wanted to drive out and see their new home again. They just wanted to walk around and get the feel of it. They met the retired meat packer neighbor Roger Laskowski and he invited them in for a cold drink.

He took then to his eating room that had a half room window and Michael was waiting for the questions to start and sure enough he started off by saying that he read both of our books and he can't wait for the next one to come out. He admired us how we were able to get at the truth and that led us into the way in solving those murder cases and he especially liked the way I caught that spy and you two are so young, God bless you. He told them that he liked our home and now that he has met us, he is looking to be a good neighbor and a good friend. He asked us if we were catholic and I told him we were neutral; he didn't know how to understand that and Michael wasn't going to explain that.

They thanked him for inviting them in his home and they have a plane to catch very early in the morning and they will make sure they meet him again the next time they come down, he walked out with them and he said he liked their car. Michael told him that they will probably buy one when they come down permanently, it's the best car they ever owned. They drove off know that their choice of the home site they chose and their home that was being built on the ocean that has its good point and bad points. They got back to the hotel and they liked stopping into the lounge again and there were Ann's parents sitting at a table with another couple. Michael told Ann not to go over to them and see who sees who first and see if they come over to us first, he told her that will answer a lot of questions about where she stands.

Michael walked by their table and brought back some cashews from the bar and they never noticed him. Ann thought that was odd and they sat there and finished their drinks. Michael asked Ann if she has seen enough and does and starting walking to her, she wants to do anything and her reply was let's go back to our room. As they stood to leave her mother called out to her saying why didn't you tell me that you were here. Ann told her that she called her a number of times and you never answered your phone, she told Ann that it is hard to believe and Ann told her that all of the phone calls that she told her are on my phone bill that we get each month just like yours. The mother had this queer look on her face Ann left her there standing with egg all over her face.

Ann walked away from her in disgust and caught up to Michael who was standing in the lobby and he could see that Ann was hurt and asked her if she was ok and he knew it will surface someday but she isn't going to wait around to see what it is. They want to go back to their room and lite up the fireplace and take the chill out of the air. The fireplace was on an 11: o'clock turn off as well as the Tv. They had breakfast and checked out and was in the air in no time, it was comforting to them to know they will be living in Florida permanently real soon. They have been giving a couple of speeches a week and their book sales are still but not as high as the other weeks. The last two weeks they sold 400,000 copies and that is a lot of books that were sold this time after its initial start.

They love giving their speeches and it gave them a chance to meet a lot of people, it seems that a lot of banks are interested in what they have to say about their computer systems and their security systems so they are asking them to come to their banks. The one thing that Michael thought of was if someone would try to hack in to the banks computers it would reverse itself back to the hackers system and totally wipe them out. The banks were paying big money for this and Michael and Ann were cashing in on the computer hacking security business and they were beginning to be known in the security world and the demand was very high for their services. It was only the two of them and they couldn't keep up with the demand to speak and visit these businesses. Michael told Ann that they can only do there best and see how it goes. There audiences loved it when they told them how they became successful in solving their cases.

In three months, they had spoken to fifty five businesses and attended their conventions. It was quite a cash flow but they would burn out if they don't slow down. They finally got the call that their home was ready for the final walkthrough. They gave everything they owned in the apartment to the salvation army, they took some clothes for five days, they would buy what they would need there from people that had the high end clothing line that they were interested in. Michael's motto was if your going to look the part then you have to dress the part. Ann knew that this is going to be a life changing move. They drove down and they would trade the car in after they settle. Michael had their route all written down all the way to Vero Beach and they got to the hotel by 1: o'clock and checked in and they rushed over to see the house and finally after a year it will be ready for them to move in.

Ann saw the house from the road and she started crying they walked around to see if they could find a door open and they did the interior was breathtaking and the first thing they remember was what Liz said that it would be a show place. Ann couldn't stop saying how beautiful it was and she can't wait to see it decorated tomorrow after they settle. Michael took Ann's hand and said they have time lets trade our car in on a Bentley, they looked in the directory and they found one in West Palm Beach and cut out to find it. When they did, they were able to walk around the lot and then inside the showroom and they found this dark two toned silver two *door convertible. I mean it was beautiful and the window sticker said $348,000 and they got a big laugh at that.*

They heard someone call out if they liked that and Michael turned around and asked him, "What was there not to like?" and he introduced himself as dick wood and Michael introduced Ann first and then himself and the salesman asked them if they would like to take it on a test drive and he would have to go with them as a company policy. That didn't matter to them so Michael took it out first and Ann droved it back to the open parking space in front of the show room and they just sat there saying how nice it was and the salesman asked them to follow him to his office and when they were seated He asked them if they wanted to drive it home today. Ann told him that there isn't anything that they would like better but it would be entirely up to you.

He told them that he is all for it and never did a couple look better than they did sitting that car, this car was made for someone like you two. Michael told him that the price was too high for their liking and his quick response was that they don't dicker on the price, company policy. Michael asked him if he was sure about that and he said his hands were tied. Ann stood up and told him that they should be a little more flexible and they started out the door. They could hear him chasing after them and they walked faster and didn't stop. They finally got to their car and out of sheer desperation he asked them to stop and make him an offer, Michael offered him $320,000 and said they couldn't do that. Michael told him that they can drive a little further south and get one on the south side of West Palm and they will make it a point to drive back and show him the car that he missed out on.

He stood there speechless and said that he would have to call the owner to get his approval, they walked back in with him and he made the call and came back out and said they will take your offer and they have a deal and how did they plan on paying for it.

Michael handed him their Swiss Card and he walked away with a sign of disbelief. When he came back, he confessed that he never held out that he had such a high rated charge card with that much cash credit. He asked them if they could spare an hour to prep their new Bentley Azure T, he did tell them that he picked the best one they had for sale here. He told them not to put the top down in the sun for any long period of time, he corrected himself and said hot sunny days because its hard on the leather. He heard Michael tell Ann that he wants to get a Escalade to knock around in.

He told them that they have an agency next door and he will give them a very good price on their top of the line Escalade. He asked Michael why doesn't he get another Bentley and Michael said they only wanted one and one Escalade, he picked up on that and he told them he would be ready when they are. Ann told him that they just had a home built on the ocean in Vero Beach and they only want the best, his reply was that they must really have good credit to buy that house and Michael told him that you don't need good credit when you can pay cash. He gulped with that when they were pulling up their cad to drive home. They decided to leave their car with the dealer to trade in on the Escalade when they return. They asked Dick if he would come to their house in Vero morning and bring them down to the caddy dealer to purchase the Escalade, he said he could pick them up at 10: o'clock and bring them down to purchase their new Escalade.

Dick went over the interior with Ann and Michael, they were a little familiar because of all the rentals that had moving down here. Michael told Ann to drive us home after they called their Insurance company and added the Bentley on to their auto policy. She found A1A and they listened to the radio all the way home to their hotel. They were starving after all that hustling at the dealership. They went up to their room to freshen up a little and went down to their casual dining room, they chose to eat in the bar lounge and they managed to get a nice view of the ocean. Donna spotted them and they did ask her to join them for dinner and Ann was excited to tell her that they just bought a new Bentley a dark silver one it is a convertible and they will store in their new garage along with he new Escalade that they are picking it up Friday, they need something to run around town in.

They told her that their settlement is tomorrow morning at the builders office and do a final walk through and then settle. They met him at the house and he started showing us the outside first and the pool was something to see and he showed them the sea wall and the grand entrance and then he opened the garage doors and they walked inside. He told them to take the elevator while him and Michael take the stairs. The interior was like a palace without any furniture the paint job was perfect and the kitchen was high end. The different views of the ocean was worth it all, he showed how to work their electric shutters, that was very impressive. The first floor master bedroom was as big as some peoples houses and their balcony was nice as well. The walk in closets were big enough for six peoples clothes.

There was recess lighting everywhere that gave the house that classic look that the builder wanted for them. The master bath was all granite and the shower were all glass, thick glass with 12" shower heads, they couldn't wait to take a shower together. The second floor was grandiose and there was expensive molding everywhere each bathroom had their own full bath and every bedroom had its own full bath. They didn't find anything wrong and they told Mr. Feeley that they liked everything but they want to have the right to have him back if there is something they missed later on, he said that he didn't have a problem with that.

They went to his office and they sat at the conference table and he opened his folder and read to them about the taxes each year and the cost of water and electricity. The taxes are $20,000 a year that *he is required to collect at settlement he said that their balance due today is $1, million 920,000. Michael reached for his Swiss card and he handed it to Mr. Feeley, it was all over in minutes and he handed them two gold keys that would open every door that has a lock. Then he gave them a house gift that consisted of a large number of assorted cheeses, fruit wines and a $500.00 visa card to use to purchase their first house food bill to stock up on their food for their new house. They thanked him very much and they told him that they will use it as soon as Liz gets the refrigerator plugged in.*

Mr. Feeley told them That Liz will be bringing her furniture moving trucks and she should be here at noon, they didn't want to be in the way so they went to Vincent's for a light lunch and back to the hotel for some afternoon delight, it was special and so would it be special the first night they spend in their new house. They were told that Liz has a big crew and they plan on working all night if they have to get them moved in. She had a team of six people hanging the drapes and another dozen unloading the furniture and placing them where she tells them to. They finally went back to the house to see how she was doing and to see all the furniture placed around in all the right places.

Liz asked them if they were going to stay tonight Ann said that they need to do some shopping for all the bath room items, shower mats and all those things from the towels to the wash cloths then they will spend their first night, probably tomorrow evening. Liz told her that it will be after midnight before she has every drape up, picture hung and every rug down where it belongs. They stayed until 9: o'clock and they left for the hotel and spend their last night there. They wanted to get an early start and pick out a service of twelve of twelve for the dinner ware formal and casual and the silver ware formal (gold) and stainless for casual. There was a great place for that at the mall and they got there when they opened. They bought everything they had in the dinner ware right down to the place mats. They loaded their truck and they followed them to the house.

There was three of them and when we got there Michael opened the garage door and he had them put everything in the elevator and take them upstairs, rather then carry them up the steps. They put all the different boxes in different places around on the granite tops so as not to over load the kitchen cabinets, that made it easier to unpack. That little shopping spree cost them $3,700.00 dollars. When they were finished, they gave each man $50.00 dollars as a sign of their appreciation, they were very happy to get that. They took a walk through the house and they couldn't get over the richness of how it looked. They walked through the house twice and Michael thought that it is as good time as ever to get some grocery shopping out of the way.

They filled up three shopping carts and one of the store associates was assigned to push a cart around for us to fill with food and other things. They checked out and the bill came to $860.00 they gave them the Publics visa card and the difference with their Swiss card. That little Bentley was packed to the roof and so was the trunk. When they got home, they backed into the garage for easy unloading in the elevator. They did check out at the hotel and when they looked in the master bed room there wasn't any doubt where they were staying tonight after seeing the king size bed in the master bedroom that was fit for Royalty. They decided to make a mad dash to the high end bath store and get all of the towels and washcloths shower mats and sink rugs and anything else they would need to finish decorating the bathrooms. They didn't get back until after 6: o'clock and both of them were dragging ass they got so tied up with unloading and putting things around the bathrooms they forgot to eat.

They had so many groceries to put away Ann was sure she could find something to eat in that lot. They couldn't believe that it was after 9: o'clock and no matter how tired they were they were going to

Cristen their new house. After they showered together, they got this sudden boost of energy and it turned their first bight to a night to remember. When they finished the both said it was worth the wait, they even had the fireplace lit and to shut off at 11: o'clock. They didn't wake up until 8: o'clock the next morning and they both agreed that they never slept so better in their whole life and it only took one night to know that. They were going to meet with the land scaper he will be someone that does more then cutting grass, he also trims all of the shrubbery and right behind him is the pool maintaince guy who will come once a week and check our water to see to it that it is germ free and he is fully licensed and backed by the state of Florida that he is certified to treat pools.

8

Michael wants to get their Escalade today that they will use for running around town on errands, they were waiting for their Bentley salesman to come and pick them up like they planned. He was there right on time and he stepped out of the car and told them how much he loved their home, he told them if he lived here, he would never want to leave it. Ann told him that if he ever wants to get a house like this one, he will have to leave it everyday to work. He told her that he just got carried away with its beauty. He told them that he was ready to go to the Cadillac dealer if they were and Michael was all for it. The ride was short and Dick was pulling into the parking lot and told them that they have six of our best Escalades to choose from.

Michael asked him what makes them to be the best ones, he said they were loaded and the best that Cadillac had to offer. Michael really looked them over and then he asked if he had any other ones to pick from, he said he had some out back and one ion the show room. He asked if he could see them now and that got Dick a little rattled. They went around back and they didn't see anything special and they started for the showroom and they spotted this pitch black Escalade with stainless rims and Michael why wasn't this one in the six pack and his reply was he didn't think that we would like black. Michael Dick if he could have a minute with his wife and when Dick was gone, he told Ann that something is up with this guy and why did he purposely didn't show us this black one. He told Ann that he is a bit dodgy and he didn't count on us looking around and why did he want to hide this better looking one from us.

Ann asked him what did he want to do and Michael said if they don't want to make a deal with them, they leave. She agreed with him and waited for Dick to return and Michael told him that it looks like the one in the showroom is there choice but not for the sticker price. They both walked over to the window where the sticker was and looked at it again and it read $87,000.00, He told them that they got him on the Bentley but not on this beauty. Michael asked for the keys to their car and they walked out of the show room and left him standing there with his mouth open. They stopped at the Cadillac dealer on US1 and they found the same Escalade for a couple thousand dollars less.

They walked around it and finally told the salesman they just left the dealership in West Palm because the salesman lied to them. That they would like to trade their car in on this black Escalade and they would like to test drive it while they are working up a trade. He went along for the ride and he could tell that these two are not the average car buyer, they went about five miles and turned around. The salesman told them that this one is loaded and the best that Cadillac had to offer. Michael told him to give them his best deal or they will have to drive to Melbourne and get one. He turned it around and asked Michael to tell him what price are you looking at. Michael to take our car and w will give them $62,000.00. he told them that he would have to get permission on that price.

He was gone for five minutes and returned with the manager and he introduced himself as Dale White and he said there has to be a little more give than take if he is to keep from driving all the way up to Melbourne. Michael told him that their offer is the best they can do and he quickly responded and said he couldn't do it; the numbers just aren't right. Just like before they both stood and asked for their car keys and he asked why can't we be a little more flexible and Michael said he was and if they have to drive to Melbourne to get a deal, they will. He asked them that you can't even give them an extra

$500.00 and Michael shook their hand and told him to prep it and get it ready to drive home.

While they waited, they sat in another Escalade and the sales men showed them everything they had to know how to safely drive their new vehicle and not have a problem and when he finished their vehicle was sitting in front of the showroom ready for their short ride home. Their salesman asked them to come inside and get the paper work out of the way and he asked them how were they going to pay and Michael told him with their Swiss visa card and her handed it to him. He left and came back in a few minutes and told them that there aren't to many people that have that high enough credit rating to buy a car on a credit card like you just did. He gave them an envelope of papers that they were to keep in the glove box. Ann said that she was going to call her insurance agent and make the change of car. Ann said let's go home they have to stop at Publics and get some more things.

The Escalade looks real good in the garage and in the drive way as well. They rode the elevator with the groceries up to the kitchen. Ann was excited in making their first meal in their new house. She decided on something simple just to get her sea legs, it was something that her mother showed her how to make it was called pig in a blanket. Michael was a little reserved but he said it was worth the wait. She cooked fat sausage links and hid them under a soft blanket of tasty dough with brown gravy and onions Michael loved the taste of the sausage and the dough and he told Ann how much he liked it. They finished dinner and decided to go skinny dipping and give the neighbors something to look at. Ann had a body that would knock anyone eyes out, with or without clothes. Michael was getting fired up and he wanted Ann more as the evening went on when he finally had her in bed and he put her fire out.

There was something about the fireplace in the bed room that added to the ambience of their bedroom experience, they were young and they could go all night. They loved their pool that they had the temperature set on 70 it was perfect for them. Liz had lounges and tables and chairs all around the pool and two hammocks if they feel like laying out some time for a short nap.

Ann was starting to notice her gaging in the morning while she was brushing her teeth, so she wanted to take the pregnancy test that she had to pee on a strip that will tell her if she is pregnant or not. It was only a few days later that she sat with Michael out back when he was sitting and watching the waved coming on the shore. He was drinking ice tea while Ann was drinking water. Michael thought that was peculiar and he asked her why the water and her reply was that the tea wasn't any good for the baby. Well he was knocked for a loop and asked her when was she going *tell him about this. She said that she went to see the highest recommended baby doctor around here and I didn't ask him to go because it was just a check up and not really knowing if she was pregnant or not. Michael asked her what can he do to help her and her reply was to relax and let it take its course.*

He planned to do just that, they were still very young and 26 is young. They will still go to the conventions and seminars and only be away and they cut it down to three a week. They still wanted to do it and it was easy because they did it. They got up with their publisher and he told them that their numbers were slowing down but there still seems to be a renewed interest in it still in the country. He gave Michael the sales count and it was 480,000 he told him that it will peter out in a month or and they were very happy with the sales so far and who wouldn't. They dot up with Roy from their Swiss bank and they downloaded another $180 million dollars into their private account. He told Michael that he would like to get one of those money trees like we have.

They are making almost $40 million dollars in interest an year, they made a deal with each other, not to worry about the money it will take care of itself and it will be a load that they will be putting *on themselves. They kept $7 million 440 thousand dollars in their everyday account. Roy from the Swiss account told Michael that he can use his Swiss card to buy a quart of milk so by leaving you money out of their Swiss account you are losing a lot of interest on that money by not putting that money in their Swiss account and that account Michael downloaded the $7 million dollars from their personal account and added it to their Swiss private account that changed their total to be $337,million dollars. They knew that Roy was correct and they were glad to add $7 million dollars into their Swiss account.*

So, they walked the beach every day to get in shape and it will make Ann's delivery a lot easier because she e will be physically strong. They have to keep their youth or they will lose their stamina and not be able to handle anything that comes their way. Ann is four months now and her doctor said she was in great shape and make her delivery a lot easier. They have gotten so use to there morning walk along the beach, rain or shine but not in any electrical storms. Ann asked Michael if he was up to having a cat, they are nice to be around. They take care of themselves and only require to be fed and they will do the rest. Michael said he would go along with it if the cat is declawed.

Michael checked with the publisher again and he said that in the last thirty days the sales have dropped off to 250,000 and they will start to slow down to a trickle soon, they expected that and they want to do another one. Ann is showing big now and at night she puts oil and creams all over her tummy that it's a wonder that she could get into bed without sliding out on the floor. She said she would do this every night rather to get stretch marks on her tummy and hips. She just had a doctors visit and he said everything was fine and we can expect a very healthy baby.

Michael hired a guy to come to the house every Thursday to feather dust their two cars and wash them if they need it. The fellow said that he had never touched a Bentley before. The only thing that Michael let him do was to back the cars out of the garage and do his cleaning if it were better for him. He said that those two vehicles are really good and well wort the money they cost.

Ann is really big and the doctor told them that Ann will be delivering soon, she still wanted to still walk in the morning, she said it made her feel healthy and when they returned, they would shower when Ann told Michael that it was time that they leave in the Escalade for the hospital. Michael called the hospital and gave them a heads up that they were on their way and they could call the doctor that we are on their way in. Michael took the Valet parking and Michael had Ann's arm and they took her away from him and they told him to have a seat in the lounge and they would come back for him, he watched them taking Ann down the hall and he wanted to be with her. He must have looked at every magazine they had and finally the nurse cam in the room and she asked him to come with her, he had to change into some hospital clothes and they took him to where Ann was and when he saw the look on her face told him that that she was in great pain.

Dr Warsal came in and said hello and he went right to Ann and he said she is dilated four centimeters and it won't be long now. Michael was holding her hand and Dr. Warsal was telling her to push some more and she did that for five minutes and the baby came right out into his hands and he told them it was a boy and they were happy to hear that. Ann said they would name him after his father Michael, Michael said they will call him Mike as a nickname. They put little Michael on Ann's chest and let little Michael suckle on his mommy's milk fresh from the breast. He looked just like Ann and he had a good skin completion. Ann crashed and so did Michael, nine months is a long time to wait.

They let Ann come home after the third day and Michael hired a Nanny and some house keepers and a cook, he said that Ann was going to be too busy to take care of the baby clean this big palace and cook all the meals. Ann was in tears that Michael could see that no one could do all the work to keep this palace clean and cook and take care of the baby. Little Mikey slept with them in their bedroom in his bassinette. They had a big screen Tv and a great fireplace and anything else if they wanted it there. The nanny would come in at 8: o'clock and she would stay until 6: o'clock. Their cook only made lunch and dinner and she cleaned up and gone by 7: o'clock. The house Keeper comes every other day except the weekends.

Their publisher told them that their book sales have all but stopped and at last count of the last batch was only six thousand. Michael spent as much time as he could holding the baby and taking him for walks in his stroller to get him some fresh air, he seemed to like it and he would fall asleep in minutes. Ann was speechless about her parents as to why they are treating her the way they are treating her as if she didn't exist. Michaels advice was to let it go and see where what happens next. This was something her parent chose to do to her. It's not Ann's place to run after them because they started this and they don't have the guts to tell her what this is all about because it is childish on their part, it is there loss and they will live to regret it.

Michael asked Ann if she was up to taking notes on them catching the lovers lane murderer and how in the end it was a little Scottie dog that sniffed him out and caught him. They worked on it a little bit each day and after four months they had enough notes for them to write the book. It could have taken longer but because of the notes were that good and he lived through that whole ordeal it was finished and ready to be read by the publisher. He finally called the publisher and he told him that he has another book, if he's interested. Interested, you two are the most famous writer we have today, he asked Michael what kind of a story is this one all about. Michael told him how Ann and he worked on these serial killings for months, until they saw a person walking this little Scottie dog and it stopped him right where one of the killings took place.

Michael asked the guy if it were at all possible for a dog to smell someone that stood there over thirty days ago. The dog owner told Michael that his little Scottie could smell drugs through nine inch es of cement. The owner bent over and he had his dog to sniff around, even out in the street away from the shooting spot and finally he started down the street away from the shooting spot. The owner would offer him some words of encouragement and after six blocks the dog stopped at a high rise apartment complex and you will read how that little Scottie dog helped us catch that serial killer. Michael told him that him and Ann have moved to Florida and he can overnight it to him.

Michael went right to fed ex and boxed it and sent it on its way. It wasn't until the second day that the publisher called and told Michael that this one will out sell all the other ones. He said he will have the dog play a big part in the advertising of the book and with all the animal lovers out there we won't be able to keep it in print and the overseas sales will go gang busters. He told Michael that he was so excited he could open up his windows and scream. He told Michael that he will advertise, if you liked this x-FBI agents first two books that they wrote you are going to love this one. He asked Michael if the same deal is ok with him and Michael said it was fine.

He said that he wants to tease the public about the book until they will be screaming to read it. When they went out, every where they went there was something about the book By Michael and Ann Smith and when it will be in the stores. There was a advertising blitz everywhere if that was possible, it has him and Ann excited. Little Mikey vis eight months old now and he is cuter than hell, he would laugh at anything. With the help that Ann is getting from the Nanny, little mikey will have a great upbringing. They were that the house cleaners are keeping the house as sparkling as the day they moved in. The cook is catching on to our taste for food and she is making an attempt to elevate us up a notch they know that she wants the best for them and if we entertain we would need to be above the level of the highest guest that might come to their home, it will make sense to them when that see how this plays out.

They even had news flashes and radio alerts that the latest book by Michael and Ann Smith will be out in two days, the news releases were 24/7 they knew that they were setting up the sale for the new book, the lover lane murders. They played up the dog part pretty big and they were hoping big enough. The day the book was released for sale it was all over the news and there was a news team right side their house asking for an interview. Michael and Ann walked outside and down the driveway and said hello.

"Someone called out and said Mr. Smith this is your third book you must be very happy with the sales."

"We are and we are flattered with the popularity of the book."

"Your books are interesting and better still they are true, your followers like the way you put your stories into words."

"Yes, they are true and we were agents with the FBI and what's in those books is true."

"Did you leave the FBI on good terms or were you fired."

"You asked for an interview and now you have turned this interview into a mud slinging debate, this will be the last interview we will ever grant your station."

"We are just trying to get to the real facts about you because we only know a little about you."

"I can assure you that you will know even less, you have ruined it for all the other news networks that want to talk to us."

"What are you going to do with all of your money."

"I should be the one asking you that stupid question, if I should see any of this interview taken bout of context on the news or in the

newspapers, I will use my money to sue you and bankrupt you out of business. Now if you don't believe me just take anything, I said to you today out of context and I will sue you out of business. Now if you think that I am blowing a lot of hot air you better read our books.

Michael and Ann walked away saying that they will never give another interview again to anyone and he meant it. They went back inside and Ann made a good breakfast for them, their cook only does lunch and dinner, they sat out back with the Nanny and little mikey by the pool. They put some music on while they were eating their sausage and eggs and an English muffin. The sound of the ocean was great with the music. Little Mikey was sitting in his highchair just enjoying being outside in the fresh air. After they finished their breakfast they just sat back and enjoyed the ocean breeze.

The Nanny took little Mikey in for a knap and Ann and Michael decided to go on their morning walk along the beach, there weren't that many people on the beach just an occasional walker. The tide was going out and the sand was very firm and easy to walk on. After an hour you can start to get a sun tan or a sunburn depending on your sun conditioner number is. They talk about that dumb Tv interview and that socialist news reporter.

Finally, after five days that their book had been released, there were people standing in line at the book store in the malls wanting to buy their book and Michael was more than anxious to see how things were going with the publisher, that when he called him the phone rang busy, he thought he would call back later. He waited until 4:0'clock and tried again and this time it rang and when it was answered I told him that it was Michael and he said Michael he hasn't taken a decent breath in a week, ever with all my employees its out of control, he asked me to wait a minute and he would get me some numbers. He started with the overseas numbers first and they were 860,000 and in the US, it was about 1,150,000 and that is some great number for the first five days, that's how popular their book is.

Those numbers were mind boggling; they were also reporting that the most popular dog to own right now is the Scottie dog. There none to be found anywhere Stan told Michael to popular to slow down, it was the most popular book in the world and that it is being sold in 108 countries. England has the most sales then France, Canada is third and so on. Michael said that they still have one more book to write after this one and that would be the end of it. They couldn't get over the intertest that these people had in these murder cases and how they got caught.

Michael thought they should join the Grand Harbor C.C. and take up golf as a past time and Ann liked that idea as well so they drove out to the Country Club and they looked for the membership office, it was down the hall and Michael walked in and told the lady at the desk that they would like to join the club as full time members. She asked them for their names and she asked them to be seated and in a few minutes another lady came in to where they were sitting and she asked them to come back to her office and join her. She had on a name tag that said Carol and she looked down on her paper with there names on it and she asked them if they were any relations to the Authors and Ann told them they were them. "Carol said o my God it's you." Your names are everywhere and your books are very popular. We would be very proud for you to be members here.

She asked them if they knew any of our members and they told her no. She said we can waive the two reference requirements because of their fame and we know you two could give us volumes of references. She told them that the membership requirements are as followed the imitation fee is $5,600.00 and the full club membership is 45,000.00 a year, payable in quarters if you should want that. There is a food requirement of a $800.00 a year. You *either use it or loose it. Golf is free on either course and women have a restricted starting time on the weekends after 11: o'clock. The cart fee is $25.00 dollars for two golfers and $15.00 for a single golfer. She told them that their dining room is highly rated and they have a 19th hole place for the golfers can stop and get something to eat and run if they have to.*

Michael asked if there is a waiting time to be approved as members and she told them she sped up their approval for them to be approved as full members. She asked them if they have chosen a method of payment and Ann said they would pay everything all at once. She apodised for not giving them a locker that carries a $150.00 a year and did they want to use a card or write a check. Ann gave her their Swiss Visa card and Carol excused herself and came back a few minutes later with a paid receipt for $10,900.00 dollars the first year and next year there will not be any initiation fee next year.

She asked them to walk with her down to the pro shop and meet the pro. His name is Rome and he's from Newark, Delaware. Michael told him he was from Newark, Delaware as well. They liked him right away and he liked them too. He went over with them in how to get a starting time, he gave him some pro shop brochures that included the dress code for playing golf and they will be billed once a month on anything they purchase from the pro shop. Michael and Ann have played a little golf so they are familiar with most of the rules and how to keep score and mostly they want to bring their game up to being a good golfer. They were happy with what they did today and they were going to rely on the Nanny to baby sit while they are out playing golf.

Now is the time to get some clubs and Michael went on line and he got Ann on a complete set of Callaway's which included a lady's professional golf bag and two pair of shoes and a complete set of Taylor made woods and a complete set of Callaway irons and *a male golf bag he wanted to purchase his golf shoes at the store in the Miracle mile shopping center. The price tag on all this came to $2,800.00 that was a bargain and it would have been doubled in the pro shop. They were given laminated membership cards and two entrance stickers that would identify them at the entrance gates as members. One thing they found out that they have this large beach complex that they call the beach property where they can use their private beach or use the faculties for their own private use. Now that was something, they didn't know they had for their members, it was only a short distance from the Disney Hotel on A1A.*

This was a good decision that they made for them to find a good outlet for their social needs. The country club and golf is a good outlet for a lot of their needs Michael knew that they will have to some practicing before they play with anyone, they will spend a lot of time on the practice rang and the putting green and then come back after dinner for a quick nine holes. Their publisher got up with them and gave them another book sale count. This one is higher and the total was 2, 600,000 sold these past ten days. The NYTimes issued a book count of sales thus far, it was all over the news and they were bombarded for interviews and they never answered one of them. They know when the news people can't have their way with you then they will try to destroy you, that is how socialism works and that makes the worst form of government there is.

Ann has mentioned to Michael the number of Harry Potter books that were sold. No one can ever top those sale numbers but it looks like their book is giving them a good race. They told their Nanny what they have done as far as joining the club and from time to time they will be using the facilities to improve their golf games. She was very happy for us and told them that she has everything under control, little Mikey is no problem to her that was the good news that she wanted to hear and that took the worry out of going to the club together and knowing that little Mikey is in good hands. Ann put a swimming suit on little Mikey and took him swimming after dinner, it was fun watching him splash around.

They found out that the three connecting lots next to them were up for sale for a $1,000,000 each. They had 160ft ocean frontage and there were about 3/4 of an acre each, and to be honest they weren't worth it. That night the temperature dropped down to the forties, so they put their bedroom fireplace on. What a night it turned out to be, can you imagine your woman in bed with you and the fire flame shadows were reflecting off the ceiling and walls it turned out to be a great night for a get together.

They keep a very low profile and the less they are recognized suits them just fine. They love going everywhere they want and not have anyone pester them. Little Mikey is sitting up now and he is crawling around a little more each day. They have barriers in each door way in each room with the intention of protecting him from getting hurt needlessly, he loves the pool and the Nanny has instructions that they will be the only ones to take him to the pool.

Michael knows that their money is collecting the best interest they could find 12% is not possible to beat by any bank. Right now, they are making $50 million dollars in interest and it grows higher each year. They are contented with that and not waste any time in worrying about it. There isn't anything we can't buy and I mean anything that can make me $50 million dollars a year and I don't have to lift one figure to do it. Michael said they are just going to let their money soak . They aren't interested in building a restaurant or hotel or anything like that and they can see their money grow a half a billion dollars in eight years, just in interest and with their base that alone would put them over a billion dollars.

They are going to enjoy life as much as they can and not decide that he wants to be a Governor or a senator or hold any public office they just want keep a low profile and play some golf and travel around a little and take an occasional vacation whenever they want to go and not be tied down to anything that would make demands on their time. I guess it's clear that they are not going to make their lives complicated, they just want to live the good life and keep it simple. They thought about an airplane and it would be a lot simpler and cheaper to charter and pay them to taker them wherever they want to go and not keep a piolet on the payroll that you might use two weeks out of the year. That will cost a lot of money for nothing.

The book is growing in popularity to where it is impossible for Ann and I to conceive of how many people are buying it, everyone wants to buy a Scottie dog and finding one like the one that helped us catch the lovers land serial killer will not be an easy task. Ann and Michael put that story together and turned it into the most popular book in the world today and it is bringing in Royalties that is hard to believe. The Country Club wanted to throw them a book recognition party and Michael told them maybe some other time, they honored their wishes and left it at that. They were not your typical glory hunters; they are perfectly happy with being one of the club members not looking for any favors or recognition from anyone.

The publisher called again and said that the book sales were over 2 million again, they just look at each other in disbelief and they realize that the public is looking to read about a great crime being solved and in this book, a little Scottie dog put the human interest in the story and made this serial killer capture unique. The news serviced are still trying for an interview from Michael and Ann they even went so far as to try and get an interview with Mr. Schriber the serial killer. They won't allow any interviews, he's hard to understand and he is very cautious when he talks. He is the last person in the world that would make a good interview. That bitch that tried to interview me a few months ago is back to trying again for a no tough question interview.

Michael told her she had a chance, she could have had an exclusive and she couldn't lose that liberal socialist style of interviewing, that they are taught that if they person being interviewed is too good to be true, then destroy them. He told her again that he will never grant her an interview and reminded her again about printing any non-truths about himself or Ann his wife. Then Good Morning America called and they told him they have been trying to get up with them and they invited them on their morning show and he reminded them what they did to Arnold Swartszineger was a disgrace and you will only realize it when the whole lot of you lose your jobs, because you will you will finally realize that you are out of step with the rest of us, that wasn't enough they keep calling us back. They don't need to be going on their show to promote their book their book promoted itself. They are livid because he is showing them that he doesn't need them, they just want to smear them as best they can on national television.

Ann and Michael feel the same about them and their destructive ways, no interviews under any circumstances, they like not being chased after, it won't take that long before the press before that start to see the picture. By not giving interviews they can survive all of the slings and arrows that will be hurled at them. They never reply to any of that mudslinging and the press and the press is helpless to do anything about it. They know that they keep slinging mud at a person that doesn't hold any office or beholding to anyone, if they didn't write those books no one would know who they are.

9

Ann's mother called and asked if they could see the baby and Ann told them straight out no, now you are interested in us when you avoided us for over a year and never told us what we supposing did to cause that. If you could be so mean to your daughter for no reason that we know of we don't want your stone age way of thinking to rub off on our child. The mother was in shock to hear Ann say that to her and finally did say to Ann that it looks like the end between us. Ann had the final word and told her that when you chose to treat us like you did then you deserve what you get and reminder her that, "turnabout is fair play." And please don't send us any cards and to remove her name that she might have with someone to call me in an emergency and if you see us out somewhere do not make any attempt to contact us and say something to us and please don't make any attempt to speak to us. Now if you do, we will bring a no contact charge against you and you will be forever marked.

Ann couldn't say anything else with out saying the same thing over and over she went to Michael and told him what happened and he told her to hold her ground and he will back her all the way. Michael said that things could never be the same after they snubbed them like she did. He asked Ann if she thinks she will ignore what she told her and Ann said that she made it perfectly clear of what her feelings were, she went on to say in so many words not to ever contact us again or there will be hell to pay.

Their income tax is coming due soon again and the way Michael figures it will be around $20,000.000 and after that everything they do and get paid for it that money will be made to the Swiss *savings account that will allow them to only pay taxes on the money that withdraw. They haven't made any friends except for the two neighbors on either side of them, they always want to get together but it never happens. They know that they will be a lot closer but right now everyone is busy, they will have to find something that they have in common and work on that to bring them closer together. They know that they are a lot younger and that is one hurdle for them to get over just like they are amazed how they can move freely among the people and not be recognized.*

They still want to play some golf so they go out to the club at least every other day and go to the range and spend an hour or so and hit some balls and finish off with thirty minutes of putting. They saw a big improvement in their ball striking and a definite improvement in their putting. Michael congratulated Ann on her golf skills and it won't be long before they can start playing a round. They are seen by all the members that come to the range or just ride by on their way to the next hole. Michael couldn't get over how they vacuum up the grass clippings after they cut it. The course is in supreme condition and the housed being built on the premises are first class and prestigious.

They just love their house and it has everything anyone could ever dream of, even though their neighbors houses are bigger they know that bigger isn't necessarily better. There house was more up to date that included electrical shutters, they even had an electric generator and they had a 500 gallon tank of gasoline buried to use just in case the blackout was extended a while longer. There generator was the size of a small car and when it ran you could hardly hear it. They weren't going to let any storm to leave them in the dark when we can afford to get our generator working to get the job done.

They loved their bedroom fireplace and they lit it a lot, it's been a month since their book has been published and their publisher told them that their numbers were still high and is almost 3 Million copies sold it was a little drop and they knew it would drop again.

It was little Mikey's birthday and they got him some clothes and some toys and a toy walker that will be a big help in assisting him in walking. He just loves his pacifier and he likes to hold his hands together like he's hugging himself. He hasn't said his first word yet but they know that its not that far away and the race is on to see if walks first or talks first. Our help has really taken a liking to him and in turn he can feel their love. They would rather not take him away on vacation just yet until he is out of diapers and he won't require any attention that you would give an infant, they did decide to take their Nanny for a distance and they would require an airplane.

Ann is starting to tell Michael that little Mikey needs a brother or sister and Michael couldn't agree more so they went at it every chance they could for a long as it takes for Ann to get pregnant again and in three weeks, she told Michael she was pregnant again. The doctors visit confirmed it and they were like two school kids know that another one was on the way; they know that little Mikey will love to have a little brother or sister. They had a nice Christmas with little Mikey and they gave all of the help $500.00 each they were taken back with their generosity. They had a twelve foot tree and they gave the help off for Christmas. They called and they had their dinner delivered by those cuisine home delivery service people. It was expensive and they knew that they were working when everyone else was off work they came and cooked the entire meal in their kitchen so that it would be fresh, there was two of them and they worked together as a team and they looked like college kids.

They did it all even the deserts and when they finished cleaning up and putting things away in the dishwasher. The meal was $120.00 dollars and Michael gave them both a $100.00 tip. Well they couldn't stop thanking them enough. They said that they had *two more meals to cook before their day was over. It turned out to be a great idea to pay someone to come to their house and cook their Christmas dinner and clean up like they were never there and by 9: o'clock they were ready to light their fireplace and do a little snuggling. Little Mikey was drained of energy and he was out by 8: o'clock, he is still sleeping with us until they can ease him into his own bed a little at a time. They keep showing him his bedroom and how his bed is and Ann a couple of times she would put him in it for a nap. He seems to love it so they want to get some listening devices in his room and theirs and it will let them hear him if he should ever cry out.*

Ann has started putting on her creams and oils to keep the stretch marks away, she was successful with the first one and she was determined to do it all over again, she said she couldn't start early enough. The doctor is pleased with her physical condition and her told her to keep it up. They still walk everyday weather permitting they are even known to walk in the rain that warm rain falling on them can be very invigorating. Ann likes to use the pool for some light exercise. Michael is with the both of them all the time. They have a good pool heater and they keep the temperature at 68⁰ to 72⁰ whatever is appropriate. The summer they don't want the water to feel warm so they change it according the heat of the day. There pool is kept immaculate and it looks brand new and their two cars are kept in showroom condition as well.

When they go to the club for dinner little Mikey just sits there and takes it all in and he is never a problem. In fact, some of the people in the dining room want to touch him and say hello. They know if he wasn't that good, he would be staying home with the Nanny. As soon as he finds out that Golf is a game, he will pursue it with a passion, in the mean time Ann the Nanny talk ton him all the time and he seems to be catching to what they are saying to him. It was just the other day he was asked where his tummy was and he touched his belly he seems like he is catching on to everything he sees Ann says that his computer mind is loading up with knowledge.

They are enjoying their life even though they don't do that much. They will find something and stay busy doing it. Right now, they are having fun walking and taking trips around Florida they even visited the golf hall of fame and loved it. It gave them a better feel for the game and be better golfers for it. There Bentley attracts a lot of attention where ever they go, people are always asking them what kind of a car is it. A lot of them have never heard of a Bentley and they just stand there in amazement. They left word with the cook before they left that they would be home for dinner, she prepared them some Veal Parmesan. That woman can cook and they show her their appreciation by paying her such a high salary and they know that some other person can't or won't pay their cook that much money.

Ann is still putting on the creams and oils and they are waiting for the day to come and it is only forty some days away. Ann can't wait for their baby to be born and only wish that it would be healthy. They have talked about a name for the baby and if it's a boy they talked about Patrick and if it's a girl they agreed on Annmarie and now all they have to do is wait. They still walk every morning and its something they look forward to doing because they know that it pays off. It is very enjoyable to walk on the beach and feel the ocean water under their feet and washing over their feet that gives them that cool feeling. On there return they can see their home from a distance and it looks awesome, they have come a long way in such a short period of time.

They don't look like they are old enough to walk out of their front door as their owner. They are still in their late twenties but boy are they successful, they have over $500 million dollars in the bank and they are making almost $60 million dollars a year in interest. With that kind of money working wouldn't do them any good except keep them busy, which they can do playing golf every other day. They *know they can get back to playing more after the baby is born, with a few weeks to go before the baby is born and they are getting very anxious.*

They had some good news today and said that the latest book sales numbers are in and their book is still number one with sales of 1, 810,000. This is mind boggling to them that they have so many books and the money keeps piling up. The publisher told them he would call again with the next batch of numbers when they come in. Well Ann woke me up early in the morning and told me it was time to go and when they got there Ann had the baby thirty minutes later and it was a beautiful and very clean. They stayed with the name AnnMarie. Ann was in great shape and her delivery was very easy for her. Michael called home and told the Nanny that they had a little girl who they called AnnMarie and she in turn told little Mikey that he has a sister now and his mommy will bring her home in a few days. He understood everything that was said to him and he was jumping up and down with delight.

The Nanny was excited as well and she told them that she can't wait for them to bring her home. The checkout was a little slow but when Michael pulled up to the entrance in his Bentley everyone stopped to see who was going to get out of that car. They were required to have an infants seat to strap the baby into and when that was done, they headed for home, the Nanny was there waiting for them looking out the dining room window and she took little Mikey to the elevator and he waited for his mother and little sister to come up. The door opened and Ann said that she has a little sister for him to play with and he ran to his mother to see her and he started kissing her all over her tiny face and he had his arms wrapped around her, he was visually overwhelmed with all of this happening to him.

It was right around noon and the cook made them some clam chowder soup and some grill cheese sandwich with tomatoes that hit the spot. Ann looked a little tired so Michael suggested that she lay down and take a nap and he would lite the fire place and she would be out in a flash. She liked that idea if Michael would lay with her and take a nap also. The Nanny had everything under control and they felt it was safe enough for them to steal a few hours and Michael was the first to come out in the kitchen and see how things were going. AnnMarie was still asleep and so was little Mikey, it must be something in the air. Ann finally woke and she came out in the kitchen and she was looking for little AnnMarie. The Nanny had her asleep in the bassinette. She just wanted to hold her and look at her face and get to know her better.

Michael was always running to the store for things for the baby and after a while they were well supplied. Little Mikey is really doing good holding on to the sofa and walk around and it won't be long before he will be able to do it on his own. The Nanny goy into a routine where one was a sleep and the other one was awake. They paid her above what a Nanny gets for that kind of work and she knows that they expect her to give the best care anybody could expect of her. Michael had a small fire in the bedroom every night and little AnnMarie was very comfortable, in there with them. Michael made sure that when little Mikey went to bed, he never went without him going to him and saying goodnight and give him a kiss on his far head and a little hug. When he wakes, he likes to watch Mr. Rogers sing, "It's a beautiful day in the neighborhood." And to watch him sitting there in all of his innocence could bring tears to your eyes.

Ann has changed after having these two children, she thinks like a mother now and she acts like a mother. The children come first in all that matters, she wants to be the best mom she can be. Ann wants to get back to walking on the beach again and Michael is happy that she wants to start that back up because he was walking by himself and he was use to Ann being with him. They did see their first shuttle launch this morning and you could hear the loud roar from the rockets from fifty miles away all the way down to our house. It drew a crown on the beach and it was out of sight in no time, its nice to live near such an historical place.

Every now and then Michael is asked to join a company as a CEO or the equivalent for some big company that inn the end that want to use his reputation for their own gain. Michael knows that and he won't lend himself to anything like that. Once Ann can free herself up, they will try and follow a routine every day so life won't get boring for them. Ann wants him to get a law degree and practice law in Vero Beach, he told her he would look into it and see what he has to do to get back to school for two years or sign up on line and take his classes on the computer and get his degree from the university of Florida law school which is nothing to throw your nose at.

Ann encouraged him to do it and he told her he would look into it; he was recognized by the college and he would have to go back to school for two years or sign up on line and take his classes on the computer. They did offer him a two year graduate course in law that he can take on the computer and for his finals he would have to come on campus to finish and graduate with his class. Ann thinks that this is perfect for him and it will keep his mind busy, he's to young not to have something serious to do. He did make some inquiries and they want him to come in one day next week for an interview.

The interview went well and they were very impressed with his computer skills as well. They gave him a hundred page catalogue to read over and see what is expected of him and how his work has to be finished in the time allocated. He would be assigned a law professor who he will have to please if he is going to have any chance in passing by following the course in every detail as he would lay it out for him to complete.

Ann told Michael that this law degree is right up his alley and if he knuckles down, he will pass with High honors and pass the bar as well. He was happy with his interview and his professor told him that he knows who he is and he likes the fact that he is a no nonsense guy and he was looking for some great things from him Michael knows that it will take two years of some grinding effort to get his degree. He worked it out with Ann that he would start very early in the morning as early as 7: o'clock and he could be easily done by 1: o'clock. That would be the minimum time he would spend studying or take class room test and quizzes. He will make a great lawyer and he will be a very popular one and be on high demand. The first month was hard and the book royalties were coming in hot and heavy. They made another 1,360,000 in book sales and that includes book sales from all over the world. They are expecting it to peter out they are hanging in there and it is still on the best sellers list after ten weeks. They do want to put their fourth and final book on the market someday. Michael is still getting praises from his law professor, he was being told that his investigation skills are helping him a lot in his first semester test Michael finished first in his class with ease, he was happy that his hard work paid off. Their book sales are down just under a million which is nothing to sneeze at.

Little mikey is two now and hid little sister is six months old. Michael is still getting good grades on his test that he seems to like a lot. He told Ann that he loves going to school on the compute, it's right up his alley. They still use the club and they manage to get in nine holes a couple times a week and they go out to the club on Sundays when the cook is off. They are very well known there even keeping a low profile. The members love seeing this young couple being this big success and bring their two children to the club for dinner with them. Every one at the club has either seen them or knows all about them being members there.

Michael is taking a break for Christmas and they can't wait to seer little Mikey open his gifts and little AnnMarie be her happy self. They liked it when they had their Christmas meal catered last year so they made arrangements to do it again and they will come later on *in the day. Michael gave Ann some perfume and a children's mother neckless that had the two children's birth stones in it and a gift card from Lord and Taylor for a $1,000.00 and buy herself something that she can pick out herself, oh I forgot he did get her some things from Victoria Secret. She got Michael two tailor made suits for his up and coming law practice and he has to go to the tailor to be fitted and some dress shirts and a smart pair of dress shoes for that special occasion and some golf shirts from the pro shop.*

Their publisher called them with their latest book sale numbers that were 980,000 and he told them that it was still number one on the best sellers list. That was a great unexpected Christmas gift. The caterer came with the Christmas meal and it turned out to be the best turkey meal they ever had. The two preparers were young college kids and they told Michael that when they grow up, they want to be just like him. They put all the dishes in the dish washer and left by way of the elevator and through the garage. They gave them both $100.00 dollars each, that really knocked them for a loop, they were genuinely happy with that. They sat around the Tv and watched the Christmas shows that have been on for years and it played perfectly on their Boes stereo surround sound speakers.

Little Mikey was starting to fall asleep so Ann took him to bed and tucked him in and Michael took AnnMarie back to their bedroom and lit the fire place to warm up their room so they could give each other their special Christmas gift. The weather outside was a freezing 42^0 *that is cold for Florida they got up early and decided to take a walk along the beach with the whole family, it turned out to be very nice and when they returned, they sat in their built in bench and platform that they used to step onto the beach in. They didn't sit there that long because the wind was starting to pick up and it wouldn't be good for the children to exposed to the wind blowing their faces and take their breath away.*

Michael wanted to start back on his computer classes so he signed on before the others did, he started to read a lot and he knew that was how he was going to be the only way he was going to learn something. He was a genius when it comes to the computer and that was a big help to him when he was doing his class assignments on the compute. His mind is wide open to the law now and he absorbs everything that he reads or hears and that is quite an accomplishment when you can key your mind on one thing and stay with it until its over. He finished his first year early and he managed to be number one in his class. His professor has nothing but praise for him and he told Michael he has a great future ahead of him.

Michael told Ann that he didn't want to be a dead beat but he did want to go places with them and still open his books for the last year. Ann told Michael flat out that what ever he wants to do now is what you'll be doing later so please don't use your school work as an excuse for studying away from us. She told Michael she wants to play golf three times a week and enjoy them selves with all that they have here. She reminded him that he finished first in his class and what else does he want to do and he told her that he would like to repeat it. She went on to tell him the school break is meant to keep Michael from being a dull boy. He looked at her and said she was right and he said let's have a great summer.

The publisher called again with some more book sales figures after about two and a half months, His numbers are going down but still high when you look at the length of time its been on the best sellers list. He told Michael that his last count on his book sales was 712,000 which includes overseas sales as well, and they are amazed how popular their books are. Their marketing is top shelf and their publisher knows the more books we sell the more he makes. They played a lot of golf and they spent a lot of time with the children. They are at the right age that they still can't go away with them because they are to young to appreciate the place they are visiting.

They don't want to wish their lives away and they will know in time they will all be able to go away and have lots of fun.

The summer is coming to the end and Michael wants to start back and get started in finishing out this important year and pass the bar AnnMarie's first birthday is coming up any day now and they will have a great time, they sang happy birthday and she dug those tiny hands into that cake and she had it all over herself. They took a lot of pictures and little Mikey was right in there with him. It was hard putting them to bed but eventually they got tired and started falling to sleep. They played hard and were pooped out. The party was over but they were only just beginning for them, Ann raced Michael to bed and it was very nice to end the day locked in each other's arms and fall fast asleep on not worrying about the fireplace because it was on timer and it will turn off by 11: o'clock for sure.

They did manage to get in a fast 18 holes before Michael started in on his studies. He was lucky that the college let him take the course that he had another degree in another subject, he told them that he has a degree in computer science, that they never checked out because we know that he dropped out when Pat passed away.

His professor knew all about his three books and he said he was completely impressed with his ability going over the crime scene and eventually figure out how the murderer did his deed and how Michael would catch them in the end. His professor told him that he has a gift and he knew how to use it and told him that he would be a success at anything he would try and do. Michael on his own was studying for the bar exam in addition in doing his class assignments. It was something he wanted to do so it was easy for him. On his spring break he went out and bought this beautiful office building on Beach land Blvd. it was close to the ocean and that was where he wanted to be and open up his new law practice. Ann liked the location very much and told him that his office would attract a lot of clients. With some heavy advertising in the right places.

They kept their plate full every day with golfing, studying and playing with the children and their mother. Ann is shooting five over par for nine holes and the women on the club golf team want her to join them and play one day a week. Ann told the nice nine hole ladies that she will have to see how things are going and set up a play day when she can come out with them, they figured that was better than no. Michael played with some retired guys and nobody his age because they were all working. Very few people ever approach him about his books or some of the cases he solved. They will want to hear from the other members how the feel about and then he will meet the ones that want to be friends with him. Hopefully there will be some young guys in that crowd, he just wants to play with a younger group of guys and mix in some retirees. They are determined to have fun and they will soon learn that he has a new law office on Beach Land Blvd. He will have to finish his classes and pass the bar first that he is working very hard on.

Michael is getting a lot of request from law firms all over the country, he figures his professor has put the word out about his legal abilities and they were making some very attractive offers for him to come and join their legal staff. Michael thanked them all he told them that he wanted to stay close to his family and open his own office in Vero Beach and how honored he was in receiving their request to join their firms.

Little Mikey just had his third birthday and eating his birthday cake and some ice cream and they had a ball and so did he. He was so excited opening up his gifts, the toys took most of his interest and the clothes got his attention for a few seconds but it was the toys that made the day.

The book sales dropped down to 50,000 and like it was predicted they were petering out. Michael was really cramming as much as he can into this last test that marked the end of his finals. His test scores were put up on his computer screen and he saw that he finished first again in his class through both of his two years in taking his law courses. The graduation ceremony for him to be a part of and Ann had the children in the audience her to see their daddy getting all these accolades that they were giving him and it went on for the longest time. They went to the club and it was festive and it topped off the whole day, they got the children home for bed. Ann told Michael that hard work really pays off and he proved it.

There was his Bar exam coming up in two weeks, he signed up for it and he spent the next two weeks cramming anything that was on previous bar exams in the last ten years. Ann thought this guy is really ready and she told him so. The next morning, he reported to the county library to sit for the test, there was a meeting room there that very few people knew about. The proctor was some kind of a beauty queen or looked like one. Michael showed her his driver' license and she smiled at him and he took a seat in the first row and sat quietly in anticipation of his upcoming test She called the roll and she told them that she would hand out the exam papers and they not to open them until she says so. She gave every one a #2 lead pencil with an eraser and she had them write their names on the inside top page and their address and phone number. She then asked if anyone has a problem hat might com up during this examination and there was silence and she went on to tell them that they had five hours to complete the exam and they can start now.

Michael looked over the questions and none of them was a surprise, he had seen them all and he memorized the answers He finished his exam in three and a half hours and he raised his hand waiting for the proctor to come to him and she asked him was he finished and he told her he was. He handed her his test booklet and gave her back his pencil and he stood and thanked her for being so nice. Her reply was he doesn't even know her and how nice she can be. His reply was it will have to stay that way. He left the room and headed straight for home where Ann and the children were waiting for him, she gave him a big hug and a kiss and asked him how it went, he told her that he finished an hour and a half early.

Now the worst part is waiting for the results, so he hired an interior decorator plush and completely finished from the telephones to the copy machines which would include a full legal library and the best tables and chairs and his desk and chair to be the best she can find. She told him that it will take a week to ten days and Michael told her that was perfect for him, he gave her an office key and told her to make his office the talk of the town and if anyone should come there, they will tell all their friends about it. He wants his secretary that can do short hand and he wants her to be able to work the phones and set up appointments that are reasonable for Michael to keep. Shed doesn't have to be Marilyn Monroe but it wouldn't hurt if she does and they can use her good looks to their advantage. Michael interviewed three girls and he finally decided on Mindy who was a graduate from the legal secretary college of Melbourne. She was a single mom with a three year old boy and she lives with her mother.

Michael never tried to find out anything about her life he knew that it wasn't any of her business and she will be evaluated by her job performance only and not her personal life. It will be them two at first and see how things go. Her still had to spend some time with his interior decorator and finish up and get some other things in the right place, his favorite picture is of Thomas Jefferson sitting at his drawing board working on some blue prints and drawings, he had pictures all over his office and some really good ones out in his office sitting area, his favorite one out there was of George Washington sitting in his tent at Valley Forge with his face in his hands, but he never gave up because he knew how important this war of independence was and it might be there only chance to defeat the British.

I think the one that really hits home is the poor mother receiving two American flags at the grave site of her two dead sons. Any one that comes in his office will feel that anguish that this country has felt since the struggle for independence and in particular from the beginning. Michael wanted to remind the people that came to his office the struggle we went through as a new nation. A registered letter came in the mail and Michael signed for it and it was clearly from the Florida bar association. He opened it up slowly and it said on the top couple of lines that he has passed the State bar exam and when he is sworn in by a sitting Judge, he will be allowed to practice law in the State of Florida. Michael told Ann that he passed and they were high fiving and all that and Ann told Michael that he worked hard for it and he deserves to have passed and now he can open his new office and start a very successful law practice here in Vero Beach.

The morning Michael was sworn in they brought the children with them to be a part of the ceremony. Ann told Michael that she wants to practice law with him, like they did as a team with the FBI and they were very successful at it. Michael told her that now was the time to do it and she said she would sign up and start her classes right away. Michael knew it would take two years if she works hard at it and he knows she will, he was definitely looking forward to working with her again. Everything was in place for them to open their doors for business. Michael had been advertising for weeks and now today was there first day to be open for business. He got some inquiries from some large companies for him to accept a retainer from them and defend them in any upcoming law suits. He turned them all down because he knew that some day he would have to go against them and he wouldn't be able to because they had a retainer with him and he didn't want to have anything from holding him back, he knew it was a clever thing to pull of and handcuff a good lawyer from going against them but Michael knew better and he passed on all of them.

He did interview some DUI cases and he asked for a $4,000.00 dollar fee up front to defend their first clients, he did have one request from a astronauts widow who husband died on the moon in one of their Moon missions and their return rocket didn't ignite to blast off and meet up with the command module that was circling the moon the whole time they were on the moon until their lift off capsule failed to ignite and her husband had no other way to get him up to the Command capsule and it was their only way to come back to Earth. She only lived about an hour away and she made plans to meet him at his office in two days. He left instructions with Mindy to bring her right back when she comes in.

Mindy walked the widow back to Michaels office and told him That Mrs. Conway was here to see him and he thanked Mindy and came around and shook Mrs. Conway's hand and he offered her a seat in front of the fireplace and he sat along side of her in his tufted high back chair like hers. She told him that she picked him and only knowing about him from his three books and she knew that no one was going to get anything over on him. Michael thanked her for that confidence she has in him. She reminded him that her husband died on the moon in the line of duty and she told him that even to this day they haven't paid her for his life insurance or his back pay and refusing to pay accidental pay which is double indemnity.

Michael was surprised to hear that and he asked her if she knew why are they doing that to her, he is a national hero and we couldn't be treating our hero's widows that way. They told her on a number of request that they were working on it and they will get back to her. Michael asked her how was she doing money wise, she said things were tough and the bank keeps pestering her for some back payments. Michael asked for a list of people that are calling her and he will talk to them. He asked her where is her husbands body now and she said that the other Astronaut that was up there with him stranded was finally rescued and he put her husband's body in a rock sample box and brought him back to Earth in the rock sample box. If it wasn't for that astronaut quick thinking he would still be up there on the moon. That astronaut was told to leave him there because there wasn't any room in the Command module, to answer your question I asked that he be buried in Arlington.

Michael asked her how is A.S.A. guilty of anything and she told him that they have not paid his widows any benefits after fifteen months or any of his back pay. They are stalling for some reason and she is in fear that they might squirm out of paying her and come up with something nasty that would give them a reason of not paying any restitution to his widow. At this point Michael was starting to get mad at hearing this terrible story of what A.S.A. is trying to pull over this poor defenseless widow. He told Mrs. Conway that he would like to give her some money to tide her over while he is straightening things out. He gave her a check for 10,000 dollars to get her through these bad times. She told him that she didn't come here to see him for a hand out and Michael told her that he could see that when he first laid eyed on her. Mindy took down everything that Mrs. Conway told him about her husband and his career at the space center and her dealings with A.S.A. and how he was not rescued for over sixty days. He feels that he has heard enough and that he would be in touch with her shortly.

Michael wants to get up with his fellow astronaut that was stranded on the Moon with him for those sixty days, while they waited to be rescued by another space capsule and lunar lander. Michael has a strong suspicion that Mr. Conway died on the moon from a severe heart attack and died fearing that he was going to die there and never see his wife again. He is sure that after he talks to John McCarthy his space partner of Mr. Conway, he will fill in all of the uncertainty in this matter. Michael went home and told Ann about the interview with the astronauts widow and how he was going to get to the bottom of it. He told Ann that he gave the woman some money that will tide her over until A.S.A. can do the right thing and take care of this woman.

Michael finally had to go through the space center to get up with the astronaut that was stuck on the moon Mr. McCarthy, he drove up and met the astronaut at his house just off the property of the space center. Michael thanked him for seeing him on such a short notice and that he has asked to see him because he is representing his partners widow Bill Conway. He told him what A.S.A. has done to his friends widow and how they don't return her phone calls or pay her his life insurance and his back pay. That really pissed him off and he told Michael that he gave up his career as an astronaut because these people have taken on this liberal thinking and they wanted him to live a lie and I refused so I resigned and left not in there good graces and right now I am starting up an aircraft manufacturing plant and I am going to make some special airplanes.

Michael said that he looked up his public record of his life up to now and there isn't anything in it that says that you have that kind of knowledge to start an airplane business, his reply was that the people he hires will. Michael also told him that he struck it big in Vegas for almost $300 million dollars. Bill said that was correct and it was before taxes. He asked him how could he win such a large amount of money and he told Michael that they kept on at him to let them get even. He told Bill that he looked at the security video footage of that night and you had someone at your side all the time.

"Yes, I did and he was someone I have known for years."

"How did you end up id Vegas with your friend and gamble on that roulette table and if you study the history of roulette that game is not a game to have any chance to win money on."

"Again, are you absolutely right that you were just having fun before you were going to leave the next day."

"Why did you want to go to Vegas to have fun after you almost died on the Moon."

My friend wanted me to go away for a few days and come back to reality Earth. I thought you wanted to talk about Bill Conway."

I did and that Vegas trip you went on was too interesting not to ask you about. I forgot to ask you your friends name"

"I am sorry I should have told you his name is Michael Deldot."

"Where is he from?"

"He comes from Canada and he studied with me at MIT and unfortunately they had a fire in their records department and all the students that graduated there in that time period and all of those students that graduated in that time period records were lost. Can we get back to why we came here and talk about Bill Conway?"

"Let's talk about Bill Conway for a few minutes and you tell me what happened up there leading up to when you couldn't blast off to meet up with the command module and are you gaged and can't tell me?"

"Sure, I can tell you and I am glad you're not a lawyer, I hold then in playing a big part in me resigning my astronaut status."

"Were you with Bill when he had his heart attack."

"I had just looked at some relay panels and they were so corroded; they could never work. I told Bill what I found and he was never the same after that he talked to himself all the time and he stared out the porthole and looked at where he thought he was going to die. The next morning, we were supposed to get some news about our rescue when he took a long deep breath and he turned purple almost immediately and he died right in front of my eyes."

"With all that time you spent on the Moon alone and had a chance to go out and look around did you find anything of any importance? You probably rode around every day just to keep from losing your mind."

"I didn't find anything that the other lunar landers had found, I am surprised that you asked that question."

"Well if you know anything about me you wouldn't be surprised."

"Tell me what I don't know about you."

"I was the leading investigator for the FBI and I caught four serial killers that every one had given up on solving."

"Are you that guy that wrote those books that are everywhere."

"Yes I 'am that guy>"

"Well it's a pleasure to meet you."

"Have you had a chance to read them?"

"Not yet but I will."

Their meeting went on for a couple of more hours and Michael thanked him for being so blunt and he appreciated it. John told Michael that he would be a wittiness for him and Mrs. Conway. That was good news for Michael to hear and he shook Johns hand and headed back to Vero Beach in time for dinner, he took the scenic route along the ocean it was very relaxing for him to do that. He called Ann on her cell phone and he told her what happened and how it went with the surviving astronaut that was going to be a wittiness for Mrs. Conway. Ann told Michael that she was happy to hear his voice and she told him that she will wait for him to come home and put some Del Monaco's on the grill for having a good day and Michael told her that he can't wait to sink his teeth into one and her later. He said he would go as fast as he could without getting a speeding ticket, he did take the Bentley and it was showroom clean.

10

Ann has the children out in the garage waiting for their daddy to drive up, it was a great sight to see those little kids cheering for him when they saw him drive up. They walked down to their beach platform and sat together on the benches for a while and Michael told Ann that his stomach was making some hungry noises that they could hear and Ann knew he was hungry and said, "Lets go you must be starving. The steaks were perfect and told the cook about it. The children are tired and so was Ann so I put little Mikey to bed and he took Ann to bed and little AnnMarie, he was asleep before the room went dark and the sound of the ocean woke them up around 7: o'clock. Their cook made them a campers breakfast consisting of eggs, sausage, hash browns and some silver dollar pancakes.

Ann wanted to eat outside this morning before it got too hot. Ann had changed the cooks schedule and they pay her for breakfast bow which includes all three meals, instead of lunch and dinner. He decided to go in the office and read over what Mrs. Conway's said to him and he also listened to what John McCarthy had to say and he decided to ask for all the files on John McCarthy as part of discovery and he will go up and pick them up. He also wanted to interview Bill's immediate supervisor after he thoroughly read through his file and there were a lot of things there that were troubling. Like why they never returned Mrs. Conway phone calls. Why doesn't his name appear on the wall of honor anywhere at the space center. Michael knew that Bill Conway was a hero like no other astronaut could ever be and a reply was that, "This would have never happened if he would have never had done his job."

Michael asked the supervisor that it wasn't Mr. Conway's responsibility to make sure that everything was in working order. His reply was that every astronaut has that responsibility to make sure everything is in working order. Michael never let on to him that it wasn't true and he has the astronauts hand book on space flight and not one word of that appears on any of the 360 pages of their hand book that each astronaut was given when they first come into the program. Michael never let on that he had the handbook that they issued to every astronaut and he has not found a single word that holds an astronaut responsible and on the space capsule or the Moon lander to be in working order. They were astronauts not mechanics and in the same breath the mechanics are not responsible for flying into space and this is a crucial point that he will bring up in court.

Michael filed a law suit against the A.S.A and the space center for the gross negligence in the death of Bill Conway in his line of duty, it didn't take long before the shit hit the fan, it was on every news program and in every news papers around the world, Michael has gotten a hot one here. Michael has sat with Mrs. Conway a half dozen times and he was ready to go to court with Mrs. Conway and get her justice for the degrading husband that is an American hero. Michael could see that the space center lawyers weren't afraid of Michael seeing as how he has never stepped one foot into a court room, he thought to himself that they have never read his book or they would have showed him a little more respect because it will be impossible for them to stop him from not getting to the truth.

Michael was notified of the court date and he practiced all the points that were vital in his case and he anticipated any question the opposition might have; he wasn't going to put Bills widow on the stand unless he has to. He thinks that she will be a good wittiness and they will hurt themselves if they try to demean her. They have to walk on egg shells throughout the whole trial. Michael got up with Mrs. Conway and he told her to get a shuttle bus ride down to his house and she can stay with them while the trial is on. She thanked him whole heartily and she will get up with the people to get her there to his house. Ann knows about Mrs. Conway coming to stay with them and she passed it on to the help that couldn't hurt they will be ready for that change in the house procedures.

Michael was practicing with Ann a much as he could and he had all of the hard questions answered and he worked on his opening statement and his summation memorized the whole case against A.S.A. and he had to show their incompetence and that won't flush with the American citizens. Bill Conway is a hero and God help anyone that will try and take that away. It was right around noon when Mrs. Conway arrived and Michael carried her bags back to her room while the girls were bonding like girls do. Michael asked them if they would like a nice cool ice tea and sit out by the pool, they thought that was a good idea and one of their help brought out a tray of drinks and ice.

They could hear the ocean and Mrs. Conway said that she has never heard that better she went on to say that their home is breathtaking and it suits them and it stands for how they live the good life and this house is a show place. Ann told her that is what the decorator told them that she would turn our home into a show place and they deserve it from what she can read from their books. Michael told her that when this is over, she might jot down her life story about Bill and herself. He told her it will be a good read and her reply was if you write it, she told Michael that she is by herself now that Bill is gone. Michael said there is no reason why you can't be happy by yourself and living without fear of losing what you have.

Michael told her she can join a travel club and travel all over the world with the club members. She said that if that was true and he told her it is, just wait and see. The cook made a great dinner before the trial starts at 9: o'clock and they will have to pick all twelve jurors and two alternates before they can start the trial. Like Michael thought they spent the day doing that and finally they picked eight women all married and six older men. Michael was happy with the jurors he picked and exactly what he was looking for. Their defense attorneys don't have don't have any idea what's in store for them, they think they can beat this rookie in his first case. It was late and the Judge told them that they will start the first thing in the morning at 9:30 and for both sides to be ready and be on time for their opening statements.

Michael asked Mr. Conway how she was doing and she said she was just fine. The defense attorney was going to make their opening statement first and he will get the feeling where they are going in their defense. Them seem confident that the causes of Bill Conway death was not their fault it was all Bill Conway's fault and not A.S.A. fault. They were unable to explain how an astronaut could be held responsible for rocket repairs and maintaince. They fumbled all though their opening statement and finally finished just before lunch. The judge told Michael that it would his turn to start his opening statement right after lunch. Mrs. Conway had a salad a d Michael had a cup of soup at the cafeteria across the street.

Michael wanted to do good on his opening statement and he told the jury that he was going to put the surviving astronaut John McCarthy that lived through his rocket malfunction for ninety days and he came back from the Moon to Earth scarcely alive. He told the jury that he will show them the astronauts hand book and the only surviving wittiness that was there with Bill Conway stuck on the Moon where he died of a massive heart attack because he thought they will never be rescued from this doomed mission. He went on to say that what killed Bill Conway was not anything he caused; he was sizing up the jury the whole time he looked at them. If you had to grade Michaels opening statement you would have to say that Michaels was more believable.

The judge called it a day and he told Michael that he would have to present his case first thing in the morning. Michael was ready and he called astronaut John McCarthy to the stand and he told it all especially how it was not the responsibility of the astronaut to repair or maintain their rocket or any rocket and Michael asked John how can he prove that and he held the astronauts hand book up high for everyone to see and I mentioned that there wasn't one word of that in the astronauts hand book which A.S.A. issued to all of the astronauts and he said it was what the astronauts had to follow in the astronauts program. Of course, the defense objected and the judge put an end to that. They were objecting to every word that Michael or John said and finally the judge told the lead defense attorney that the next time they raise an invalid objection he would fine them $10,000 dollars and he would have them jailed for contempt of court.

This defense team are digging their own grave and they are helping Michael win his first case. Michael asked John why isn't he still an astronaut and John's reply was something that the jury wasn't prepare to hear, He said they would do anything to make those officers look good and they will lie and defame Bill Conway's good name. The court room was real quiet and that meant only one thing that John had told the jury the truth because he was there next to him when he died. He went on to tell the jury that he could no longer serve his country with people that weren't interested in serving their country. He went on to say that they did a poor job in smearing his name with blowing out of whack his partying at school from over ten years back. Michael told the jury that Bill was tops in his class for four straight years and he was tops in his ROTC classes and tops in his astronaut training class and Michael turned to the jury and asked them does that sound like a party guy.

Michael told the jury that John graded test papers for some professors and the administration office for three years and it is pat of his record in college that he was the best grader they ever had. In all that Michael could see the defense was finished, John stepped down and Michael thanked him for his service to his country and for his input in this trial. The judge asked either side if they had any other wittiness's and they both said no. The judge told them that they will hear closing statements tomorrow morning at 9: o'clock sharp. The lead attorney asked Michael before they started their closing statements if they could talk outside. They offered Michael a million dollars if he would settle here and now and he thanked them for their generous offer and turned and walked back in the court room, back to Mrs. Conway seated at the table with him.

The defense went first and they were very weak on their defense and they only took an hour. And now it was Michaels turn and he let it all go and he took over three hours and he blasted A.S.A. and he told them that they should be ashamed of themselves for treating this poor widow the way they did her. Her lawsuit was for $3 million dollars. The judge explained to the jury what it is to be expected of them and for them to look at the evidence and make a decision. Michael left the courtroom with Mrs. Conway and Michael called home and he told Ann that he was finished and he would be home in twenty minutes. Michael was in the Escalade and she loved sitting up high and seeing the road better than in her car.

Michael gave them two phone numbers that they can contact him on when they want him to return because they have made a decision. Michael knew the only decision they could come up with was that A.S.A. was guilty of not inspecting all of the working mechanisms of the lunar lander that it would be able to blast off into orbit from the surface of the moon and join up with the command module and come home. They had a nice dinner at home and Mrs. Conway told Ann that Michael defended hers and Bills honor like only a person with a warm heart could do, he is a great lawyer. She went on to say that when Michael spoke, she looked over at the jury and they were hypnotized with every word he spoke.

Michael went into his office the next day and he came home a little early he figured that they might be getting ready to announce their verdict. He went in again early the next day and worked on some DUI's and get ready for court when the phone rang asking him to bring his client to the court as soon as possible. He called home and toll Ann to tell Mrs. Conway to get dressed they have to go to the court for the verdict. They started up the court room steps when the lead attorney from A.S.A. made Michael an offer of $2 million dollars and Michael told him that wasn't enough. Michael left him standing there with his mouth open and speechless.

Michael walked in with Mrs. Conway and took their seat and soon after that they were asked to stand for the judge. He entered soon after that and they were asked to be seated, when the jury started filing in and they took their seats. The judge asked them if they have come to an unanimous verdict and they said they have. The judge asked the Forman to rise and read their verdict. He pit on his reading glasses and read from the paper he was holding and he said that we the jury in full agreement here by find for the plaintiff be awarded $3 million dollars for damages against her husband's reputation and of false actuations that were made against him, then the Forman then went on to say that they wish to award Mrs. Conway punitive damages to the sum of $50 million dollars. Well the defense team jumped to their feet and started yelling objection to that large sum of money being awarded to that woman and they wish to file an appeal right now. The judge asked them who were they referring to when they said that woman. The defense attorney said the plaintiff your honor, then the judge asked him isn't that better then saying that woman and with a deep struggle they said yes. He still wanted to say that the decision was excessive and no one could spend that much money in a life time.

They sat back down and the judge told the lead defense attorney that they had ten days to present their case and they failed miserably because you didn't have a case against the plaintiff but he proved with out a shadow of a doubt and won his case fair and square. He went on to tell them that if the plaintiff isn't paid in three days, he will levy a fine against them for a million dollars a day until it is paid in full. He banged his gavel down on his desk and said these proceedings are over. He stood and left the court room then Mrs. Conway stood and hugged Michael and thanked him for helping this old woman in her hour of need. Michael told her that she was not an old woman so don't refer to yourself that way. The opposing attorney never shook his hand or say goodbye or even looked over at them. He suspects that they will be let go by A.S.A. they cost them too much money.

Michael called home with the news and Ann was so happy for Mrs. Conway and she told Michael to come right home that the steaks are being prepared for our celebration. He told Mrs. Conway about Ann having the steaks on the grill and she smiled and said she was starving. They talked on the way home and she should wait until the money has been placed in his account then he will transfer her share into her private account. The celebration was great even the children were excited and jovial and the evening was really great he told Mrs. Conway that they will drive her home to the cape when the money comes in. He gave Mrs. Conway a check for $ 26,500,000 and he told her that she can live in peace now, she thanked him again and they all piled into the Escalade and went up the ocean rd. A1A and it took about an hour and she had to vouch to security whop we were. He congratulated on her court win and he told her to have a nice day, news travels fast.

Michael asked her what she was going to do and she told him joining that vacation club sounded good to her, she went on to say that after giving them a good whooping as bad as they did she said she would put the house up for sale and move out to another place where one of her friends closer to the ocean. Probably not that far from John McCarthy his wife and I get along real good. She was in tears thanking Michael for all that he did for her she told him that she will never forget Ann and the children. They stopped at Mamma Mia's on the way home, just the smell of the Sause could make you want to stop there tonight. Michael was sorry for not taking Mrs. Conway thereon the way home, it is impossible to get a bad meal there.

Ann held Michaels hand all through dinner and all the way home and she asked him how did we do today and he burst out laughing and said he was proud of her for being able to hold off so long he told her $26,500,000 dollars, you won all that money on your first case in court. Michael told her that the bigger the case the bigger the settlement. They finally got home around 8: o'clock and the children were sound asleep and they both had a child and they had them in bed in minutes. Michael told Ann that he wants security at night because they are becoming too big to be normal and there is nothing normal around here. They can sit in a car in the driveway and do a foot patrol around the house every thirty minutes. Ann liked that and they can feel moiré relaxed with security at night.

The security patrol would have to check in at certain post to verify that they were there at that station and at what time, it will be kept on a company log. Michael kept this security on low profile and it wasn't easy to cover up a security vehicle in your driveway every night, for as famous as they are no body seems to know them. Their Bentley is noticed by everyone and they both like driving it, it is the best vehicle they will ever own.

Little Mikey is around four and AnnMarie is two and a half, Ann is beginning to look for a very private school and a highly rated one at that. They did find one that backs up to the Riomar C.C, that is very highly rated and they have good security team that *protects those children from just about anything. The tuition for the first grade was $18,000.00 a year they run through then seventh grade through high school and it is on A1A. they did have a school bus for $150.00 a month, their high tuition keeps the riffraff away. The school goes by the name St. Edwards and it has a five star rating. They feel good that this school is so close to their home and easy to drive to if they have too.*

Michael had a hankering to surf fish so he bought a license, pole and reel and he decided to try his hand at it early in the morning. He did practice his casting for a few days and now he is ready. He made a good cast and not to long after that he felt a tug pulling away on his line. It started to feel heavy and after fifteen minutes he could finally see this long fish and when he was able to pull him out of the water and it was a small shark about two feet long. He didn't know what to do about this shark so he thought if he gave it back it could kill someone some day so he decided to kill it. He felt justified about that decision and he buried it deep in the sand hoping that it will disappear soon.

He couldn't wait to tell Ann about it, it was his first fish he ever caught and who would ever believe that it would be a shark. He doesn't know how he can top that and he figures he couldn't, he told Ann that he wants to do it again and she told him that it wouldn't hurt.

Michael got in his office early and he had had a message to call Bruce Ellis, he called the number given him and someone picked up the phone and said hello and Michael said who he was and the person on the other end said he was Bruce Ellis.

"What can I do for you Mr. Ellis?"

"I have a grievance with my employer who have done me and the other employees dirty and unfair tactics against us over a last couple of years."

"How dirty is dirty."

"They fired everyone before we can collect our retirement and pension checks."

"I have an office in Vero Beach and if you want me to listen more, I want you to bring all that you have to my office tomorrow."

"I can do that and is 10: o'clock good for you?"

I'll be here and to bring everything that you have that will help you to prove your point, every single piece of paper you can find."

Michael didn't know who his employer was to him it didn't matter because no employer has the right to do unlawful practices, he wanted to get the whole story. Bruce was right on time and he was escorted back to one of the meeting rooms. He was carrying a brief case and he stood it up right on the floor. Michael asked him again what have you brought to show me how I can help him. He said that he worked at the space center for thirty three years and they fired me for not doing my job satisfactorily. Michael asked him what was he doing wrong and he quickly replied nothing and I will show you that. They gave me rave reviews every year, I read each one and I signed every one of those reviews.

"When I look at them what will they say about you."

"Nothing that wouldn't be the truth."

"Are you the only one with such a grievance?"

"I have had some meetings for breakfast with loads of employees, that say the same thing."

"Ok let me get this straight, you were fired a few months before you were scheduled to retire."

"Yes, that's correct."

"How many other employees are there with the same story and can they prove their grievances like you can?"

"I think there are at least 70 people that are willing to bring charges like I have done."

That really knocked Michael back on his feet that this could be happening right under our eyes. Michael had his secretary tape every word that Mr. Ellis had to say, he asked him for the names of his supervisors that he worked for or with. He told Mr. Ellis that he would take it from here and he was going to do what he does best and look and see how this could have happened and when he gets a little deeper, he will get back in touch with him. He took a day and figured if he went to the Cape making an inquiry he will be stonewalled because he will be telling them what he would be looking for. He also had his secretary draw up the papers for the court and he would file a suit the next morning and FedEx his suit to the space center Human Resources Department. He drove up to the Cape and he was escorted to the Human Resources offices, where he was asked to take a seat.

He waited about fifteen minutes and finally he was taken back to a meeting room where there were three well dressed men sitting there waiting for him, they said that they represented the space center. Michael asked them are they aware that Bruce Willis is suing them for wrongful dismissal. They said that they just found that out late yesterday. They asked Michael what does he expect to get out of this. Michael is a cool guy and he told them that he is determined to get this mans name cleared of any wrongdoing.

"Are you aware that this man Mr. Ellis signed a contract when he was hired and that he could be fired for any wrongdoing on the job or fob related."

"Well that is good news, I am sure that you can supply me with a copy of that and all his job performances and interviews for the past thirty three years and I also want his attendance record for thirty three years. I want the names, addresses and phone numbers of all his supervisors. Please don't tell me you can't do that because if you do that, I will hold you in contempt and disrupting an ongoing legal investigation."

"We will need some time for that."

"I will give you one week and that is five working days and if you try to delay anything that I ask you for I will bring it up to the judge and in my opening statement and my summation and you will look like shit to the jurors."

"Now Mr. Smith you don't have to go on the defense, we know the law and we know what is expected of us. Aren't you the one that wrote those books on how you were the one that caught those serial murderers?"

"Now that it seems that I am always tracking down the bad guys, not referring to you of course."

Michael gave them his business card and he said that his address is clearly on his card and they know now they are in the fight of there life They said that the best way to describe him is that he is like a mountain lion with an abscess tooth. Michael thanked them for their time and he gave them a list of all the people that he wanted to depose. He told them that he might be adding and removing some names and that he will be letting them know by mail usually by overnight mail services and he asked them for the same courtesy. They never let on that they heard him. He thought to himself that if these guys are their best defense team that he will be going up against then they won't have much of a defense.

He got up with Bruce and he told him what he has just done and how he went to the cape and spoke to their attorneys and how he asked for the entire file that they had on him. He told Bruce that they seem to put a lot of weight on the contract he signed when you were first hired and that you can be fired at any time for a bad job performance. Bruce was quick to say that he never has a bad performance review and he went on to say that he only missed five days in those thirty three years and one of them was to bury his little girl that died by being hit by a car. That really hurt to hear him say that and that was the fuel he would need to go on and get this poor man Justice.

The things that Michael asked for came one morning early and Michael had a full day to review the materials, he asked Mindy to hold all calls to him that he would be reading over some materials that just came in. He found the contract that they put on top of the papers. Then he found all of his yearly reviews and job performances and each one had high praise for Bruce and his work. His attendance record did show that he missed five days in thirty three years. Now according to polls taken across the country that he was reading showed the national job attendance that the average employee missed five days a year and in Bruce's case he could have missed one hundred and sixty five days over the last thirty three years that was accepted according to the national average but in Bruce's case he only missed five days and one of them was to bury his little girl.

Michael looked at his reviews and they were outstanding even all the way through up too and including his final year. Technically speaking they broke their own rule about getting fired and Michael was going to make sure that the jury would hear that more then once. They almost destroyed this poor man and he came to Michael as his last hope, for a while there Michael thought there was something wrong with him. Michael knew that when they bring up that Bruce was fired and they had a contract that allowed that. Michael will maneuver them into that contract waiving it high in the court room. A few of his old supervisors have passed away but his last two supervisors are still around and Michael has plans to depose them.

He has made plans to depose them here at his office in Vero Beach and he told Bruce that he should be here to wittiness what they are saying about him. The three lawyers that he met at the space center also came along for the deposition. Michael looked at the crowd of people there and asked who is Steve Grant? This fellow put up his hand and Michael explained to him to him that anything he says here can be used in a court of law and he asked Mr. Grant if he now ready to answer his questions honestly, he said he was and

Michael was holding about a half dozen of Bruce's evaluations and he asked Mr. Grant how was Bruce Grant as an employee?"

"He said he was alright."

"Come come Mr. Grant that's not what you wrote in your review of Mr. Ellis when he worked under your supervision, look we just want you to tell the truth. Would you like me to review what you wrote about Mr. Ellis? You seem to be having a case of selected amnesia I have it all here everything you had to say about Mr. Ellis."

"Go a head if you can you must have some of his evaluations."

"I am holding every evaluation here in my hand that you signed and you had Mr. Ellis sign and not once did you say he was alright. In fact, when he had to take the day off to bury his little girl you put in his evaluation how you never realized great of an employee he was."

"I remember saying that and I am sorry for that."

"Do you still think he is great?"

"Yes, I do."

"If I didn't have this evaluation, we would have been left with alright and never knowing the truth."

"What made him so great?"

"He was reliable and you could count on him in a pinch."

"Michael thanked him for coming to Vero Beach today and he would be excused, the three attorneys were speechless and they didn't have anything to say. Michael called Bruce's last supervisor and he asked him how could he allow his supervisor fire such a valuable employee."

"I had nothing to do with his firing."

"That is not true and I disagree with you on that Mr. Herr and I have read your last review of Mr. Ellis and you wrote down that you were going to nominate Mr. Ellis as employee of the year, is that correct?"

"Now that you say that, I do remember that now."

"I'll ask you again why didn't you stop this awful firing of this poor unselfish man who had nothing else in this world but his job at the space center who went to bed early every night just to show up at work early and sharp and ready for all the problems that come up at the space center who you were going to nominate as employee of the year. This man was fired by telling the worst lies you can say about someone and I have the letter here that he was given when he was fired spelling out things that just weren't true. When I read it, I got sick to my stomach? You never know how low people can stoop until you work at the space center, how can you sleep at night know that you wrote those reviews and read them and you are completely disgusting.

Michael asked if Michael was the only ones fired because of poor job performance and right away the other side objected to that line of questioning because how would Mr. Herr know that answer and that told Michael that there must be more. He did say that he didn't have anything else and that he was finished and that the wittiness can be excused. He told them that he would send them a copy of the transcript as soon as he gets them and he will send it overnight. They thanked him and left. Michael told Bruce that they made him so mad that he could have kicked them out ofc his office. Bruce thanked him for defending him and he is starting to feel better about himself. He said that they have the contract and that will be very hard to overcome and Michael said on the contrary it will be our best weapon in beating these people.

Michael asked Mr. Ellis if he was ok going home and he said he would take the ocean road and he will be home in no time. Michael told him that they will be getting a court date soon and the next day it was all over the news that the space center was firing their employees illegally. This bad press is good for their case against the huge space center. It was on the news every night and the news vans were starting to park all along both sides of the street just wait to sink their teeth into some flesh and they don't care who's. They were looking for interviews or anything that they can use to keep the momentum going on this big story. They even called Ann's parents and asked for an interview and they were turned down. They were running stories on Michael hoping to get more viewers.

As you well know that Michael has a policy that he doesn't give interviews especially with the press. The trial date was set for two days and Michael was suing the space center for personal damages of $12 million dollars, no one ever gave it a thought that he would get a verdict that high and Michael was a bit skeptical. The space center didn't have a defense for what they did for Mr. Ellis and some of their other poor employees that this was done too as well.

Mr. Ellis drove down to Vero and he booked a room in the Vero hotel on the ocean, Michael went to his room the night before his trial and they talked for hours. He told Michael his wife left him when he told her that he was fired for a poor job performance. He told Michael that she went home to her parents in Michigan. She told him that she wasn't going to live poor again and snuck out on him one day when he was at the doctors for a checkup. He told Michael that he would never take her back and when she snuck out on him like that, she proved to him that she never loved him. Michael told him that when he wins his case and we will win; she will be on the first greyhound back to you. He said he can't stop her from getting on that bus but he will refuge to talk to her.

Michael was glad that Bruce opened up to him and he is feeling more confident every day and he can handle anything that they might say about him. He went home and he and Ann hit the sack and Michael set the alarm for 7: o'clock and Ann will send him out to court with a full stomach. He told Ann that they will probably spend the whole day selecting jurors. Michael wanted some old people on the jury and some men that might identify with being fired or fired by wrongful dismissal. They had sixty potential jurors to choose from to get twelve and two alternates and it was cut throat the whole day and in the end, Michael got the edge with seven older men and seven women two of which were alternates.

The judge told them that they can start in the morning at 9:30 sharp; Michael was happy with Bruce and how and how calm he appeared. The Judged asked Michael to start with his opening statement he planned to take his time and make a slower pace to explain to the jury what the space center did exactly to Mr. Ellis and how as a result of them falsely firing Mr. Ellis it broke up his marriage, he lost his house because no one would give him a job and he was forced to move into a used trailer that wasn't any bigger then a utility shed. All of his credit cards were canceled for no activity. His day consisted of sitting at the run down park on an old wooden bench and eat his tuna fish sandwich that he made for lunch before he went to the park. His day consisted of sitting there watching the people walking and he would often wonder how they were doing, even the runners and the mothers pushing their little babies in their strollers, sometimes he would doze off because he didn't sleep that good on his mattress that had springs coming through and it made it difficult to find a comfortable spot.

Michael finished his opening statement by saying that he admires Mr. Ellis for not getting into trouble with the law in this horrendous time that was forced on him, he thanked for their time and he walked to his seat. The Judge said they should break for lunch and they can start back at 2: o'clock this was music to Michaels ears and now if they don't speed up their opening statement, they will piss off some jurors for being kept after there dinner time. They finished around 4: o'clock and only taking two hours on their opening statement. Michael could see after that display that they have no case and not one chance of winning.

Tomorrow Michael was going to start calling wittiness's and he is going to crush the opposition like they deserve to be, he doesn't plan to take any prisoners and they won't be getting any let up from him not after what they did to Bruce Ellis and he is going to make them pay for it. He will belittle them the way they did Mr. Ellis . The press were outside in the street waiting to interview Michael and Mr. Ellis and all of their request fell on death ears, even the morning news channels were offering $250,000 dollars for a three minute interview and Michael never answered.

11

Michael called John McCarthy to the stand as his first wittiness and he had him on the stand for two hours and he got them to admit that he did have to admit that the maintaince men were top notch and he remembers Mr. Ellis working on the launch pad and how thorough he was. Michael asked him how could he remember this man he said that was easy his work was clean and neat of course the opposition were attacking Michael every chance they could get and they failed with every objection. Michael asked him why did he resign the space program after he came home from the Moon and he said simply they are more interested in how does it look and not how it is.

Then Michael called Mr. Steve Grant to the stand and he reminded him that they have spoken before and he would like to go over that conversation and what you told me in deposition. He asked him what kind of an employee was Mr. Ellis and he said he was a good employee and he said he wrote that in his evaluation that way. He asked him if he had to criticize him of anything what would he say about him. He thought for a moment and said that he worked too many hours without a break. Michael asked Mr. Grant if it were possible to be fired and work as hard as Mr. Ellis did day in and day out and his reply was not under his supervision. The defense brought up that Mr. Ellis was fired under someone's supervision; they didn't realize it that they were opening the door up for the next wittiness.

Michael called Mr. Ellis's supervisor that he worked for when he was fired, he looked pitiful when he walked to the wittiness stand. Michael reminded him that they have spoken before in deposition and he said he remembered, Michael said good then he will continue. Michael held up Michael's last six reviews and he asked him if he has read them and signed them and he said he did and did he mean it when he said that he was going to nominate Mr. Ellis for employee of the year. He said he did and Michael said and yet this man was fired for a bad job performance and no consideration was given for what was in his last job performance interview, he went on to say that he didn't know, he didn't have any say in his firing Mr. Ellis.

"Look we are not blaming you for firing Mr. Ellis, in fact you praised him to the hilt for being an outstanding employee, isn't that so."

"Yes, I did."

"Then how did this one of a kind employee get fired after reading this good employee's review."

"Maybe someone didn't read it."

"Maybe if someone didn't read it because if they did, he would still be there, is that about right."

"I think so."

"Do you know who fired him?"

"It was someone from the employees relations section."

"Did you know that there was a fire in that building a year ago and I guess we will never know who the genius was that fired Mr. Ellis. Now Mr. Herr are you aware of how Mr. Ellis's life detreated after he was fired or because he was fired. Do you remember me telling you that his wife left him and how he lost his house and how he how to live in a trailer not much bigger than a shed and how he went to the park every day, weather permitting and just watched the faces of the people passing by him?"

"Yes, I remember all that."

"What was your reaction when you heard Mr. Ellis was fired?"

"To tell you the truth I cried for him and I knew I could be next."

"Is this why you didn't go to your immediate supervisor and complain or protest his firing."

"You could say that."

"So, you agree that he should have never been fired."

"Yes, I do."

The opposition was coming at him from all over the place and that tried to show that Mr. Herr's statement was an opinion and it doesn't have much value in this case. Michael spoke out and said that if the defense had any justification of why Mr. Ellis was fired, they would have showed us already. He told them that the defense was slinging dirt all over the place and Michael said that it was a desperate attempt in destroying Mr. Ellis further than they have tried all along. The next day was their closing statements and the defense went first and they took a few hours. The judge said in all fairness they should give the plaintiff enough time to make their closing statement without having the lunchtime break split it.

They took the lunchtime break and went down the street they got a sandwich and walked back to the court room with time to spare. Michael knew what he was going to say and he was prepared to say it. He started off by reminding the jury what Mr. Herr said and how he reacted when he heard that Mr. Ellis was fired, he said he cried and I am sure when you get a free moment you might cry. This poor man was degraded down to a new low, they left him with no daughter no wife and no job to go to in the morning, no place to live but in a trailer park and live on a tuna fish sandwich every day, this was the payback for being nominated employee of the year. He thanked them for listening and he said that he gave them all the facts that should make their decision easy.

Michael went and sat next to Mr. Ellis and the judge told the jury that their decision had to be unanimous. The jury left the court room and so did Michael and Bruce they went out through a side door and walked quickly to his escalade and took Mr. Ellis to his hotel and when he was leaving him off, he told him to order room service and sit by the pool or something like that and not to draw attention to himself. He assured Michael that he wouldn't and Michael told him that he would be in touch with him soon He reminded him that they wouldn't get much notice that the jury has come to a decision and they would have to go back to the court house.

Michael went home and there was Ann waiting for him with the children. She wanted to hear how it went and he filled her in on everything. He told her that now it's a waiting game and poor Mr. Ellis was waiting in his room all by himself and Ann said to go there where he is and bring him home with us for dinner. Michael immediately jumped up and he headed straight to the hotel to get Mr. Ellis before he ordered room service and bring him home with him.

He was able to get up with Mr. Ellis and he told him that he was wanting to bring him home with us and spend the evening with them. He was taken back with that but he never the less came with Michael and when they arrived little Mikey ran to him and gave him and shook his hand and gave him a big hug. This was a very emotional moment for Mr. Ellis. Well he couldn't hold back his emotions and started crying. Ann got him some Kleenex and in a few moments, he was able to compose himself, he apologized for that and Michael told him not to be he had them crying too.

The cook made them some Yorkshire pudding with all the trimmings. He was speechless and it was easy to see how much he appreciated his hospitality. They went out back and sat on the landing and watched the waves crash on the shore. They had some real cold glasses of ice tea and enjoyed the stars in this unusually clear sky and Mr. Ellis called out that he has just saw his first shooting star. Ann told him that was a good omen. Michael saw him starting to doze so he said that he better get Mr. Ellis back to the hotel for a good night sleep. When Michael returned the children were in bed and so was Ann with the fireplace lit and lieing there in the buff waiting for her man to join her. Michael isn't known to waste any time so he went to bed and took care of business and passed out.

Michael got up and ran some errands and he didn't get back until 11: o'clock and still no call so he told Mr. Ellis that he was going to pick him up for dinner again at a restaurant that was casual dress. Michael wanted to take him to Vincent's and start off with their bowl of Pasta Frijole, they all loaded in the car and took the five minute ride to the restaurant in the miracle mile shopping center. They were happy to see us come back we were given a seat at a booth and little AnnMarie was seated in a high chair. Michael talked Mr. Ellis into trying a bowl of Pasta Frijole and Ann wanted to try one too. It definitely was worth waiting for and Mr. Ellis loved his very much. Michael had two dozen mussels in Marinara Sause and Mr. Ellis ordered the Veal Parmesan with marinara Sause. Ann ordered the Veal as well and she ordered a couple slices of pizza for the kids.

Michael had some concerns for Mr. Ellis and it was nice to see Mr. Ellis enjoy himself and it made Michael feel good to see Mr. Ellis let himself go. He is a very likable guy who probably had a right not to be. They stopped at Rita's on the way home and that hit the spot. They took Mr. Ellis back to his hotel and Michael told him that in all likely hood we might get called in to the court room for their decision. They got the children in bed and they preferred to finish their evening in their bed room rather to look for something on their bedroom Tv. Michael got up early again and went in his office and he started to make plans that if enough of these fires space center employees are interested in suing, he would have all that was needed to file a law suit. It was around 2: o'clock when he was asked to come to the court in an hour, he swung by Mr. Ellis hotel and he was waiting at the entrance for him.

Mr. Ellis got in and Michael told him that this is it and we will know soon how well we did. The news vans were all over the place, they must have been alerted because they were everywhere sometimes blocking the street entrance. Michael has plans when it's over to talk to the press all about the others employees that were fired illegally by the space center. They entered the court room and they were seated when they were asked to rise for the judge. The judge just sat there and waited for the jurors too start filing into the court room and be seated. The judge looked over at them and asked them if they and the head juror stood up and said they have.

He put on his reading glasses and spoke loud enough for the entire courtroom to hear him and said we have found the defense of the space center guilty of wrongful dismissal and they award the plaintiff the sum of $6 million dollars and they wish to add to that sum $55 million dollars for punitive damages. The judge asked them if that was their unanimous decision and they all said they were. Of course the opposition were in a rage and they said they were going to appeal, when the judge told that they had ten days to defend their position and they failed to do that miserly and then he told them not to hold up this payment and that if it wasn't paid in three days they will be fined $3 million dollars for every day over that time limit.

The court was filing out in the street and there was pandemonium out there in the street. Michael and Mr. Ellis walked out front and thanked the news media for being patience, he told them, that he was happy for Mr. Ellis and he is sorry but there are a lot more people out there that were wrongfully dismissed by the space center and all they need to do is to contact him for his help. Michael knew that this will get back to those people that were wrongfully fired and he knows that the space center is going to have a big problem on their hands. Michael answered some questions and he told them that he has a meeting to attend to but he told them that they will meet again. They weren't to happy about that but they had no choice but to suck it up that's how it is in the news media world.

Michael's interview on the court house steps was all over the news and he was hoping that some of those fired for poor job performance would see it on the news or hear it on the radio or even get around by word or mouth, he thinks that it will draw a crowd of some very unhappy space employees. He checks his account every day and finally the money suddenly appears. He called Mr. Ellis and gave him the good news and told him that he wants to deposit but you will have to go to the and sit with the bank manager and have him call me for a money transfer. It was only an hour later when the bank manager called Michael and Michael told him that he has $30, 500,000 dollars enrooted to his account and to leave $500,000 out in an interest bearing checking/savings account in the highest interest rate they can offer him.

Michael told him that he was Mr. Ellis's attorney and he will be dropping in on him from time to time and can he let him talk to Mr. Ellis. I told him that he has $500,000 dollars in a high interest checking/savings account and that he has $30,000,000 in a high interest bearing account and enjoy himself and be careful of the sleaze bags and if they make it sound to good to be true he can rest assure that is will be and by the way remember what I said about him having a visitor pop in on him from her Greyhound bus ride be careful how popular he will now be to some people. He told Mr. Ellis not to be afraid to call him id he needs him or just an opinion and that he will always be there for him. Bruce was very happy about what has just happened to him that will turn his life around and he told Michael, "God bless You." Michael went home early and he asked Ann if she felt like dinner out at the club and he said the Nanny can watch the children while they are at the club, to celebrate their win over the space center and the new life that Mr. Ellis will now have.

When they walked into the dining room the place broke out in applause and in a spontaneous ovation. It stopped them in their tracks and they nodded to them that they appreciate their recognition and the dining Maître D escorted them to a seat overlooking one of the holes and told them that he was happy that they came to the club for dinner this evening. They nodded their heads again and mouthed thankyou to the room their fellow club members. He also told them that they saw him so much on Television that it was nice to see him in person. Michael told him that they like coming to the club for dinner when they can. Michael ordered the Veal smothered in marinara sauce with a small order of spaghetti also in marinara Sauce. Ann fancied the lobster ravioli's and for an appetizer they split a dozen oyster Rockefellers.

It turns out to be a great evening and they took their time eating their meals and they didn't get home until just after 9: o'clock they saved desert until they got home and it was worth the wait. The office phones were coming in one right behind another and I four days they had 80 request asking Michael to help them and take their case against the space center. He, Ann and Mindy would get back to every one of them and they were asked about twenty questions about their employment record like when they started and when they were fired. Who was their supervisor and did they ever receive any awards and so on and did they ever keep some of their performance reviews, they were ok if they didn't because he can get a complete copy of everyone's employment service reviews?

Now they have their work cut out for them and if they work together, they can make it happen. Michael rented a hotel meeting room near the cape and they interviewed every one of their future clients and they knew which one of the people interviewed which one of them had a case or not. There were two that tried to sneak in but the system that Michael set up would pick out the fraudulent ones leaving 78 bona fide complaints. Michael knew that the space center will go all out not to lose this one and they knew that the precedent has already been set. It was only a question of time and the games *that they might want to play, either to string it out or delay the enviable which Michael knew would cost them more money in the end. They will have to wait and see if they want to talk. Michael went to the court house and filed a lawsuit against A.S.A and or the space center naming all the fired employees alphabetically and asked for damages of $880 million dollars either for the employees if alive or their next of kin if they have passed away and he asked for double the shared amount if anyone of the complainants had committed suicide.*

He over knighted a copy of the law suite to the space center legal department knowing when they see it, they will want to talk. They finally called about a week later and they asked Michael if they can talk about this lawsuit. He told their lawyer that they could if he will supply him with a complete copy of each employees employment file named in the suit. To this day it has taken Michael, Ann and Mindy ninety days and an uncountable number of hours that they have spent on this and its still far from being over. Thank God these people wanted to be found or they would have never gotten this far. What happened to these poor employees happened to Mr. Ellis and probably the same sad ending for most of them. The reason why Michael was asking for so much money is because they decided to eliminate the punitive damages for a quick settlement, Ann called it like throwing them a bone.

They had to go to the cape and Ann and Mindy went with them, they knew at the main gate that they will be coming. Mindy had her distraction clothes on and they won't be able to concentrate while she is moving around. They were met at the front entrance and escorted back to a meeting room where they were seated and moments later their legal team walked in and started introducing them selves and Michael introduced his wife Ann and his secretary Mindy. They congratulated Michael on his win for Mr. Ellis. He told Michael that all they have to do is to change the name of the space center to the space launch center and you won't get a single penny out of this case.

"When you first came in you congratulated me on my win for Mr. Ellis, did you mean that by me beating you head to head or that you just felt bad for Mr. Ellis and that you were happy that he got something for his pain and suffering."

"Look I said nice win, I don't t that I have to go in detail and explain myself."

"I wasn't asking you to explain yourself, I was just curious to hear you say how you personally felt about the win."

"We can put an end to this frivolous law suit at the stroke of a pen."

"It will take more than a change of name of the space center to another name. You will need approval from the United States Senate and then the President so please don't take us as dummies and don't piss down our necks and tell us it's raining. We have more experience at this then anyone that you will ever meet for the rest of your life."

"You sound pretty confident about that."

"A ten year old child would know that and I am surprised that you take me for younger than ten years old."

"Do you think that you can produce a ten year old child that would know that."

"It would take some time but I probably could. I know that I can produce 78 employees that were unlawfully fired so the space center could save millions of dollars not caring what was going to happen to these poor loyal employees, just fire them and get them out of here was probably the way it went. If you think I was good at Mr. Ellis's case I plan on making you pay restitution to every one of these poor people and when I tell all of the sob stories to the jury the punitive damages will go through the roof. This case will cost you billions of dollars and a lot od space peoples jobs and when it gets out how you treated a large number of employees the American people will want this

place closed and padlocked. After they see that you will have to spend all of their billions of tax dollars on something like this despicable inhumane treatment of your employees there will be record number of people on unemployment."

"Did you drive up here to flex your mussels and threaten us like you just did."

"No, we didn't but we do want you to know what game your playing and better still the rules of the game your in. We don't play slow pitch so if you think, and if you think that you are going to scare us by saying that you are going to change the name of the space center to get out of paying damages to these unlawfully employees then all bets are off. If that is how you are trying to scare us in to believing and we will file for an interview with the judge in this case and you tell him that you don't want to pay restitution, you want to make false statements and get out of settling this god awful injustice, Come on girls let go and talk to the judge."

"Now wait a minute we are not finished."

"When you tell us lies were finished as far as we are concerned."

"Now you know that lawyers will always put out feelers to test the waters."

"Do you have the information and files we requested from you."

"We do and there are over a hundred boxes that would only fit in a cargo van."

"We want them loaded on one of your cargo vans and brought to my office in Vero Beach today, now."

"We are not in the package delivery business."

"Ok I'll call the motor pool and ask them to bring a cargo van here at the space center office fort a delivery to my office in Vero Beach."

"This is going to take some time and every thing around her closes at 5:05 pm, ok then you will have to put them under your roof and guard over them until I officially take the responsibility

for them. I gave you a week notice that I was coming and you never lifted a finger to call me and tell me that we would need a cargo van to transport these file boxes out of here. This kind of treatment only comes from someone that's doesn't want to cooperate and it is crystal clear to us that is what our trying to do. You haven't counted on me helping you out and you were right on that one."

"Let me call the motor pool and see what they have available to get these files out of here."

They just sat there and waited for him to return and he told them that their cargo van will be here in fifteen minutes. Michael was thoroughly disgusted with this so called lawyer and he has decided to keep notes on all of his juvenile stall tactics and have them written down to show the judge or the Florida State bar association. Michael didn't know who orders this guy was following but if this keeps up someone was going to pay for it. When they were leaving he was writing down all of those nasty lies that he was telling us and he tried to use them as stall tactics and when we have a couple of more pages filled we are going before the judge in our opening statement and we will need a full day in court just for that and the jury will be sickened when they hear that, so clean up your actor I will tell the world how uncouth you are. Don't take it out on me because you have a piss poor case to defend.

Michael knew that if that didn't turn him around then nothing will. The cargo followed them back to Vero Beach, the driver wouldn't help them with the boxes, it took them over an hour just to get them off the side walk and safely locked away in the office. Michael said that he would to start looking at them tomorrow and set up an alphabetical list of names and place stickers on the tops of each one of the boxes. He crashed when they got home and he went in the office early to start the tedious job of sorting out what he would need for each one of his clients. He noticed almost immediately that every employee fired had a good employee review and he was shocked to see how thee good employees were fired he spent a day going through the boxes and he called the space center legal dept. and told the lawyer that answer the phone who he was and he gave him a list ofc people he wanted to depose. They were the immediate supervisors of the following fired employees, there were eight of them and he had set up a time for the court reporter to record all of the depositions.

When Michael got to the space center with Ann, they were escorted to a meeting room and the defense attorneys started filing in and they sat across from Michael and Ann and looked at them for a long time when Michael asked them where are the eight supervisors that he asked to have here for this deposition. They told him that they could only get up with three of them. The other five have either passed away or they don't have any address for them. Michael asked the defense attorney a letter explaining why he only has three of the eight supervisors and ow they couldn't locate them, he told him that he needs that letter for the file and the court if necessary, of the explanation as to why these five people aren't here this morning. Of course, they protested and Michael told them what is wrong in putting the truth in writing.

The defense attorney said again that they could only get three out of the eight supervisors that you ask for. Michael told him to put it in writing or they will go back to Vero now and go straight to the court and that you have to refused to give him a letter of explanation how you attempted to get up with the missing five supervisors for this deposition. Michael stood up with Ann and walked out of the room and they headed for the parking lot.

The lead defense attorney was chasing after Michael and Ann and asked Michael why doesn't he depose the three that are here he told the attorney that he no longer trusts him to tell him the truth. They left and a few days later they received phone call from the legal department at the cape and they asked him if they can come down and talk to him. Michael said he didn't mind just as long as you don't bring your lead attorney in this case with you, he told him that they have compiled about four pages of lies and stall things that he tried to pull on them in this case so far and I know the judge will want to see how you people operate when it comes to the law.

They told Michael they wouldn't and can they meet with him tomorrow morning around 10: o'clock at his office. Michael said that would be fine and Ann came to the office with Michael this morning and they sat in the meeting room for them to show up. Mindy came back and told them they were here and she escorted them back to where we were. There were two of them and the one that looked important enough introduced himself as Jack Collins and he introduced himself as Mike Waltz. He didn't waste any time for apologizing for them getting off on the wrong foot. He asked Michael is there a way they can show him that they are taking these claims very serious. Michael told this guy that they can't win this law suit because he just beat them out of $63,000,000 and the best, they can hope for is that there aren't any casualties. The best they can hope for is to keep it out of the billions of dollars.

Michael asked him is he aware that he just won this identical case against them for $63.000.000 foe Mr. Ellis, he said he was aware of it and Michael told hm that if he were to multiply that by 78 you come up with $4,914,000.000.

"I can tell by the look on your face that you can't believe what you just heard"

"That kind of money would close the space center down."

"Well I am all ears how you want to solve this suit; I think I have a way you can solve this suit, most of the money handed down was for punitive damages and I can assure you the same thing can happen all over again. If you would agree to pay each fired employee $12,500,000, we would waive the punitive damage sand you settle this case and every claimant will sign a gag order then you will save your client $4,000,000,000 Once the court date is set all bets

are off. He sat there for a moment to digest all those numbers that Michael told them about, He asked Michael if he would mind if him and Mike could go outside and talk it over and they will need to contact our office at the cape and see how they feel."

"I can't object to that and Ann and I will go up the street at Mulligans and get something to eat like fish and chips, its not that far away and service is fast."

"That was fine with them and if we have time, we might grab something as well."

It was nice to have lunch on the ocean, Ann asked Michael if he thinks they will take that offer and his reply to her was if they like the space program they will. They were gone about forty five minutes when Jack and Mike were walking back to the office. They walked in together and back to the meeting room. Jack told them that they spoke to his legal department and they told him they would settle these claims if every one of your clients would sign a gag order. Michael got up and left the room and he came back with this box of 78 gag orders that Michael had what they were asking for, Michael said that he anticipated this request so he had all 78 of his clients sign a gag order when he interviewed them separately

Michael took them out of the box and told Jack that he figured that he would want them as part of a settlement so I put them away for this very moment and Him and Ann also signed a gag ordered. That knocked Jack back on his heels for a loop and said he was impressed and he was also afraid to ask what else he anticipated. Michael laughed and told Jack what he doesn't know won't hurt him. Michael told Jack that he has already made copies of these files are their copies are from the original. Michael gave Jack an overnight box to put them in. He said he would have to go back and lay this out to the higher ups and they will be the ones that will make the final decision. Michael reminded them that that they were on the clock so please don't let your decision take too long.

They stood and shook hands and Michael walked out with them and he watched them drive away and went back in where Ann was waiting to tell Michael that he is one of a kind and that you have almost made a half a billion dollars when this lawsuit is over. Michael wants to take Ann out for dinner tonight at the club and ran home to get things ready for the Nanny could stay for a while and watch the children. They were warmly welcomed to the club and was seated by a window, they both ordered surf and turf and it was as usual. The club always has the best food that money can buy and it tasted like it. Michael gave Mindy a paid week vacation anywhere in the world or a $10,000 dollar bonus. She took the bonus and told Michael that she can use the money for other things.

Michael knew it would take some time for Jack to make those heard heads seethe point about wasting time, this will turn out to be the biggest fight of his life. Jack and Mike had to go before a review board and discuss what happened and what will happen if the court sets a date for the trial to start. They had heated discussions for hours at the cape and Jack reminded them that this man beat us in one case for $61,000,000 and he has promised me that he will give us a $4,000,000,000 dollar savings if we settle before the court sets a date for us to appear in court, he told them that he has the claimants signed gag orders and the lawyer and his wife.

Finally asked the board for their decision and they all voted to settle for the agreed price that the opposing attorney offered. Jack called Michael and asked him to come to the cape tomorrow morning to finally settle this case. He and Ann drove up early and were there easily by 9: o'clock. They were escorted back to the same meeting room they were at before, Jack walked in with a folder and he shook their hands and he congratulated them on their huge settlement. He opened the folder and he handed and he presented them with a check for $975,000,000 dollars. Michael asked him if they could wire this money to their bank and he gave him his routing number. When *he returned the check was stamped paid on both sides and a receipt that the money was received by their bank.*

When they returned the first thing, they did was to write each claimant a letter they are invited to meet them at the hotel they previously met before and receive their case settlement. He said he would meet them in four days at noon to sign for their settlement money. It took almost half a day making up making out each persons check for $6,250,000. They were done that task and headed for that hotel at the cape and arrived before noon and wait for the anxious recipients to come for their long overdue settlement money. They opened the doors at noon and they all had their drivers license in hand. They had to sign their name for their check and a thumb print just under their name and Ann was talking a mug shot of everyone that showed up to collect their over due money for the wrong that was done to them.

Ann attached everyone's picture to their check receipt and felt safe that the money went to the right person. The room was in a festive mood and they all wanted to shake Michaels hand and couldn't thank him enough. There was one person that didn't show up, they waited for him until 5: o'clock and in the middle of packing up when the missing recipient finally showed up and he apologized for running late, he started balling like a baby, Ann was looking for some Kleenex and she was able to get him calmed down and told him goodbye and when he was ok they left for Vero. Michael will have to wait but he did want to wire $700,000,000 dollars that they had accumulated to their Swiss account in Zurich. They replied thanking him for their large deposit and Michael thought to himself that their interest is thanks enough.

Michael wanted to do something for Vero so they got the leaders together in Indian River County to approve a pier that the public can fish from it would go out 800 ft in the ocean so the people could fish for fish that they don't usually get a chance to catch that far out in *the ocean. This pier will be very popular and Michael and Ann will cover the cost. It would take two years but in the meantime they will pay for the updating of all the parks along the ocean that included the playgrounds as well and bath houses, bath houses and boat ramps and all new picnic tables and double the size of all the parking lots, they also paid for some new play house and art museums. He and Ann couldn't wait to see all this happen. The total bill totaled up to $120,000,000 and they knew that money well spent. They also wanted their names to be anonymous.*

The new construction was started to show and the news media were beginning to ask questions like where is this money coming from and other than that it was business as usual, the people went along minding their own business almost expecting these things to be built. Where ever it was possible they asked to have a board walk built if it was at all possible to give the walkers some place to walk along the ocean and sit on benches and relax looking out over the ocean, they also put small ocean front eating places along the ocean that can pay to stay open by the small profits and after paying the salaries they make. They were going to charge a fee for parking and to walk out on the pier to fish. This will help on the maintaince cost to keep the pier safe but only a modest fee just enough to pay for all the expenses.

There was a while to go before this could be finished, it is quite an undertaking. It would have been a disgrace to have all their money and not help the people of Vero Beach and the surrounding counties. Ann and Michael went to the county board and they will pay to have a new children's wing built on the existing hospital we have now and it will be as big or even bigger than the our existing we have now. They asked Ann and Michael if they would have a problem if it should cost $150,000,000 and maybe a touch more. Michael said they would pay for it but they would have to review the entire construction coast and they would have a watch dog to over see the entire construction job and be responsible for the money being *spent on the project. They said they will pay for any audit on every ninety days until this project is finished. The county approved of everything and set the start date to be in sixty days.*

In the mean time Michael and Ann are enjoying an interest rate of 12% on their money in their private Swiss private savings account. Their money is growing at an alarming rate and they are only giving away their interest, they have accumulated over a billion dollars now it is climbing so fast that it will double in less that seven years. The club that they love so much has fallen on hard times so they bought it for $20,000,000 and there are still 400 building sites available and for sale and that alone will make them millions. They really didn't want the country club but he really didn't want anyone else to have it either, he kept the name and made the club house second to none.

Ann really liked the idea of them owning the country club and it was only fitting that they bought it. It was totally done over and the members loved it and they were proud to be a member. With their purchase that now have a beach club right on the ocean that they turned into a spectactical get away for the day. They had 300 feet of ocean front and a casual dining room that was open that was open on Friday and Saturday for lunch and dinner by reservations and they were going to try something different and open on Sundays brunch for a breakfast buffet that would stay open till 2: o'clock. It was the place for anyone that was something to have dinner at the new casual restaurant on the ocean and the public were invited to be a part of this private setting.

12

Michael has this lucrative law practice and Ann worked very hard and she passed her bar exam and Michael wanted to show his devotion to he so they gathered up the children and went out for dinner at the beach club that they are very proud of and everyone there knew who they were, the children had a ball, their meal was a bit pricey they wanted the restaurant to take care of itself and not need a handout from the club to keep them afloat. The restaurant was son popular and busy that some of the reservations were after 9:o'clock. It got great reviews and it was the place to eat at on the ocean on the weekend in Vero Beach.

They would come from all over Florida just to experience eating on the ocean like that. There were a lot of demands for an interview and he always said he was too busy; he just didn't trust them to be fair in an interview like they weren't before. Little Mikey is in the first grade now and he loves it and his sister is gearing up for her first grade when it cones. Michael told Ann that the children seem smarter than he was at their age, they love living in Florida and hope that they will never move.

When they purchased the country club, they put a spark into the outdoor life in Vero Beach. They loved playing golf on their top rated golf in Florida. One night when they were sitting out back Ann told Michael that she was pregnant again and Michael thought that was great news, he asked her when the baby was due and she said not for a while yet but probably sometime around Christmas. They loved sitting out back and this one time while sitting on their bench looking out bon the ocean and enjoying their ice tea when Michael spotted this girl coming out of the ocean and just stand at the water edge. He picked up his binoculars and he wanted to get a better look at her. She was about six foot tall with a beautiful body with short hair.

Michael gave the binoculars to Ann for her to have a look at what just walked out of the ocean and to see what she thought. She looked for a few seconds and told Michael that she is quite the woman. She just stood there and finally she spotted them looking at her and she started walking towards them and stopped at the beach bench steps and she looked at them and she started to cry and Ann rushed down to her and asked her what is wrong. She said she was lost and right away Michael thought that was unusual to be lost coming out of the ocean. Ann brought he up and sat her on the bench with them, she was upset that she didn't know where she was. Michael told her she was in Vero Beach Florida just south of the Kennedy space center. Michael noticed that her hands were beautifully manicured and her features were perfect.

Ann wanted to know, "Were you swimming by yourself?"

"Yes, I was."

"You should always be with someone when your swimming in the ocean, to many things can happen to you out there all alone."

She corrected herself and said, "That she was with a small party and she got separated from them and she swam here where she could see some buildings"

"Were you in a boat out there fishing?"

"It wasn't a boat it was a small craft."

"Did it capsize or did you fall overboard undenounced to the other fishermen?"

"No, it started sinking and I floated away to safety."

"How many people were with you on your craft?"

"We had a crew of six."

"Do you always call your friends a crew?"

"Well yes I do when I am explaining them to you."

"I think we should notify the coast guard to be on the lookout for your crew."

"I wish that you wouldn't do that because they won't want to be found, they prefer to be on their own."

"What about you do you feel that way as well?"

"I don't know how I feel, right now you seem to be friendly and I feel comfortable being around you."

"Do our children bother you?"

"No, this is my first time to be inContact with the young ones."

"Well if you don't know where you are and you don't have a place to change out of your wet suit into some dry clothes then you can come with me up to the house and change into some dry clothes and maybe get you something to eat if that is alright with you."

Ann took her by the hand and they walked to the house and she asked Ann when the baby was due? Well Ann almost fell over with that and asked her how she knew she was pregnant and she told Ann that she could see that with no problem. Ann took her to the bedroom and she said she would get her some dry clothes and when she returned, she was standing in the bathroom stark naked she thought from what she saw that she was a perfect specimen of any woman she has ever seen. She wasn't shy and coving her self up, nothing like that and Ann handed her some ladies panties and she told her to put them on and she asked Ann how can she put them on. Now Ann went along with this and she wanted to see where this was going. Her breast were so perfect that she didn't need a bra for support but never the less Ann asked her if she wore a bra.

Ann stopped and said that she didn't even know her name and she looked dumfounded and asked Ann and asked her do you mean what I answer to and Ann said yes. They call me Venus and Ann asked her where she was from and she told her she was from Tapolia.

"Where is that ?"

"I am from a place that is real far away from here."

She is standing there still naked and Ann is still trying to have a conversation with her and she is not inhibited at all. Tell me Venus can you be a little more explicit about where Tapolia is. She pointed up at the ceiling and p[pointed up there far away and Ann asked her how far away is that and her reply was two light years from here. Ann trying to get her wits about herself said to her let me understand you, Tapolia where you come from is two light years away.

"What are you doing here on Earth?"

"We have coming here for thousands of years studying your species."

"We can't travel to your planet and when you come here, you prove that you are a hell of a lot smarter than us. Please put those shorts on and that blouse before my husband walks in on us."

"Are you that long out the stone age and ice age that a whole you are barely civilized."

"Were not hurting you are we, and wouldn't us uncivilized humans would have already hurt you."

"not yet but we know min time you will, you have evolved from apes and you tend to be animalistic and that is something wed cannot put up with."

"We can't go out in space like you can for at least twenty thousand or more, we are no threat to you and if you stay with us you will find that out. Please stop hiding behind that shield that we are uncivilized and we come from apes."

"It is nice of you to offer me a place to stay, it won't be that long before my crew finds me and takes home."

Ann asked her again if she wanted to wear a bra and she lifted up her shirt and showed her what it looked like on. Ann thought those things stand straight out and they don't need any support. Ann explained to Venus that it is a custom here on Earth to cover those things up, Ann helped her with some adjustments and said there's how that.

"It feels uncomfortable to me."

"You will get used to it in a few days, we usually take it off when we go to bed. My name is Ann and my husbands name is Michael. I will have to tell him about you so please don't be alarmed."

"I won't be, he seems friendly enough."

Just then there was a tap on the door and Michael asked if he could come in and Ann said, "It's Ok."

"I was wondering where you two were."

"We were just talking and Venus told me a lot."

"What are you going to do about the children going to bed."

"I'll take Venus and she can help me put the children to bed."

Ann took Venus's hand and found the children in there bed rooms and Ann tucked them in and they gave Venus a kiss and it was heartwarming and it took Venus by surprise. Both children gave Venus a kiss and Ann took Venus again and they walked out in the kitchen and they found Michael at the table with a glass of ice tea. Ann introduced Michael to Venus and Venus to Michael and they sat down.

"Venus is going to stay with us until her crew finds her."

"What crew is that?"

"The crew she came here with."

"Do you mead like a race boat crew, like those big sail boats?"

"No, I am talking about a space ship crew that was lost at sea, Venus was one of the crew of six."

"Are you telling me that she is not from around here?"

"I am saying that, she comes from two light years away and if her crew members don't find her, she will be applying for a green card and applying for American citizenship. He said he was joking and

he knows that it wouldn't be that simple. In the end he said he would protect her from anything bad that could happen to her."

"No one has to know anything about her, she will have to be one of our relatives living with us and no one can prove anything different."

Michael couldn't stress enough to Venus that she can never tell anyone anything about where she's from we will have to keep that a secret or she will see first hand just how uncivilized we can be. Not him or Ann but the others out there. Michael asked her if she was hungry and she said she wasn't. Ann took Venus by the hand back to her bedroom and showed how the shower works and where the soap was and how to put the toothpaste on the brush and how to apply her deodorant and why we use it and she showed Venus how to use the toilet and flush.

She watched Venus get in bed, she tucked her in and she kissed her on the cheek like the children did earlier. Ann told her they will be up at 7: o'clock and we can meet in the kitchen for breakfast. Ann said good night and closed her door and she went to her room and she felt better if she closed her door as well. She said to Michael can you believe what has just happened to us?

Michael was sitting in front of the fire place and said that he didn't believe it. Ann told Michael that she saw her naked and he can take it from her she is a very healthy young lady and she is all girl from her head to her toes. She is not like any woman from around here.

"What are we going to do?"

"That's a good question, we are not breaking any laws by letting her live with us and if it should ever get out what you know about mankind will not last very long. There will be Ciaos and all of the financial institutions will collapse because their people out there that are smarter than us and they proved it by coming here."

"I will have to tell our help that she is a relative of mine and I will have to stress to Venus not to say a single word to anyone about herself."

"I think that she knows all about that what you said, that's why they never want to be seen or captured. What you can't see would be hard to believe in an extraterrestrial life flying around and being seen by everyone."

After a good night sleep and they went out in the kitchen and Venus was not there Ann walked back to her room and she wasn't there either. She ran to Michael and told him that Venus is no where to be found. Michael told Ann that if she doesn't want the safety of our home then it is right that she has left. She was surprised to hear Michael sound like that, she knew it was true. Mikael had showered and on his way in the office by 9: o'clock. It wasn't long after that Ann called and said she saw Venus walking up from the beach and sat in a chair and started crying, she couldn't believe the predicament she was in. Your family are the only people she knows or trust with her life. Ann told her if she means it, she should never disappear like that again.

Ann reminded her that most of the people around here are not as broadminded as we are. She did ask where Michael was and she told her that we have a law practice in town and Michael is a very good attorney, he loves to come to the aid of someone that was wrongfully accused or cheated out of their legal rights. Venus liked that and she knew he was successful when she first laid eyes on him. I could feel the electricity coming from him. Ann asked Venus to promise that she will never leave the house alone again or unless she tells one of us. She said that she promises and Ann believed her. Ann sat with her and asked her if she was married and she said no because I was always busy at work in the space program.

:Have you ever had sex with one of your young men."

"No not yet, I hear its devine and I am looking forward to it."

"How old are you Venus?"

"I am fifty years old according to your Earth time and only eighteen years old on Tapolia time."

"That is remarkable and you have a body of an eighteen year old."

"I guess I take it for granted and I don't realize it until someone like you a stranger tells me."

"Is there anything that you haven't told me that I should know, now is the time to tell us rather then to find out something that you should have told us."

"There are so many things that I could tell you, but there just isn't enough time for me to do that."

"How were you able to tell me that I was going to have a baby? That is something that us humans on Earth are not capable of doing"

"I have been trained for decades to see what no one else can see."

"Wouldn't it take more than training, and wouldn't you also have that ability to have that kind of vision."

"Yes, most everyone on our planet has that ability but very few have that ability to know how to use it."

"Do you have the ability to tell what people are thinking? Can you tell what people are talking about just as if they are standing next to you?"

"Yes, I have that capability to do that."

"I guess Michael and I better be careful when we are in our bedroom talking, you might be able to hear what we're talking about."

"I could but I respect your privacy."

"I guess you can tell when a person is lying to you?"

"Oh yes, very easily."

Venus asked Ann if she could become a attorney and Ann told her that anyone can if they pass the bar exam. Ann went on to tell her that you can pass the bar exam but you have to have an understanding of the law and our way of life. She told Ann that she has been studying the people of Earth and the united states for thirty five years and with some coaching from you two I could be good at it. Ann told her to read these books and I will quiz you to see what you can remember, she thought that was a good idea. Ann told Venus that she will have to get her an identity. She told Ann that her identity can be traced all the way back to Plymouth rock. Ann thought that was great and by her having that kind of identity it was going to make it easy to get her those important documents that she will need to go through our society.

Ann couldn't wait for Michael to come home and give him all of the that she has leant about Venus. When Michael came in Venus apologized to him for disappearing like that and not telling them where she was going and she knows now how bad that would haver been for them. Ann told Michael in front of Venus all that she told her about having proof of citizenship and even a SS# and she wants to be a lawyer like us and work in our firm with us. Michael told her that she will have to do a lot of studying and some classroom work to be a lawyer. Venus said she can pass the test just give her the books to read over. Michael left the room and came back with a dozen books in a carrying case and he told her she can use the library to study in.

Both Michael and Ann knew she could do it or she would have never said so. Venus loved talking to them, about the law and they were amazed to hear her rattle on. There was one thing that puzzled Michael and that was what interest could we be to such an superior intelligent people. She told them that we have been watching you for a very long time and instead of us seeing some improvement you seem to be getting worse and that concerns us and how much worse can you people get is our dilemma . You will not be allowed to come out in space and stagnate any life that is out there.

"So, tell me Venus with all this intellectual superiority you have you end up in the ocean and none of your crew around to help you or keep you with them and you end up living with these uncivilized people that hasn't ate you or killed you. That is a mystery to me and I don't think that you have told us everything we need to know about the real reason why you came here."

She sat up in her chair and she told them they were on a mission and take back their findings weather humans should be extinguished and start all over again. Michael asked her what were her findings to this point before she was lost at sea. She told them because of all the crime and wars and civil unrest all over your planet that the recommendation was going to be to extinguish life as you know it here on earth. If you can see how life it is on Tapolia you would understand what I 'am telling you. He asked her wasn't there any good happening here on Earth to stop this elimination of mankind. There might be but your good doesn't out weigh the bad. Your family is good and there some others that are good too, but that doesn't stop the huge blocks of evil people all around you that you can only destroy each other and eventually your planet. This keeps going on because these evil ones think that they don't have anyone to answer too.

"They would change their ways if they could hear what you just told me, they could answer to your leader and he could tell them to stop this uncivilized behavior or perish. Michael said that sounds like something that God would say that you call another name."

"I don't know who God is but it sounds like he thinks like us."

"I would like to know where the rest ofc your crew is?"

"I would like to know that answer as well, we knew about your claims about the Bermuda triangle and something very odd knocked us out of the sky when we were just gliding over the water about a hundred feet or so sending messages home."

"How long would it take for them to receive them?"

"To calculate that into your time it would take about ninety days or so."

"That is a long time to wait for a reply."

"When you think about how far it has to travel at four times the speed of light that time is ok."

"To get back to how you were complicating on the destruction of life Earth because of how uncivilized we are, there are a lot of good people on Earth."

"Your right and I am sitting with some and you are the exception and there aren't enough of you out there to change that decision and just as an example we watched your advertisements and every single company that advertises misleads the public into buying their products and it is an excepted practice through that industry, in fact you teach it in your school and other untruths."

"How long do you think it would be before they send down a space crew here to bring you home?"

"There can be a number to that question but time will tell."

"What would you do if they come here to take you home?"

"That would all depend on what would be the circumstances in my life at the time they come."

"I understand what you're saying I am amazed at this that someone who wants to destroy life as we know it on Earth and we are no threat to you what so ever."

"I agree, it is a little strong but they don't want your way of life infecting their way of life and soon your Star Wars would become a reality."

"What do you call your leader when you refer to him?"

"There more than more than one and a total of twelve to run a tight ship."

"Are they elected by the people like we do here on Earth?"

"No, they sit on a board for a four year term and keep the system working with no problems."

"Do you have prisons like we have here on Earth."

"No, we don't and we also don't have crime like you have here. Your way of life could only destroy any civilized way of life, it would only be a matter of time before your infectious ways destroy everything that is good."

"Your people must be deathly afraid of us and blind to the good we have on Earth."

"Your country alone has made 25,000 atomic bombs and your biggest enemy has done the same, now that is insane and if you were to try and it was detected by us, they will reduce your planet to a bunch of small particles of dust floating in space till the end of time."

"Is that what you were doing here looking for the soft spot of our belly?"

"They have known where that is for years, I was here on a mission to see if your planet was worth saving."

"Where is the harm in letting us destroy ourselves or don't you think that good can defeat evil. We have plenty of evidence of good winning over of evil."

"Well then who won over evil at those Roman coliseum lion slaughters?"

"That is the only record of anything like that happening on our planet."

"What business of yours what we do on our planet with our lives, who put you in charge of our welfare or who put you in charge of what we do here on our planet. We are too far away from you to be any threat to you and we could never travel at those speeds to even find you."

"You do have a gift of getting your point over and you have done that in your successful law practice, we are not intimidated by some one that has a gift of persuasion. The ones were afraid of are the ones that are not like you."

"The ones that your afraid of are the evil ones and they don't have any way of coming out in space for 20,000 years."

"We are afraid of that leader from N. Korea, we feel if given a chance could turn out to be worse then that Germans leader that killed all those people and made a good attempt of Ethnic cleansing a race of people out of existence. That is what we are afraid of if those kinds of people should come out here and infect us like their failed attempts on Earth."

"Just because we can go to the moon and back doesn't make us space travelers, you haven't taken into consideration that the older we get as a planet the better we will become. We have only just gotten out of the caves and you are telling me how scared you are of us. That tells me a lot about your inabilities to handle anything different from what your use to and not in charge of."

"Good point, its hard to believe that they haven't thought of that."

"It seems to me that they are making decisions without having all the facts and in our case, you need to do some more homework and talk to some of our good Earthlings. Imagine if you can that you don't like us and you want to kill us under the disguise that we are uncivilized. That would not withstand the scrutiny of any court of law on any planet in the total universe, would it?"

"I am not an attorney and I really don't know, but it is a good point that your making."

"You don't have to be an attorney you only have to know the difference between right and wrong. Killing people is a very serious offence and someone will have to answer to someone for this crime against humanity. That German fellow you talked about do you think that he had to answer to anyone, I'll bet that he didn't and he found out that he started something he couldn't finish. We all have to answer to someone and those people on your planet that think that they don't have to answer to anyone and they are so richest and they

can erase an entire planer t of human life when ever they think that its time to get rid of the trash."

"I only know about that thinking because I grew up hearing that thinking all around me, so I guess I was brain washed like you like to call some people when you can't find another word to describe someone."

"So did those German grow up with that thinking but it didn't stop them for doing the dirty work for that crazy man. Don't blame us we were only following orders was their excuse and it was not accepted by the war tribunal and those killers were found guilty of war crimes and some of them were put to death."

"You know Ann how lucky you are to be married to such a man that he is, I could listen to him all day."

That was quite a meeting and Michael spoke his mind and told Venus how he feels about her planets barbaric thinking and it was no different from that German's fellow thinking it only proves that sick minds think a like even if it is two light years away.

Michael if she still wanted to be an attorney and she said yes. Please feel free to ask Ann or myself if you need any help on anything. She told him that she would and she told him that she would be in the study reading over all those books you gave me to read. Michael told her that she should stop in the evenings and take a break, so as not to wear yourself out, she thanked him for that advice and left the room. He knew her would never have a case like the space center one again. The fishing pier and the ocean front parks are going really well and the children's new wing on the hospital is also doing really well. Michael knows that the pier out on the ocean will be a lot of fun to fish off of and walk out on. Michael said that he wanted to walk out on it to the very end and Ann asked him if he has any idea how deep the water is out there at the end of the pier. Michael told her that it will be deep enough to anchor an ocean liner to.

Michael is getting a request for him to sell his ocean front restaurant for some big money and money is the last thing he needs more of; he knew that the new owner will go in there and screw things up trying to make a bigger profit. If they are good in running a restaurant let them start one up on there own and not buy into an established business after we have done all the road work to get here on the ocean. The Tv station called and they wanted to do a story on how charitable we are and when would be a good time to come out for a talk. Ann told her that they know that we don't do interviews because you can't be trusted to be honest when you put it on the air. Of course she became very defensive and the girl barked at Ann how would you know and Ann not being a push over Ann told her that you have a reputation of not showing an interview as it was originally taped and you also lie about the people you interview which tells me that you don't get any repeat interviews, you know it and you don't give the news on people that you protect and cover up all their lies. Ann told her not to call us again, it will not help you and definitely hurt you.

Michael goes in the office every day and does everything from Wills, divorces to DUI's and all in between. Michael knows that if he has a retainer with a company and someone comes to him wanting to file a law suit against them he would have a conflict of interest in a lawsuit against the company that he has a retainer for. They will not defend any company that is being sued by an employee, they found out that an employee doesn't sue their employee for no reason, just like in the space center lawsuit.

Michael was talking about how her studies were going and she said she was ready for him to test her. Michael asked her if he could ask her one question and it won't be easy and she told him to ask her anything. Michel asked her to explain, uninsured motorist and underinsured motorist. She did it with ease and she told him what book it was in and what page it was on and what line it was on. He *was shocked at the memory she had and he told her he would look into when the next bar exam will be It turns out that it was in six days at the library in town in the meeting room. They paid $250.00 test fee and she casually waited for the day to come, Ann said that she would drive her down to the library and she can call her when she's ready to be picked up. Ann got home and in an hour, Venus called her for a ride home. Ann was in shock and speechless when she was driving to the library to pick her up. She told Ann that she remembers reading all the materials and the test was easy when you study properly.*

Ann stopped at the red light and said to Venus, we can study properly but we don't have the memory or the recall that you have. They waited for a week and a letter came in the mail from the Florida bar association it was addressed to Venus and she gave it to Michael to open, he took it out of the envelope and unfolded it and looked at the top and it said congratulations you have passed the Florida bar exam with a perfect score of 100 and you may begin to practice law in Florida after you have a judge swear you in and take the oath that you will faithfully discharge the duties of an attorney or counsel at law to the best of my abilities in the course of the practice of law, after that you can practice law in Florida.

Michael handed her the letter and he told her to place it behind the license they sent her framed. They both congratulated her on her perfect score and Michael asked her if she was raring to go out and she said she was. She told them that she was coming in the office tomorrow and you will have your own office and your license hanging on the wall, Ann said that we all have a license to practice law now in the State of Florida and we will make a great team. Michael gave a good point to remember and that was that she will have to argue a point no matter how difficult and painful it may be if you can do that you will be hard to beat. Follow your instincts and I know that you have some very sensitive instincts that will put you above anyone that you come in contact with and you will be a tremendous asset to this firm.

Ann wants to leave right away and get Venus some great outfits to work in and some slack outfits where a dress would not be appropriate to work in Ann left going on a shopping spree with Venus that every woman would die for, she knows to get everything she will need and then some and don't forget to get herself something..

13

Venus received a letter from the Florida bar association asking her for an interview. Michael wanted to go with her because he smells something fishy. They arrived at the office and they were escorted in to a small meeting room and a Mr. Ramos came in and introduced himself to them and he said that they wanted to talk to Venus alone.

"Unless you have some legal right to only want to talk to Venus alone, she is my employee and I will sit here with he at her request and she asked me to accompany her here today."

"Are you concerned for her safety or something else or are you afraid that she can't sit with me and have a conversation with me one on one."

"I don't think that she has anything to be scared of with you and you will see if you want her to, she can talk circles around you. She is a very intelligent young lady so please start the interview or we will have to leave."

"Venus you scored a perfect score on your bar exam and that is unheard of coming from a person with no background in law or law school or any school so can you tell us how you scored a perfect score."

"I studied hard for this test and I wanted to pass it the first time."

"You scored a perfect 100 you got every question correct."

"That was my goal and that was what I worked hard to do."

"I asked the proctor if she remembered you and she said how could anyone not ever remember a young lady like her, she remembers you only taking an hour from the time allocated was five hours and you only took one hour. If we tested someone that had all the

answers, they would take more than an hour. You had to read the question and answer the question one behind the other and you took as little of the time needed to write the answer down and still score a perfect 100.

"I want to say something about what I am hearing here today and that is you seem to bed suspicious of Venus's testing skills and you would have been a little happier if she took the allotted time and got some of the answers wrong. Look you sent her as license that she earned to practice law and letter congratulating her on scoring a perfect 100. What happened from that time until now that you want to talk to her?"

"There some people who are in disbelief that this could ever happen."

"Where are these people and who are these people that are in disbelief, we want them here to stand in front of us and cast their dispersions and ask those questions of disbelief and challenge Venus's abilities to pass this bar exam test or any other test."

"Look this was only meant to be a friendly conversation about Venus and her perfect test score."

"I believe that you put some doubt on that after someone got in your ear and made you have doubts that a person couldn't finish that test in an hour and you actually called Venus in here and watch you dance around this distasteful interview"

"I am sorry if I have offended you Venus please accept my apologies and I wish you all the luck in the world with your new law career."

They stood and walked towards the door when Mr. Ramos told Michael that he read all three of his books and he was deeply impressed how he and his wife with your investigative skills. Michael nodded to him in a thank you for that compliment and left for their car that he was lucky enough to find a parking spot right in front of the building. Venus asked Michael what was that all about and he told her they were snooping around trying to find something wrong with your testing abilities and he finally waited to the end before he told you that your score and time was a remarkable feat. She told him that she memorized every word and she has a photographic mind recall, she said that she can give the page number and what is on them. Michael took a big gulp and he knew that there wasn't anyone like her on the planet and she is friends with them, she could solve every crime that is still open and unsolved.

They got back to the office and he asked Venus if she would sit with him for a few minutes and she said of course. Ann wanted to be there too so they all sat at the table in their small meeting room and Michael asked her point blank and he asked her if she was able to score a 100 in her bar exam, if she wouldn't mind telling him.

"I have a photographic memory and I am able to recall with ease and in very precise detail."

"What else can you do?"

"I can read minds and I can go to a crime scene and through my mind's eye I can see how the crime was perpetrated. I get this feeling of being there and I can see it all. I can also tell when a person is lying or not. I can also predict the winning numbers that you play at your gambling places and win every time and I can make the lottery numbers you play appear that you have chosen as the winning numbers.

"Wow you can do almost anything."

"Almost."

"What can't you do."

"I can diagnose someone's illness but I can't cure them of it."

"Are you saying that you can talk or meet a person and you can detect that person has a physical impairment that they don't even know they have."

"You can tell if an airplane pilot is healthy enough to fly or weather our astronauts are healthy enough to go into space and so on.

You can even read the minds of our enemies; we probably wouldn't want to know what they're thinking."

"I don't want to practice that; it is something I stay away from."

"I just wanted to know what your capabilities are in case we need some help on something."

"Now you know."

"Ann and I are so happy that you are living with us and we know that the children love you very much."

"I feel very comfortable here with you and I love the children too and I want to stay with you if you let me."

"Of course, we'll let you stay with us weather you like that or not, you are now a part of our family and that is the most valued thing you can have."

"You are the only family have here on Earth."

"Good I want to get you a car do you have one in mind that you like very much. She said she would love a black Bentley just like the one we have."

The next morning we'll go down to the dealer and get you one, she said she couldn't wait. They pulled up to the dealer showroom, they went inside and this salesman said he remembered him and Ann and Michael told him that he wanted the same deal that you gave us the last time we were here for our relative who will pick one out. He showed us this pearl two door convertible that Venus fell in love with right then and there and he made the price right for us and while they were prepping it for her and they worked on all the paperwork and Michael told Venus that he will have to get her a driver's license right away. Ann drove her car to the Vero Beach motor vehicle and they allowed Venus to sign up and for Venus to come back for the written test and the driver's test as well. God help the instructor when he sees Venus get I for her test drive in a short skirt.

Ann spent the whole week with her and she was ready to be tested. Ann waited for her in a waiting room and when the instructor saw Venus sitting behind the wheel with her legs apart in her short skirt, she wasn't going to Havre any problem passing the road test. He took her inside for the written test and she passed that as well they took her picture and Venus drove Ann home. It was to late to get anything done at the office so they headed for home and waited for Michael for Michael to come in and they decided to go out to the club for dinner. The nanny was watching over the children and they were going to celebrate Venus passing her motor vehicle test and getting her derivers license. After dinner they decided to go over to their beach restaurant for a cold drink on the ocean.

Venus told Ann And Michael that she couldn't believe they own the country club and ocean restaurant it must be a dream come through for them to sit and have dinner in their restaurant on the ocean. They all ordered ice teas for something to drink and they sat outside where the air smelt salty and the waves crashed on the shore, it was a very nice experience for Venus and she couldn't help but to tell them how she felt. They weren't in any hurry to leave they were just happy to be in each other's company. Venus thanked them again for the car and she promised to keep it as clean as they keep theirs. Michael told her it will be included in the car cleaning rotation each week and not to worry about it. He told her that it won't be too long before people see her driving it around town and associate her with it. They will ask who is that beautiful girl in that shiny Bentley. Venus laughed at that and Michael told her to wait and see.

Michael told her she will be the talk of the town and he told her to be careful of those old gray wolfs that want to neat up little girls like you. That seemed to alarm her but she did get the message pretty quickly. She wanted Ann to take her golfing and they spent a few days hitting some balls when Ann told Michael she is a pro; she has never seen any woman hit golf ball like that before. She either pars or birdies every hole, she can drive the ball almost three hundred yards and she puts like a pro.

Michael was very happy to hear that and he told Ann that she is to shield Venus from those peering eyes of the storytellers and have it all over the club how good a golfer she is and draws to much attention to her self and maybe that person will want to peer deeper into her life past. He went on to tell her not to turn in any score cards and don't tell anyone how good she is, she needs her privacy and let us not forget where she comes from. Ann asked Michael to go out with them the next time they go out for a round, he told her he wouldn't miss it for the world. It was only a few days later they teed off and Michael couldn't out drive her on any hole, she hit every green in regulation and she ended up shooting two under par and they both congratulated her on her great round of golf and they headed home for the great meal their cook promised them she would have it waiting for them to enjoy.

Venus was starting to get this very rich persons tan and she looked better if that was possible. She was coming in the office every day now and she was reading anything on the law she could find. She was extremely intelligent and she knew the law inside and out and Michael was anxious to see how she can handle herself in a court room. One day this little old lady came in to the office and she asked if there was anyone here that would listen to her story about her son who was the father od two girls and a sick wife. Venus took her back to her office and she asked this nice old lady to take a seat and she would listen to what she had to say about her son.

She said her son worked for the power company and while they were out one day working on some lines he was electrocuted and he died a very painful death. Venus asked her how did he die and she told her that the electricity arched from the high voltage line over to the line he was working on and electrocuted him. She thought that was strange in this day and age of high voltage safety procedures. Venus spent a lot of time with this old woman until she got the whole story about as correct as it could be. She went to Michael and told him that he told this old lady that the power company isn't responsible for electrical arching. Then she told Michael that they aren't responsible for any employees death for arching and they never return her phone calls, she showed Venus her phone bill where she called the power company thirty seven times, it was clearly on the phone bill and it was proof that they were clearly receiving all those calls and not calling her back.

Venus was told that this old lady's name was Susan White and that she needs to sue these people and she will file the papers right away. She went ton the court house and filed a law suit against the power company for the plaintiff Susan White for $5,000,000 then she waited a few days and called the power company's legal office that would represent the power company. They were extremely rude on the phone to Venus and she asked them if they wanted to talk and their reply was that there was nothing to talk about and they hung up on her. So, she had them served with a subpoena for the attached people to appear with out fail for a deposition in one week at the law offices of Smith and associates. Michael was looking over Venus's shoulder just to guide her and see that she is on the right tract.

The morning of the deposition the court stenographer was set up and ready to go, the power companies lawyers were almost an hour late and they only had three of the six people that Venus asked to depose. Michael immediately intervened and told the power company lawyers that he was going to notify the court of them being an hour late and they only showed up with three of the six requested and never apologized for being so late which in the legal world is a great big no no. The power company lawyer said that they couldn't find the other three. What they didn't know that Venus can read their minds and she knows that they never even tried to get them to appear. She told the lead attorney that he never even tried to round up the missing names on her deposition list and if she could quote him precisely, "Fuck them I aint doing nothing to help them." Is that about right in how you felt about this law suit, am I quoting you correctly.

He was speechless and said that it wasn't true and Venus responded and asked him and asked him if he told those three people that came with you here today that you told them in your office before you came here not to tell us anything, we are not going to help them, is that about what you said to them this morning Mr. Miles and you instructed the people in the records department to bury anything that pertains to arching. Is that about right and did you tell those people that or am I just hallucinating those things.

"Not the way you just stated it."

"Please tell me where I have misstated it."

"I don't remember."

"Do you know the way you have acted so far in this deposition and behind the scenes that I can have you disbarred from practicing the law anywhere. I promise you I will work hard on having you disbarred because you are not a good representative of the American justice system."

He just sat there knowing he was up against a tough group today. Venus asked the three people present if they were ever told about arching and all three4 of them said yes and that was all they heard about it. Doesn't your manual tell you about arching and that you are to cover those high tension lines with those five foot long orange rubber sleeves that protect you from arching, they all said that they have never seen a manual. Venus thanked them for coming here this morning and she told the attorney after the wittiness's left the room he told him that he would see him in court if he is allowed to still practice law. He was one shook up dude at this point. After they all left Michael was praising Venus on how she handled herself and for it being her first case she was excellent.

Michael told her that she was going to eat this guy up in the court room, he doesn't have any chance against her. Venus was in touch with Mrs. White and she gave her a heads up that her case is going to be heard in three days and she told Venus she will be ready. The morning of the trial they waited for Mrs. White to walk in with her as a sign of solidarity. Venus was picking jurors that were either widows or widowers. They broke for lunch and when they returned the power company was up first to make their opening statement. They made their opening statement far to short because they didn't have a case and it was in Venus's advantage because the next morning Venus took three hours burning home the point that the power company never trained their men properly or even give them a manual that they could use on the job and they will produce wittiness's from the power company to that effect.

Venus brought up other young men that died suspiciously and they covered it up like they tried to cove up Mr. Whites death. It took this little old lady to make them pay for this and some of their other past sins. The judge who id getting the feel of this told the court that he would rather start fresh in the morning and Venus left there knowing that the jury would never side with the power company when she gets done proving her points and proof. The judge wanted them to start at 9: 30 sharp. Venus called her only wittiness to the stand and all three of them repeated everything they said in the deposition. That was so devastating them that the defense attorney fumbled miserably to change their story.

On the third day it was time for the closing statements and Venus got to go last. Again, the defense only took amount of time to sum up their case, while Venus told the jury how Mrs. Whites daughter in law killed herself after the death of her husband and how she is left with the two grandchildren and the burden of raising the two grandchildren. Then she held up the phone bill of where it showed thirty seven phone calls to the power company and not one return call back, no wonder these people are finding themselves in a court room. Facing this poor mother who is still waiting for someone from the power company to call her back. Venus walked up to the jury box and looked at the juror's and told them that she hopes that they will return Mrs. Whites call to them and walked away with the phone bill in her hand.

She walked back and took her seat at the plaintiffs table, Michael leaned over and told Venus that she has just ripped those crooks a new ass. The judge gave the jury his instructions. They left the court room and Michael told Mrs. White not to stray far because we will only be given an hour to come back to the court room. Michael looked at her when she walked away and thought how pitiful she looked and she didn't have very much to live for. The next day at the office they received their phone call to come back to the court for the verdict, now that was fast, they waited for Mrs. White to show up so they could all walk in together. There were a lot of reporters there and it was so quiet you could hear a pin drop. This was going to be big if the power company loses this case.

They were asked to rise for the judge when he entered the court room and he asked them to be seated, the jury filed in and took their seats. It seemed like a long time but it was only seconds that all that happened and the judge asked them if they have come to a decision and the hear juror said that they have. The judge asked him to read it out loud to the court. He put on his reading glasses and read from his paper, we the jury have found the power company responsible for the death of William white while in employment of the power company, he went on to read that their judgement against the power company for the plaintiff for $5,000,000 you could hear the defense shuffling their papers at their desk, then the Forman told the judge because of the was they treated this old woman in her desperate hour they wish to add punitive damages to Mrs. White the sum of $20,000,000.

Well the defense erupted in to loud objections and they want to file an appeal. The judge told the lead defense attorney that they had a week to prove their case and they didn't because they didn't have one. Then he went on and told them that this award isn't paid in 72 hours he would fine them a $1,000,000 a day starting *back to the first day so please and not waste any time to settle this case. The judge told Venus to let the court know if they don't meet their deadline. They have left the court room and the reporters were swarming on the courtroom steps clambering around for an interview with Venus, she did say she was very happy for Mrs. White and sorry for anyone else that lost their life working for the power company.*

She walked away with Michael and congratulated her on a great win and how she made the firm $12,500,000 Venus said that she doesn't need any money and he has given her all that anyone could ever want. He asked her, "Do you mean that you don't want your share?" Her reply was the same and money doesn't mean anything to her and she is perfectly happy living with her new family. She went on to say that she lives in a mansion on the ocean and drives one of the most expensive cars around. Michael told her that he was uneasy with that but he will go along with her decision.

They decided to go out for dinner and celebrate their win at their ocean front restaurant and as they were seated, they heard someone call out Venus they looked around and they didn't see anyone they recognized. They were seated when this nice looking woman staggered up to them don't you say hello to your friend. I guess you don't recognize me not looking like an old woman, I am Mrs. White the old woman you just made $12,500,000. Don't you remember that Venus and Michael said that he remembered her but not the woman standing in front of them now and all made up and half drunk. He told her if this is the real you then you fooled a lot of people including her lawyer and the jury.

She told them, let me put you at ease everything about my case was true and do you think the jury would have given me punitive damages if I didn't wear a disguise and look so pitiful. She directed her next comment to Venus don't feel bad about the real me I am still the same person you defended in that court room and if they excuse her, she is going to get drunk. Well you could have knocked them over with that bit of news so they decided to leave there and go down to P.V. Martins and pick up their celebration with a better atmosphere. They were still in shock a few hours later and even on their drive home they were still talking about how clever she was.

The money was paid on time and they forwarded her share to her bank with the routing number she gave them. He took a moment about what she did and she appealed to the sympathy of the jury for them to feel sorry for her and maybe be awarded more money. It worked beautifully, he thought what would the jury think if they could see her now. All that was out of their control, the woman had a grievance with the power company and Venus brought them to task for it. In this case the worst you look can't hurt you. Michael assured Venus that this ending will be only one of many endings that they will experience over the years.

Michael assured Venus that she can have anything she desires and she told him not to worry about her she is a big girl now. With that Michael let it pass away now. With that they both felt that if Venus was happy with her life with them then so be it. Venus never went out at night or anything she only would go out with Ann or Michael and they knew why. Let us not forget that she was an alien and nothing good can come from mixing with us Earthlings and only God knows what could happen to her. She wasn't hip to the silver tongue sex talking wolves that are always looking for that vulnerable nice girl that they can turn into a sperm dumpster. Michael imagined her sitting in a restaurant or bar sitting by herself she would draw a crown of men wanting to talk to her and ask her all kinds of questions that seem to be innocent that a lot of girls lose their innocence to.

Michael and Ann have taken on the responsibility for protecting Venus from any harm, Heavens knows what powers she possesses and she told them of a few and they are sure that she hasn't told them of a few others she is capable of. It looks like she is stranded here and if there is someone coming to take her home a lot of years will have to go by before anyone comes here and find her, Earth is a big place, we might all be dead before anyone could travel back here to fetch her. While one life is traveling at the speed of light time slows down for them bur the people not traveling at the speed of light hundreds of years might go by before anyone could come here. Only the people on Earth their time wouldn't affected by someone's else traveling at the speed of light.

Michael wants to sit with Venus and learn more about her way of life on Tapolia, there are so many questions that he wants to ask her. The only reason he hasn't done it up to now was because he was hoping that when they sat sometime, she might just let it come out freely without questioning her. It would be interesting to compare her way of life with ours and if she was able to travel here to Earth then we don't have that much to compare to.

We have never found any life outside our planet and yet her planet has thousands of years ago and they are able to come here at some unbelievable speeds and survive the trip unharmed and they are eons in intelligence ahead of us. To compare us to them there is no comparison. Our bodies are not capable of traveling in space and survive, yet she has, that something that they have conquered that has enabled them to travel through space with out any consequence. Michael feels that Venus isn't going to divulge that or anyone else, she must have a good reason.

After winning her first law suit there won't be any stopping her now. She possesses physic abilities that are not imaginable and she hides it very well. I wonder about her side kicks and where they are. She demonstrated that she could question a trained professional like her last legal opponent and she was able to see how much he had lied to her and what he had said about her many miles away and turned him into an worthless lawyer.

We have to make a decision about our law firm and do we want to expand like it is and we can take some time of when we want to and not get tied down. We don't need the money that's for sure. The pier is opening up today to the public and the county wants to walk first and see how it feels like to walk over the ocean 300 feet out and imagine the dept of the water and feel the salty mist in our faces. It was quite an eventful day and even more for the fishermen that were raring to cast for the big ones, the parks along the ocean are a big hit and everyone goes there after work and on the weekends for sure the hospital has about another nine months to go before they can open their doors and it will be a great celebration when that happens .

We have been asked to put on a golf tournament at the club for the seniors that will be televised all around the world. I turned them down on the grounds that the public would trample our beautiful grass to death. They said they would pay him anything to have this four day event here on his course, he told them that it wasn't the money it's the cost to repair the damage to the property in general and the membership wouldn't be allowed to use the club for months before the tournament and after. The members have paid good money for the privilege foe being a member and I owe them that. It didn't go over that good with the Public Golfing Association, Michael felt that they would get over it in time.

Venus didn't get up this morning so Ann went back to her bedroom to see if anything was wrong. She was lying there with her eyes open and Ann asked her if she was alright. She hesitated and said that she was very ill and Ann immediately called an ambulance and get her to the hospital. She didn't say no and the ambulance was there in minutes and it wasn't that long before they assigned a doctor to her. She talked to the doctor for the longest time and she told him what medicine he should give her; he was quite taken back by the patient prescribing her medicine.

He hesitated and Ann told him that we are the ones that are paying for the new children's wing. He asked her if her name was Smith and she said she was Ann smith. He was gone for almost thirty minutes when he came back with a syringe and he gave her a shot in the arm and he said that he hopes this works. Ann thanked him very much and she stayed with Venus and Michael came in to join her and they slept in the chair all night. It was the sun shining through the window that woke them up. Venus sat up and thanked Ann and Michael for bringing her here, she told Ann that she would need another day or so and she will be just like new.

Michael asked her what happened and she told him that her shots she had before she came here had wore off and she was in dire need for a booster or she would have passed away. Ann asked her when would she need another one and she said not for a long time from now, even sick she looks beautiful. Michael left Ann there and went home and got Venus some clothes and was back with a sausage and Egg McMuffin and her favorite cup of coffee. Venus was being her old self again and she told them that she would be alright here and for us to go home. Ann told Venus when you go, I'll go. Michael left for the office and Ann called him and said that Venus can be discharged in the morning and she will stay with her until then. Michael understood about the attachment because he had it as well.

It was a festive moment to ger her discharged and back home, Ann asked her where she would like to sit an she said she would love to sit on the deck that overlooks the ocean, so Ann made some ice tea and walked down there with her and they sat on the benches and were hypnotized watching the waves breaking on the shore. After a while she started talking to Ann how she really ended up in the ocean. The crew wanted her to have sex with some Earthlings and see if you can manipulate them and see if she can make then do whatever she would ask them to do. She said she refused and they slowed down and threw her out of the space ship as it was a few feet above the water and sped off not caring weather she lived or died.

"What does that say of the people of Earth that we have these heartless invaders looking for ways to get something over on us Earthlings, no matter what the outcome would be."

"With that impulse they were capable of causing havoc on earth. How did she escape being raped? How are these people recruited and trained to be part of your planets space program?"

"I can only tell you about my recruitment and training and it was very extensive and how my crew changed into this lawless bunch or renegades is a mystery to her."

"Could these crewmen get out of control and cause some very bad problems."

"They probably could but when they return they will be severely punished and they will have to explain what happened to me and they have the same abilities that I do being able to read their minds and it will go on until the whole truth comes out, I don't think they can pass that investigation."

"What do you call punishment in your case for invading a sovern country who was never a threat to them."

"They will no longer to be trusted to serve and they would be sent out on a small missal to the sun and die a horrible death."

"Would they come looking for you?"

"That's hard to say we will have to wait and see. They will know that nothing would be the same as it was when they came here. That is what space travel does, it speeds up for some and slows down for others. I will say that the cost doesn't support the risk and they will probably not come back for me, at least I hope they don't."

"So now we have you with us for the rest of your life."

"It seems that way."

"Let me assure you that the children and Michael and ne love you very much like a family and we don't want you to ever leave us, I

guess you could say were selfish. When we use the term family with us that is the highest level there is when it comes to us."

"As much as you love me as family and I feel the same about you but that doesn't stop me from being homesick."

"Do you want to meet someone here and get married and have children."

"If I say I would love that or if IO should answer that I don't want to meet anyone, either way I can't win or as you say, "Dammed if I do and dammed if I don't."

"Look we believe you and what ever you decide to do we will be 100 % behind you, tell me Venus don't you miss not having a partner like a nice young man to snuggle up to."

"I'll be honest with you I don't know how that feels."

"I can tell you if you should meet someone and you love him like love is, love can turn your world up side down and you will have feelings that you may have never had before."

"All of this will come if I meet the right man?"

"Yes, you can count on it to change your life."

"I don't think I will ever meet a man; I am too busy."

"You think your to busy but there is someone out there that you are destined to meet."

"I am happy with what I am doing here with you and at the law firm."

"We are putting you on as a partner in the firm that you deserve to be."

"Thank you very much for that and I will never let you down."

"Now please promise us that you will always confide in us and tell us if you have any issues about how we are running our business, or how personal of an issue that you might have."

"I will always tell you how I feel about anything that can affect our relationship."

"I know you will and I agree with you to keep our law firm the size it is now and not grow so big that we lose touch with each other and our clients because that is the nucleolus of our business."

"I think we can give our clients better service that way."

Michael and Ann were given notice of the ribbon cutting ceremony at the hospital in a few days, they were very excited and Venus wanted to go with them. When they arrived, the Governor was there and he wanted his picture taken with them. They were introduced by the Governor and presented the scissors to cut the ribbon and a round of applause broke out for the longest time. The chief medical doctor said some nice things and now it was time for the tour. Ann noticed right away that the new addition had everything they had plenty of mobile chairs to get anyone around in. It probably won't be that long before the new wing will start filling up. They are short of staff and they will have to come up with some incentives to attract some people to pack up and come to Vero Beach. The biggest attraction for that to happen is money, they will have to pay certain positions more money.

Vero Beach is a nice place to live and housing is cheap as well, like everywhere else you have to be very careful where you buy, the hospital planners will have to come up with a package that will entice the professionals to come to Vero Beach to live, in other words they have to offer them an opportunity they can't turn down. Venus told them that she would like to work as a volunteer at the hospital on the weekends, they know she will be a very big hit there. If the truth be known she could probably preform miracles and in a few weeks the word would be out about the volunteer that the volunteer working in the children's wing. She was being observed by some of the hospital staff and they all concluded that she had supernatural powers to help cure these children that were dying of cancer. Unbeknownst to anyone in the hospital she would prescribe a mixture of drugs that would show that the children that Venus worked with were in remission.

Venus was called in to meet with the head physician at the hospital and he asked her point blank where did she get her medical knowledge, what school did she go too" He told her that she is responsible for the cure of four children cases and they are starting to say that you are capable of performing miracles. From hearing him say that she could see that she was drawing too much attention to herself so she made the decision to stop coming to the hospital as a volunteer that stopped all that talk about her. Michael received a phone call from the head physician asking him if he could stop by the hospital for a chat. Michael told him that he would meet him at 3: o'clock and he told Ann where he was going and he was anxious to hear what he wanted to chat about.

Michael walked in the entrance and stopped at the information desk and he told them who he was and he was here to meet Dr. Nelson and that had someone there to take him back to the doctor's office and he said his name was Dr. Nelson. Michael sat there and he had planned to let the doctor take the lead. He told Michael that the young lady that lives with him and she was volunteering here at the hospital children's wing. She stopped coming on the weekends and does he know why. Now he's really thinking to himself weather he should fill him on the missing pieces that is his dilemma.

Michael asked him if he had her phone number and why doesn't he call and ask her."

"To tell you the truth she seems to on another plat toe and way out of his league."

Michael asked him, "How did he arrive at that observation in such a short time?"

"It didn't take that long before we could see that. You should read all the reports about her, they all say the same thing, she saved their

child's life and now all these reports can't be wrong, there are too many people that are saying the same thing about her."

"I know that she has certain abilities but saving children's lives is a stretch."

"We miss her and we want her to come back, can you help us?"

"Venus didn't mean to attract that much attention and she feels best to stay away and hot have stories about her by the press that they would try to destroy Florence Nightingale and the new children's wing, if you think about it this could get pretty ugly. I have met some of those reporters will either destroy her or have her or she would be the second coming of Christ."

"You are probably correct bur never the less we still miss her. Is she any relation to you if I might ask?"

"She is my niece of my parents that died in an airplane crash."

"We enjoyed having her here at the hospital and she put a lot of life in the children's wing."

"Our two children love her very much."

The doctor was hoping that he could talk Venus into coming back on the weekends, Michael told him that as much as it is what he doesn't want to hear, you and the hospital are better off without her. Just think if the word got out that you were performing miracles at the Vero children's hospital and some child should die because there wasn't any miracle for that child, you would be sued for hundreds of millions of dollars. He looked up at Michael and said you are a lawyer and I believe every word you said and if I would think about it that is what would happen.

"Please don't try and contact her and please put some of these stories to rest just like the Air Force puts those flying saucers sightings to rest, he told Michael that he understands what he's saying."

On hid drive home Michael thought that he made it easy to get his point over by saying something about Venus's medical miracles without having to go any deeper into the subject and scare that doctor to death. Venus say that what she saw from the reaction from what she was doing with those poor children they were calling them miracles and she had to stop going to the children's hospital because of her advance medical knowledge was being blown out of proportion and called a miracle. She told Ann and Michael how easy it is to cure these children but because of our ignorance it prevented Venus from helping some children that were in dire need of her knowledge of medicine.

Michael told her that she is an angle of mercy and she will have to stop or be found out about. Michael told her that we sent a satellite into deep space with the history of mankind on Earth engraved on it and it was attached to one if its supports and it read, "We have come in Peace." And if someone from out there were to come here with that in hand he would probably be shot dead holding the record up that they took from the support it was attached to in his hand, that's how far we have come from out of the caves to now and I don't think that there is any difference we are just wearing different looking clothes and we buy our food from the super market.

14

It was a crying shame that Venus had to stop going to the hospital but she knows it was for the better and in time she will get over it and she told us later on that she wasn't surprised about the outcome. She went on to say that we are from two different worlds and it isn't easy for me to try and live in yours, everything you do is completely different from what she was ever exposed to. Michael told her not to let things get her down because she will have to adapt or be eaten up the difference of her life experiences. Michael told her not to lose sight of who she is to use and the children and that she is a partner in a law firm and she will be play a small part in correcting some of the injustices that are all around us.

Ann asked her was she working on anything interesting and she told Ann that she has a meeting with this old man that claims that he invented this gadget that would keep a car going at the same speed that the driver would set it on. Michael told her that it's been on automobiles for years and she told Michael that he claims he was the man that invented it and that his invention was stolen from him. She told Michael that she will know more when he comes here today.

Mindy told Venus that her 1: o'clock appointment is here and she told her to escort him right back. When he walked into Venus's office, he introduced himself as Craig Cruse, to be very frank he looked like a tramp and he smelt like a rotten garbage can. Venus stayed very calm at what she was looking at knowing there has to be a reason for this, she politely asked him to be seated. She caught herself staring at him and broke the silence and asked him how she can help him. He broke down and started crying and he told this beautiful angle that she was his last chance of any hope of getting back to his rights to what is his and only his invention.

She asked him what gives you that right to make that claim and come in here today crying for help. He reached for his wallet and he pulled out this dirty wrinkled piece of paper that had a number on it that you could barely read he said that this number was given to him when he registered his invention of the Cruise Control and he wrote it down on this piece of paper because his x wife took and tore up all the papers that has this number on it, in one of her insane tyrants and threw all of his papers in the trash, that was my proof of my invention.

She asked him where did he file his invention and he said in the Library of Congress well over twenty years ago and then what happened?

"I saw an advertisement that there is a car now that the driver can set a control and set the speed that he wants his car to run at and they called it Cruise control."

"She said, she will have to look up the first time it was put on any vehicle and that will be the first hurdler that she will have to get over and see if what he is telling her is the truth and please don't think that I am calling you a liar I have to think like a lawyer does and what they might put me through to discredit everything you have to say."

He told her that he has lost his wife and children because of this stealing of my invention, he lost his home and he spent all of his money in fighting with these automobile manufactures that showed me their paper work that they superseded his filing. Venus asked him if he had a lawyer present when he went before them and he said he couldn't afford one. She asked him does that mean that he can't afford one now. I can't afford you either but if you believe me and you check me out to see if I have told you the truth, then we will beat them and that is how I'll be able to afford you.

Venus asked Mindy to come back and record everything that Mr. Cruise tells her about his life as far back as what he can remember up to now and to please give her all of the detail he can growing up in the city tinkering with as many cars he could get his hands on and sometimes with only a flashlight to see with and some worn out tools. He told Venus he kept thinking what if a car could run on its own by merely setting a control and it would stay at the speed until it was changed and he first called it a speed control. He said that he went to Washington D.C. she asked him to go on about his family. He told her that he met this very nice girl at the park and they became good. Her said he kept telling her about his dream to invent a speed control for a car for the driver to set it at a speed that he would want his car to travel at a steady speed.

He told Venus that he immediately went to the Library of Congress and filed a registered sketch of his dream speed control, they never told him that he was at the wrong office and he needs to take it somewhere else. They gave him the number and a sheet of paper that serves as a receipt and they are holding his invention on this day of Feb.28th 1958.

"Where is this letter that they gave you now?" "At first my x-wife said that she didn't have it but later on I found out that she tore up and threw all of my paperwork in the trash."

"Why would she do that very mean thing to you?"

"She grew over time to be so mad at me for trying to prove that the cruise control was my invention and how I kept fighting with these manufacturers that I was ignoring my family over nothing that I couldn't prove."

"Let me ask you how did your marriage to this nice girl that you met in the park, that's quite a turnaround."

"I guess I let my struggle with the automobile manufactures consume a large part of my life. I was so focused in on my problem and I wasn't able to see anything going on around me and in her

eyes, she was fed up, rather than help me and be a lot more successful in proving my case against them. They all said the same thing, "Show us the proof?" know that they blocked every avenue I would use to do that they must have had something rigged so I couldn't prove my case and when my x-wife tore up all of my papers she in so many words helped them against me."

"Why didn't you go to the Library of Congress and have them give you a copy of the filing that you had earlier?"

"I went back there and they told me that they don't do patent filings. I told her that it wasn't a patent but proof that I had invented this cruise control first and somehow the automobile manufacturers got a hold of it and that was always a mystery to me."

"Did you know that if you want the exclusive rights to something that you have to file for a patent which prevents the very thing that happened to you. They didn't tell me that at the time. They just took my sketch and notes and gave me a receipt with that number on it."

"I am very surprised that you could remember that number after all these years."

"When I found out my x-wife had thrown out all my papers I wrote the number down and I put it in my wallet for safe keeping."

"This is the eight digit number I can see why you wrote it down. Life must have gotten pretty rough for you, losing your wife children, house and car and all of your money and living in the streets fighting with all these companies that literally stole your speed control.

"He told Venus that his health is starting to fail and he wants to make these people pay for what they did to him. They lied all the time and they did anything they could to get out of owning up to what they did to him. They lied and they would do anything to get out of owning up to this out right theft of someone's else's work."

He asked her if he could beat them, she said she would like to try if he would let her. That's when he broke down and cried, he was hoping she would say that.

Venus asked Craig how could she get up with him, he told her that he doesn't know where he would be from day to day. She went in to her cash reserves and she gave him $300.00 to get a ride to Walmart an get some clothes and toiletries and save the rest for some food. She called the Frontier Hotel on the ocean and she told them that she wanted to book a room indefinitely for a Mr. Craig Cruise and she will give them her card number until further notice and for them to take the money for the room weekly. She had all the information to identify him to anyone. When he was leaving, she told him that his room was being paid for by the firm and for him to try and clean himself up. She recommended that he take a cab to Walmart and ask him to wait so he could take him back to the hotel. She told him not to drink or get in any trouble or they will drop him and his case like a hoy penny.

He was far different leaving than he was showing up for his appointment he was joyous that Venus was going to take his case. Michael stopped in Venus's office and he asked Venus who was that guy who just left her office, she told him would he believer that he is the original inventor of the speed control device that is called today by all the automobile manufacturers as the Cruise control and the manufacturers have ruined his life lying to him for years and when all of this was going on for over twenty years he had lost everything and he is homeless. She told Michael that she got him a room at the frontier so he can have a decent clean place to sleep and hang out and stay out of trouble. She told Michael that she gave him $300.00 dollars out of her petty cash and get him cleaned up and look a little more presentable. Michael told her that he was proud of her and not surprised at all that she helped him get on his feet and cleaned up.

She asked Michael if he would accompany her to D.C. and drop in on the Library of Congress, he said he would be glad too. They left the next day and Ann wanted to come as well. It's been a while since they have been in Washington. Every one that needs to know where they were going and they had all the numbers they would need to get up with them if it became necessary. They decided to wait until the next morning before that go to the Library of Congress and they would use this time now to talk over what they were going to use as a strategy to try and get them to cooperate with them. This will be the most important evidence that they can find to win this case for Mr. Cruse. They loved their two bedroom suite and Venus could stay with them just like a family. They went out for dinner in George Town and it brought back some great memories.

Their hotel served a great breakfast the next morning and they did an inventory of things and headed for the Library of Congress. They went and they identified themselves as lawyers and they would need some assistance in locating the file # 13551492 this rude girl walked away and said that there isn't any file here under that number. Right away Venus knew she was lying and trying to cover up the fact there isn't such a file. Venus told her to look under #10802050 and try again. She was gone for a few minutes and came back and said that there isn't any such file for that number. Venus got angry and called the woman a liar, she walked away and came back with a gentleman who looked scared to death. Now don't forget that Venus can read minds and she can tell if she is being lied or not.

She explained to this scardy cat that she won't leave here until they produce the file #13551492 that you gave him that number on Feb. 28th 1958 and he was given a receipt for his paper work. She told Venus that they don't have that receipt but we do have that number and that number is a good number. He came back and he said that the 1958 files have been purged and they are in the basement and it would take a team of ten people a year to find it. Venus said she could find it if he would allow her the time, he apologized and told Venus that no one is allowed down there without supervision and that's when he said maybe tomorrow and Venus told him in her strongest voice that they are not leaving here without that receipt. And when we come back tomorrow the 1958 files would have disappeared and you would be the leader in the disappearance and you know it.

He told Venus that she had no right to speak to him like that. Venus told him straight up that she knows what he thinking and the supervisor requirements can be waived under special circumstances Venus told him that were here because you have lied to this poor man for years and now, we are here to tell you that the jig is up and he quickly replies what are they. The fact that that woman and him lied to us three times and she can prove it. He excused himself and walked away so he thought that Venus couldn't hear him talking to that woman a little farther away. She could over hear him call her a bitch and they have instructions not to show anyone that file that they are asking for they walked back to Venus and she told the scardy cat that she was a female and not a bitch. She wanted to know the person that gave the order not to show anyone that file, isn't that what you just told that bitch?

He just rocked back a little and said that the file cannot be shown to anyone and Venus asked if it could be shown to the person that filed it and Venus showed them a sealed document paper asking for that file to be released to her, his attorney and I am that person. The scardy cat walked away and came back with the folder that Venus could see that the Christlor company is on it and they are the ones that asked for the file to be held in secrecy. There was a poor attempt to erase it. Venus opened the folder and there was Craig's sketch dated Feb. 28th 1958 she asked for a copy of everything including the folder both inside and out they came back with all the copies and a new folder to put the copies in.

Venus looked over all the original copies to make sure that nothing was excluded. Venus thanked them for not cooperating with them, she told them they are a disgrace to common decency, the hardship that you cased this gentle man is almost too sad to discuss with you but you will hear it in court, and if and when it will be in the newspapers you all will have to hide in disgrace. Venus turned and walked out with Ann and Michael when they got outside Ann was happy that they got the receipt and couldn't how much of a fight they put up to protect the bad guys.

This paper if we are lucky can win us our case against Christlor Motors. She said that they have a long bumpy road ahead of them before they can get in a court room. Michael told them that there will be opposition coming at us from everywhere and who we will least expect it from. This case will be so big that it will be on national news for six months and because you took the time to listen to this scruff and smelly old man.

They decided to stay over and visit a few museums and to catch the 6:05 to Melbourne and it would get them home by 9: o'clock and plan their next strategy and they all agreed to file the law suit right away. They will sue the Christlor Motors first for stealing the cruise control system from Craig in August of 1858 and it was an outright theft of his invention and they spent the next twenty years of denying it and even went so far of bribing some employees at the Library of Congress. They all drove down to the court house and filed the lawsuit, knowing that this one was not going to be easy. Michael told them that they have deep pockets and no ethics to guide them. There biggest excuse is that they did it for the stockholder.

They stayed busy working on the case and lining up all their ducks and be ready for the onslaught. Michael let Venus run the show, she is the one that he asked to see. They can't wait for the depositions and really press them on important issues in the case. Michael knows that they are not ready for his cross examination he can be brutal at times with his lethal tongue. Finally, the phone call that they were waiting for came in from Michigan for Venus and they actually asked if they could talk to Venus and she said that she will talk to them if they come to her office on Thursday at 10: o'clock, they said they would be there. They showed up on time with their six lawyers and when they saw Venus, they knew they were I deep shit. She had the stature about her that she could persuade the jury into anything.

Michael asked the lead attorney William what is it they would like to discuss, they told Venus that this case could be considered frivolous and her immediate reply was that this case will be heard all over the world the worst example of how this big conglomerate has ever done to someone just to hide the truth and believe we will name names. Your company is as lowdown and rotten to its core.

"It will be easy for us to prove that this case is frivolous and it will be a failed attempt to bilk this American company out of this observed amount of money."

"It will be just as easy for us to prove that you lied to our client and you cheated him out of Millions of dollars and by that you destroyed this gentle old man's life and now it's time to destroy yours. This case will show the public how low you can stoop and your car sales will plummet down to a trickle and in time you will be just another name like Studebaker. Venus said that it will be her dream to destroy them if they continue on this course of lieing and cheating their way through this suit.

"We were hoping that it wouldn't come to this piss war where everyone gets pissed on."

"You will need more then piss to put our fire out to win this unwinnable case that we are going to bring against you. Venus handed William a sheet of paper with the names of people that they wish to depose within the next ten days.

"Who do you think we are to get these people ready for deposition in ten days."

"In answer to your question about who do we think you are, we know who you are and we know what you are and both of them will

be clearly in every newspaper in the world. We are well aware how you work out of sight lurking in the dark and trying to hide behind those dirty people that you paid to lie for you. We know how you have tried to cover up and bribe people so you can lie to the American public. When this case is over, we will be able to submit the proper legal complaints charging you with lying, cheating and taking part in the worst crime ever committed against one little old man who never hurt a fly. I could throw up just talking about it and we will be pushing for disbarment on every one of you and you have ten days to produce these people for deposition or we will file charges against all six of you and you will have to stand before the judge and explain to him why you didn't complete our request for deposition by the gig deadline we gave you."

"You have made it clear to us that you think that you scare us with your baseless threats and nothing to back them up with."

Venus didn't want to give her away about visiting the Library of Congress and how their company name is right on the folder and they specific instructions that they were to seal from any request for anyone to ask to see it. They finally stood and told Venus that they would get back to her. Venus told them to huddle with their client and come up with a better strategy to win this case because they will need one. They left the room as fast as six men could leave. For the next week they worked on questions to ask the people they were deposing. They really had some good ones and one of them would play the role of the one being deposed. It was very effective for them to do that and when it will be time to question the wittiness's they would be ready having a good idea what their replies would be. This kind of strategy will give them the upper edge in this case.

They knew that their opposition isn't doing those things and if the truth be known they are spending a lot of time putting lies into their answers that Venus will easily see that right away. They all flew to Michigan and booked another three bedroom suite at the Hilton down town. They took dinner in the dining room and put themselves on the wake up for 6:30, by the time they got their showers out of the way and a light breakfast they will be ready to start their day. The deposition was to start at 10: o'clock, they got there early and they were escorted into the meeting room where they were going to have the deposition. The stenographer came in a few minutes later and she got herself set up before the 10: o'clock start time. The opposition didn't show up until 10:21 they were twenty one minutes late and never once said a word about it.

Venus asked the stenographer to note the time the defense attorneys came in the room to start the deposition. They immediately objected to that. Venus asked the lead attorney how could he object to something that was a clear fact. He said out of frustration you're not the one paying her, we are. Venus told this looser that he better get used to it because this is only the beginning of the cost you will be paying in this case.

Venus took the list of names of the people that they were supposed to produce for deposition she asked them to bring in Jan Morris and the lead attorney said that they looked for him everywhere for him and he left the company over ten years ago. Venus could read his mind and she corrected him by saying that was a lie be4cause she can prove that he's been gone for only two weeks. Your company records will show that, why are you continuing to lie to us"

"I made a mistake on the date."

Venus told him that the only mistake here is him since day one. He completely lost it and his other attorneys had to step in and face Venus when she asked for the next person on the list Bill Ford. She was told that Mr. Ford had a stroke and he is unable to attend today. Venus smiled and she told him that was a lie as well and that he has moved to Seattle and the stroke you just lied to us about was not a stroke but a bad case of indigestion and there is a big difference between those two. Venus asked to depose the girl at the Library of

Congress Kay Star, they told her that it was her responsibility to have her here and not theirs.

Venus asked them why didn't you call us and tell us how you feel about her being here. Venus told them that this makes three people not here to depose and you lied about two of the three. These are serious complaints that will lead to your disbarments and we will push this complaint when the time comes. Venus was visually disturbed with these so called lawyers and she asked them who do they have that is on the list for her to depose. They say that they were able to get up with the engineer who invented the cruise control system and Venus asked them to bring him in. He was almost seventy years old and Venus planned to get to the truth even if he has a heart attack. He gave his name as brad Shaw and Venus asked him if he brought any notes or sketches with him today and he said he did. Venus asked him was this his entire package of notes and sketches that he has on his invention and he said it was.

Venus asked if she could take a second to look them over.

"No please do."

"Are these papers the original papers or are they copies."

"The company keeps them in a safe and they gave them to me."

"How do you know that to be a fact."

"Only because they told me so."

"What would you say if I were to tell you that they don't keep them in a safe but a three draw steel case metal cabinet with sliding draws? There is no safe. Why do you think they would lie to you like that? It's not the first time that they lied to you like that."

"What are the other times they lied to me?"

"They told me my cruise control was the first one."

"Do you remember when that was?"

"Yes, I do because it was my birthday 4/4 1958."

"Do your originals have a date on them?"

"I know they all had a date on them."

"What is your date on your cruise control papers show."

"That is easy for me to remember that date because it was on April fool's day 4/1 1958."

"You have a good memory on dates, don't you?"

"I always did, I always have to me it's fun I have been doing that for years. I always associate the dates with something in my life or something important."

"What would you say if I told you that someone filed for protection at the Library of Congress on 2/28 1958 about 31 days before you."

"I am not surprised because they told me what to draw up."

"How were you able to do that?"

"They gave me a sketch on a piece of paper to cop[y off of."

"Is this the sketch that they showed you."

"That's the one I am sure of it."

"Why are you so sure of it?"

"I had it in my possession for a few weeks. I remember the date 2/28 1958 was underlined just like it is now on this piece of paper. I told you I was good on dates and how I find a good way to remember them."

"What will you associate todays date with?"

"I was finally able to get something off my chest that has been bothering me for years and I will tell you anything you want to ask me. One thing for sure I feel better telling someone the truth about this big heist that they perpetrated against the original inventor of that speed control device, I will never forget meeting someone as nice as you are."

"Thank you for that, I appreciate that because I know that is how you feel."

Venus excused Mr. Shaw and told him that we will meet again soon, he said he will be looking forward to it. Venus folded up her paper, she stood and told the six that she was going to report these unlawful tactics to the court as soon as she gets back to Florida. They couldn't wait to get out of that building and breathe some fresh air, the stench in that building might give you a lung disease. Outside Ann told Venus how great she was and she had those so called lawyers by the balls, Venus blushed and decided to leave quickly before she turned into a beat.

Michael gave the stenographer their office address and he gave her $300.00 dollars to send them three copies by overnight mail, Venus gave her a $50.00 tip on top of that expense. They paid extra money for three seats on a flight out of Michigan right away and they were home by 6: o'clock. They caught the shuttle back to Vero and Ann got the children ready and they went out for dinner at their famous restaurant on the ocean P.V. Martins.

The children had a ball and Venus was just chilling, Michael said it was nice to see her call on some of her powers to assist her in the deposition. She confessed to them that it didn't hurt and she liked our chances of winning this case for Mr. Cruse. Venus will be outstanding in court and the jury will melt in her hands She has a look about her that makes you feel relaxed when she talks to you like she did to Mr. Shaw at the deposition. Michael drove out to see Craig and he was watching the price was right and Michael stayed there with him and play along with the price is right and Craig loved him for that.

Michael asked him how his money was holding up and he told Michael that after he bought some clothes that he only had $60.00 dollars left. Michael slipped him another $50.00 dollars and he told him that their Michigan meeting and how Venus got them real good, he was very happy to hear that because it was better news that he has had in the last twenty some years. Michael told him to stay out of trouble and have dinner on them tonight and he gave him another $20.00 dollars for that.

He was really happy to hear the good news of their visit to Michigan and they were making some headway in his case. They sat together again and they went over all they had and they hoped they could overcome anything they throw at them. They did file a complaint to the court about what they did at the deposition. They were caught in two lies and lied about the whereabouts of the wittiness's that were not there how they showed up for the deposition twenty one minutes later and never said a word as to why.

They called Venus in a few days and said they wanted to depose Mr. Cruse and Venus told them they know where their office is. They made a date for one week later at 10: o'clock . They brought Craig in the office every day for hours going over the evidence and what they were going to ask him and try to trip him up. He just loved Venus and he really felt good in her company and she was happy he knew everything frontwards and backwards and he was ready as ever.

She told him that whenever he talks about his family and how he lost everything it wouldn't hurt if he got emotional talking about it. Craig showed up in a collared shirt with dockers trousers on, he was clean shaven and his nails were cut and he had a nice haircut. He knew how important this case was going to be and only answer the question and only answer the question and only give them anymore then they asked him for and not to believe it if they should flatter him because they won't mean it.

Craig assured them that he wouldn't and they will ask you a lot of questions. Ann told him that they will try and trip him up and even try to insinuate some things in his life that he caused that he called his family trouble that led to his downfalls in his life. They will bring up that he caused his own problems by insinuating that Christlor Motors stole from him and he has no evidence to back up his claim. They told Craig that they have the evidence from the Library of Congress to back up his claim. The morning of the deposition every one that was supposed to be there were early and the stenographer was there and ready to go. Their lead attorney saw Craig sitting in a chair alone at the table and he approached Craig and he shook his hand and said that it was nice to meet him.

He started off by asking how can a man with no training ever invent something so intricate as this control system that allowed a car to run at the same speed the driver chooses to set it at, he went on to say that he couldn't do that even if you put all the parts in front of him. He replied quickly that he tinkered at it for years until he got it right.

"What do you mean by tinker."

"Just doing a number of different things with the throttle."

"Just what different things are you talking about."

"I was just adding different parts that I made in my garage and I kept adding different parts until I got it right to work."

"What did you work on to make this thing work?"

"My old 1953 Chev. Nova."

"Do you still have that car?"

"Venus objected to asking him that question."

"I still have it in storage in a garage here in Florida."

"What kind of condition is it in, is it still drivable?"

"Its old but the cruise control is still on and it still works."

"How did you manage to lose everything you owned that you held dearly to your heart.?"

"Because I was always trying to get a meeting with you and you made it very hard for me to make an appointment for the last twenty three years."

"Come come Mr. Cruse no one can get turned down for a meeting for twenty three years."

"Well I did and I have my telephone logs and the voice tapes of me trying to get you to return my calls and me leaving my name with your secretaries and they assured me every time that they would have

someone get back to me right away and I would always leave my name and phone number just to be sure how to get up with me and I would wait for their return call and I am still waiting for that call that I was assured or even promised that I would get a call by those secretaries."

They could clearly see that they weren't getting anywhere with Craig so they told Venus that they were finished. There weren't any claims about the authenticity of Craig's claim and things like that. Venus said that she was going to ask Craig some questions. She asked the lead attorney if he honestly believes that Mr. Cruise is lying about his experience with his company and that this is just a scam on his part to bilk you out of some money and we would be a party to that.

"I am not the one being deposed here save it for your reconciliation speech and save your temper tantrums for the court."

"Don't you think that all we wanted to know what your opinion was and you made it obvious what your opinion is."

"I don't have an opinion my job is to get to the truth."

"We have the same job then to get to the truth no matter what it is."

Venus went back to Craig and she asked him how they stole his invention from him?"

"I believe what you found out at the Library of Congress that they let someone copy the sketch. He said that he had a misspelled word in his write up, I spelt the word lying wrong and I spelled it lieing."

Venus held up the sketch and sure enough the word was misspelled wrong and they are going to where they filed their patent and see how they wrote up their summery lying or lieing. She told Craig she was finished and she asked him if he could wait outside in the hallway for a few minutes she would be right with him. Craig left the room and Venus said that she still wants the stenographer to record everything that is being said. That scared them not to say another word for fear that it might come back to haunt them. They packed their bags and they left without even saying goodbye. They all three concluded that the defense hasn't a leg to stand on. Michael warned them to be on the lookout for some desperate thing that might come their way.

Venus went out to thank Craig for his great deposition and she asked him how was he doing and then asked him how was he doing with his money and he said that he has a few dollars left so she took out $120.00 from her petty cash fund and she told him to stay healthy because the day he was waiting for is coming shortly with that he left for the hotel and to get something to eat.

15

Venus went back to Michael and Ann and they were very happy how the deposition went. Venus thought with her specialties she will know when the defense attorneys speak that she will know whether or not they are lying or not and even how he's thinking. She told them that she will even be able to hear them talking at their table and maybe even hear them talking about their strategies they are planning to pull on us. Ann said that she wishes she had those abilities. Venus said that there weren't that many people on her planet that do.

Michael drops in on Craig from time to time to see how he's doing, he told Michael that he feels real good and he is back to sleeping better again. He is anxious for his court date. The next day they were notified that their case is scheduled to be heard in one week.

They went into full lockdown and reviewed all their papers and they read the deposition over and over, well Venus didn't have to and they talked strategy. Venus wanted Michael to make the opening statement and she would question the witnesses and make the closing statement. They all agreed to that plan. They had to be in court by 9: o'clock sharp as well. They had to pick the jury and they think that it won't take that long. Venus looked sharp in her knee high skirt and with a slit up the back. These people are only use to seeing something beautiful like Venus in the movies. All eyes will be focused on her and her melting smile that she will be giving out most of the day.

Craig was standing on the court house steps waiting for them to show up. He was very clean looking and he wore a navy blue double breasted jacket with gold looking buttons and a very nice pair of gray slacks that went with the Navy blue jacket. The defense attorneys never said hello or even look at them. It didn't take that long to select the jury and they were finished by 10: 30. The defense started the opening statement by saying that this case is cut and dry and that there isn't anything Earth shattering so they will be brief. They weren't kidding they finished by lunch and they started back up at 1: 30.Michael told the jury that this case and they will prove how low these people can stoop for money. They never returned this poor man's phone calls for twenty three years and they have the phone bills to prove it and to this day they still haven't returned this man's phones calls and twenty three years of audios of Mr. Cruse being assured that someone will return his phone call.

We have all these records and you will get meet their so called inventor admitting to you that he copied his invention on a paper given to him that came from the Library of Congress that our client gave them for safe keeping. This coverup goes right to the root to where Mr. Cruse filed his invention with the Library of Congress. This cover up prevented Mr. Cruse from seeing his own filing and he that he requested time after time to see his own invention and year after year until it reached twenty three years and they told him every time that they can't find it anywhere in their files. They told him that it was lost in the basement with all the other files of that time, these people were bold face liars.

Someone was paying them to do that because this kind of treatment that Mr. Cruse was given came from people that had something to hide. Michael went on and told them how Mr. Cruse never gave up but his family did and eventually he lost his wife, his children his home and what little money he had. You will hear it from his own lips how this man suffered from those corporate thieves that respect nothing but the almighty dollar.

How can any company do this to a single law abiding citizen with no axe to grind with anyone, he only wants his just dues for his invention that has been put on every car for the last twenty three years? Michael looked at his watch and he thanked the jury for listening to him and he took his seat at the table. The judge said that was enough for the day and we can start in the morning at 9:30 sharp. They stayed seated at their table and thought their day went well Mr. Cruse Thanked Michael for that great opening statement, they wanted to give Mr. Cruse a ride back to his hotel and he was happy they offered and he didn't think that he could handle that long walk back. To the hotel this evening after that long day in court. Ann called home and she told everyone that they were going to eat out and they would be home before 8: o'clock.

Their ocean restaurant was closed during the week so they went to the Vero hotel that was on the ocean as well, they loved the sound of the waves breaking while they were talking and easting. Venus thought that Michaels opening statement was the best she has ever heard, she said that she watched the jurors they were mesmerized and listened very intently to every word that you said Ann said that she noticed the same about the jurors as Venus did. They respected Venus for not drinking any alcohol so they didn't drink it either. They all three had the surf and turf with the baked potato with some red sauce also with some chopped beacon mixed in. They played some beautiful music that was appropriate for that kind of dining they finished their meals and headed for home after a very trying day.

The children were already in bed, Venus said she was going to bed as well, so Ann and Michael went to bed but not to sleep. Ann was all over him and Michael liked it when Ann got very aggressive especially in bed, Michael asked Ann if she ever mentioned to Venus about having a boyfriend. She told Michael that she is not your typical woman she not only has brains and a great personality and a body second to none and no man will ever get to see or touch because men are the furtherest thing from her mind. When she is grocery shopping with me, I see all the men both young and old practically falling aver the displays that they have in the isles. She is a magnificent speculum of a woman and she is as pure as the driven snow. He told Ann that was quite a report and he respects what she has to say about her.

The next morning that had a light breakfast and their coffee to go. Venus had a glass of orange juice. Mr. Cruse was waiting on the steps again for them and they all walked in together. Venus called the girl that tried not to help them from the Library of Congress to the stand and she gave her a thrashing and the defense attorney fumbled through questioning her and what she had to say and he couldn't bring himself to talk about the Cruse file and why it was so hard to find. They broke for lunch and when they returned Venus put on the stand their so called inventor of the Cruse control, Venus asked him if he remembers talking to her at his deposition a few weeks ago and he said he did.

She showed him the paper that he filed his invention on dated 4/1 1985 and she asked why he underlined the date on the paper. He paused for a second and said, it was already underlined, he didn't do it, it was already on the paper he copied off of. Then she asked him why did he take all the credit for this invention all these years. His reply was that nobody cared anymore. She asked him if they paid him a lot of money for that, he looked at Venus and told her with his eyes full of water waiting to spill over that he lives in a one bedroom apartment on the east side, you tell me.

"That's it, all you can afford is a one bedroom apartment."

"The company told him that copping a sketch doesn't make him the inventor."

Venus got what she wanted and she excused him from any more questions from her. The defense asked him if he is in the habit of lieing, he looked stunned but he didn't answer. This time the attorney said loud enough to hear that wasn't he kicked out of school for lieing, he nervously said he was and the defense attorney said he didn't have any more questions. Venus immediately stood and asked Mr. Shaw why was he kicked out of school for one day for lieing. He tried to get his composure and he said he lied about why he was late for school that day.

"Why were you late for school every day for a week?"

"He said my father was drunk and he was hitting my mother and beating us for no reason and when we finally fell asleep it was 2: or 3; o'clock in the morning and too tired to wake up in time for school and we were late the whole week."

"So, you were embarrassed about your home life so you lied about why you were late."

"Yes."

"How long ago was this?"

"It was almost fifty years ago."

"Venus was having a hard time from crying after seeing his lawyer throw him under the bus, they used him and discarded him trying to get you to discredit the evidence he just swore to and took an oath to tell the truth and the whole truth. their client who proved our case against the Automobile company and they wanted to destroy him for telling because he was embarrassed about his home life. Venus leaned against the jury rail rather than lose her balance and said the jury has just saw how low people can stoop. This incident had no reason to be brought up in this case. This was a young teenager that every one of us would have done the same thing."

"She excused Mr. Cruse and he walked out of the court room having been belittled by the same peopled that were supposed to be defending him. The judge adjourned for the day and they will start back again tomorrow morning bright and early at 9:30. Tomorrow was going to be a big day for Mr. Cruse and he will clinch his case for them. When they approached the court house they could see Mr. Cruse waiting for them and he looked like he was ready to go. Venus took his hand and walked in with him, that was very touching for

them to see. Venus didn't waste any time putting Mr. Cruse on the stand, she went through his life before and after his invention. She asked him if he ever had a drinking problem and he said he did about five years ago and she asked him if he was ever arrested and he said a few times for being intoxicated in public. She asked him if he ever spent any time in jail and he said only when they were booking me in for being drunk in public.

She told him, that in essence that he was not a criminal and all you are guilty of is that you have shown us the scars of what a big corporation can pay people off to go against you and lie and cover up the biggest theft ever perpetrated in this country. She looked over at the judge and told that she was finished with the wittiness and now it was the oppositions turn to try and destroy Mr. Cruse testimony. The first thing the opposition went after was that filing with the Library of Congress doesn't validate his so called invention. You have to apply for a patent. He responded by saying that the Library of Congress accepted it as proof and they took my sketches and gave me a number to back it up. The defense attorney turned to the judge that his claim of registry is not a patent and they are asking the court to halt this case now for the lack of evidence and they wish to file for a frivolous claim against the plaintiff and we feel that this is the appropriate time to do it.

The judge said that there was ample proof that the Library of Congress accepted his sketch and even gave him a file number, he walked to his table knowing that he has just cemented the case against them and it's just a matter of giving the closing statements before it's over. The judge wants to start at 9: 30 sharp in the morning and start their closing statements. You can bet your life that Venus, Michael and Ann will be ready as well. Venus has been waiting for that day for a long time. The defense started off by calling Mr. Cruse a liar and a convicted drunk, he couldn't hold a job and he didn't have any friends, he thinks that he can get some from this honorable company that has a history of being honest and giving everyone a fair deal.

Now it was Venus's turn, she brought up all of the lies and how they bribed the Library of Congress file clerk and all of the twenty three years of no return phone calls and the audio recordings of the people at the corporation telling Mr. Cruse that someone would get back to him shortly. The engineer that worked for them and they were crediting as the one that invented the Cruise control that he admitted under oath that he copied Mr. Cruse's sketch right down to the underlined date on the sketch, she went on to say that no one should be subjected to such inhuman behavior. She looked at the jury an asked them to give Mr. Cruse back his dignity and some life that he may have left. He came to us penniless and we were his last hope to get the credit that he tried for over twenty three years to get. She thanked them for their public service and the hardship that some of you might have had being assigned as a juror.

Venus walked back to her desk like she could only do and Ann and Michael gave her a big hug, the judge waited for a few seconds and he instructed the jury what he expects from them and consider all of the evidence and come to a decision. They left the courtroom and still no recognition from the recognition. Ann called them a disgrace to the name lawyer. They gave Mr. Cruse a ride back to the hotel and they told him that it was in the hands of the jury to finally show the world that crime doesn't pay. They went home after leaving Mr. Cruse off and they had a great meal outside at the picnic table by the pool. Their cook out did herself with the Veal Pharmashon and three different pastas and their favorite Italian sauces.

They sat outside with the smell of salt air like only you can get from the ocean, Venus was saying how sorry she felt for Mr. Cruse and all this would have not happened if only they did the right thing. Mr. Cruse would have had some kind of a normal life and not have suffered as much as he did. Venus said that she is practicing law and helping the downtrodden get back on their feet. Michael said he is going to go in early and he would come home for lunch, he was home by 12:30 and he was happy they could get together again.

Mindy told Michael that she missed all the running around and hustle bustle. She knew they were waiting for the decision that is pending. Ann said let's put the children in the pool for a swim and their cook wanted to give them a surprise with their favorite roast beef dinner with all the trimmings. It was a nice way to end the day and they went to bed early for what they hoped would be a big day tomorrow. The children were in great spirits and happy that they will be going to St Edwards. Michael went in first and they received the call they were waiting from the court for them to come in right away for the decision in their case. They swung by Mr. Cruse's hotel and gave him a lift and we all will be in the courtroom at the same time.

They were all seated and it was very quiet, there were plenty of reporters around just looking for someone to say something that they can take out of context and misquote them. The Bailiff called out, "Please rise." And the judge walked in and told everyone to be seated. Then the jurors filed in that took a few minutes until they were seated. The judge looked over at them and he asked them if they have come to a verdict in this case. The head juror stood and told the judge that they have and he went on to say that they find on behalf the sum of $200,000,000 and because of what has come out in this case with all the lies and cover up they want to award Mr. Cruse for an additional $400,000,000 and if they are allowed they wish to award Mr. Cruse an additional $350,000,000 With that decision the defense started screaming that this was ridiculous ani it was excessive and he will not be able to spend that money in ten lifetimes.

They said that they will appeal decision and especially the money they awarded the plaintiff. The judge admonished them for allowing this case to ever come to court.

"I listened and watched this trial intently and you did not have one single thread of evidence to back up you defense that you were the actual first ones that invented the cruise control system that what this trial was all about. The Plaintiff proved without a doubt and he went on to tell them that they have three days to put this money into the attorneys account or pay a fine of $10,000,000 he hit his gavel down hard and he left the court room. Michael wouldn't even look at the opposition attorneys and none of his team did. They all gave Mr. Cruse a hug and he started crying and he said he had to take a seat because he felt nauseous and sick to his stomach . They got him a cold drink of water and let him sit for a few minutes and he stood after that little rest and Venus holding his hand, he told them that this day will be the beginning of a new life.

The reporters were all over him and asked him, how he felt and he said he feels like he has been finally recognized as the true inventor of the Cruise Control He went on to thank my lead attorney Venus who was a genius in this case proving how I was cheated out of my rightful recognition as the inventor and not to leave out my two other attorneys that were geniuses as well. Of course, one of the airhead reporters asked him what was he going to do with all his money. Mr. Cruse being quick on his feet said that he hasn't gotten it yet. That flushed her toilet that she was standing in and disappeared out of nowhere. It was only a matter of time when these reporters saw that this guy needs some bad press from them and now they are shouting questions out over the other question being asked but nothing could top what came next from some hidden reported in the crowd that called out, "If he was going to take his wife back?" They have no shame and they help each other steam roller over anyone just to get a story that nobody would be interested in. He clearly won his case and justice prevailed.

Ann told Mr. Cruse that they were going to pick him up at 6:30 for a celebration for the best celebration that they could give him. He asked them what will the dress code for this celebration and Michael told him that a collar shirt would be alright and to bring a sweater in case the air changes and gets cold. Then Michael reminded Mr. Cruse to open up an account to put his money in for the time being until he gets his sea legs back. They ran home and showered and put their golf outfits on and they swung by the hotel to pick up Mr. Cruse and go to the Vero hotel for an elaborate celebration where nothing was off limits or out of bounds for this celebration and treat him like royalty. None of them drank alcohol but never the less they will be on a natural high this whole evening.

Mr. Cruse wanted to get serious and he took Venus's hand and said that if it wasn't for her this might have never happened. She gave me the time when I wasn't that presentable and looking bad enough to scare any woman. She gave me the time to tell my story and asking me questions to see just how real I was and after a while I could see that she believed me. I deeply for her putting me up at the hotel and paying for my meals and my clothes. He said he would never forget us and he turned and looked at Venus and said you for making me feel important again and giving me back my self-respect and let me walk with my head up.

They drank ice teas and Virgin Mary's all evening and when it dawned on them, they looked around the dining room and it was empty. They stood and they had a big team hug and they took Mr. Cruse back to his hotel and when the stopped at his hotel entrance, he told Michael that he was going to get a Bentley like his. He reminded him to open an account so they can rout his share of the money he was awarded he told Mr. Cruse that it would be $450,000,000 and she told Mr. Cruse to spend it as he sees fit. When Michael got a chance, Michael told Venus that she earned a share in this win.

She told him that she is sharing in their lives and they have given her a wonderful life here with them and knowing that their two children love her with all their hearts. She went on to say that she doesn't need money and she still has the charge card that he gave her when we first met, I use it when I need it. The next day was Thursday and they only have two business days left to fulfill the judge's order. Saturday is not a banking day and this was their problem and not ours.

The money came in Friday morning and they called Mr. Cruse and they gave him the good news about the money coming in and they asked Mr. Cruse for his routing number so they can rout his share of the money to his bank. Michael asked him to come in to his office after he sees his money has been put into his account and to come in and sign some papers that will put this baby to sleep. It wasn't that long before Mr. Cruse was at the office.

Venus took him back to her office and she had him sign all the release papers and a gag order not to talk to anyone about this case and that means anyone. He told her they can count on him, he said goodbye and he gave everyone a hug and he said the first thing he was going to do is to buy a Bentley and he likes Vero Beach and he was going to build a house on the ocean that he has fell in love with and live the good life. He asked Michael if he was going to go after the other manufacturers like they just did The Christlor Motor company because they all as guilty as Christlor Motors were.

Ann told him that they all will have to pay for using his invention illegally, we will send them all a letter first telling them of the loss that Christlor just had and if they don't respond in a reasonable amount of time and take them all of the way through the legal system and defeat them like they did Christlor. He did tell them that they can save a lot of money by contacting them and talk about settling this case out of court and saving a large number of millions of dollars. They sent a letter to ten manufacturers, he told them to make a decision and to call his office what their decision might be. Ann asked him to stay around Vero because we are going to take this *to another level. The numbers that we are looking at average around $500,000,000 individually.*

They sent out all the letters and they waited to hear from all of the manufactures. There were only a few days left in the dead line they gave them and the phone started ringing off the wall. These companies were asking Michael to come to their corporate headquarters and talk. Michael told all the callers that it would be easier for them to come to his office. It took about a month and thousands of air miles before they all settled for $5,000,000,000. Mr. Cruse couldn't believe the outcome of going after those other manufactures Michael told him that they had squeezed all of the juice out of the grapes there were They routed his share of that money in his bank of record that made him another $2,500,000,000 richer and they hope he has a good head on his shoulders and stays as cool as he has shown them. Michael and Ann's money in his Swiss account has totaled to $6,500,000,000 and they will make interest of around $700,000,000 dollars a year.

Where does one go from here, don they keep working or take the children all around the country, the answer was simple they decided to stay in Vero Beach and keep a simple law practice and let the children live a peaceful life and they would have no idea how well off they were. They didn't own a plane or a yacht and housed all over the world they just had their beautiful house on the ocean. They did everything for Vero even building all the schools and computers in every classroom he built all their football and baseball fields and all of the teachers were give scores a $15,000.00 pay raise, provided they could improve their students test. As you might know it was leaked out that Michael and Ann were the ones that are responsible and they were un indated with all of the news services wanting an exclusive interview and Michael turned them all down flat, they cased this and they deserve no having an interview with them. Mr. Cruse stopped by the office and he wanted them to see his new

Bentley, his was pearl in color and a four door. He was like a new man; they were happy for him that he has gotten his life back. He didn't say anything about his dream house on the ocean but they were sure he was going to get one.

Venus had someone stop by the office and they stayed for almost an hour, Michael was talking to someone on the phone about changing a few holes and he said that he would make an appointment in a few days and come out and talk about it. Venus tapped on his door and she asked Michael if he has a few minutes. He told her to have a seat and she asked him if he saw that man she was talking to in her office. He said he was sorry but he was on the phone and what would she like to talk about.

"He was one of the crew members that I was with when I was thrown out in the ocean to either as you would say, "Sink or swim." Until you saw me walk out of the ocean in front of you."

"Did he offer to take you home with him."

"It wasn't an offer it was more or less a demand."

"Tell me Venus how did the demand go?"

"He insisted that I go back with him or have a very good reason not to."

"How can an entire Planet miss one of its citizens so bad that they send a space craft two light years away and bring her back home and what is it about her that they would go through all this trouble to bring her home?"

"Precisely, this is something that this individual wants to happen for some undisclosed reason and can get away of using his space ship for this individual pick that is no threat to anyone."

"What did you tell him about this unusual threat for you to come with him right away."

"I told him that I have made a new life here, without and help from, when you threw me out of that craft I could have drowned with no problem and I can still hear the other crew members laughing,

that this was funny to them. I told him if I end up back on Tripoli I will not stop until they all get the death sentence"

"Let me guess he didn't care because he has a better plan for you."

"He said he didn't care at all and he would get back to her in a few days"

"It sounds like he wants to talk this over with someone, I would think that it would take months before he could get a message from your planet. How can he make you go with him if you don't want to go?"

"He can threaten to harm your family, not leaving me much of a choice but to go with him."

"Do you think he would do that to us and the children? I can't help but to remember how you thought we were uncivilized, now who do you think is uncivilized us or them."

"That is a good point that you bring up and very timely, he will do anything to get his way and for me to go back with him."

"I am not sure what I want to do, I have a device that can destroy their spaceship with just a touch of my figure this will all go away."

"If you haven't made up your mind then they are free to take you back with them. I would have liked you to see you make a life here and raise a family."

"I don't have time here to find anyone to fit that scenario."

"Sure, you do and if anyone has more time it you, there are plenty of young men here that would love to meet you but you seem to be shying away from that. There not as many people that can handle the fact that you come from another planet."

She got very quiet and Michael told her that they love her very much and we always hoped that you would never leave us. She walked away and Michael didn't see her until dinner and seemed relaxed and cheerful. She told Michael that the visitor told Venus that they would wait behind the moon and they will come back for their answer. Michael looked at her and told her that she looks like her old self again and that's when she told him that she took care of that business she had told him about. Michael knew what she meant, but Ann didn't, but he will fill her in when they are alone.

Twelve years have gone by now when they were sitting out back when Venus and Little Mikey came out to join them and Little Mikey said that him and Venus want to get married and they almost fell over. But it was clear for them to see just the way they were hanging on to each other that they were in love. Michael asked Little Mikey when do they want to get married and his reply was as soon as possible, Venus thinks that she is pregnant. Well finally Venus found that man that she didn't think she would ever find that she would want to marry and raise a family with. I wonder if she will tell him where she is from.

The End

Printed in the United States
By Bookmasters